The Kremlin and the West

By Wolfgang Leonhard

CHILD OF THE REVOLUTION

THE KREMLIN SINCE STALIN

THREE FACES OF MARXISM

EUROCOMMUNISM

The Kremlin and the West

A Realistic Approach

WOLFGANG LEONHARD

Translated by

HOUCHANG E. CHEHABI

W·W·NORTON & COMPANY

New York   London

The text of this book is composed in Vermillion, with display type set in Antikva
Margaret. Composition and manufacturing by The Haddon Craftsmen, Inc.
Book design by Jacques Chazaud

First published in the United States in 1986

ISBN 0-393-02372-9

W. W. Norton & Company, Inc., 500 Fifth Avenue,
New York, N. Y. 10110
W. W. Norton & Company Ltd., 37 Great Russell Street,
London WC1B 3NU

1 2 3 4 5 6 7 8 9 0

Contents

AUTHOR'S NOTE   *ix*

1:   The Soviet Power Pyramid   *3*

   The Soviet Population   *4*
   The Ruling Party   *8*
   The Four Power Bases of the Regime   *13*
   Who Are the Soviet Officials?   *16*
   The New Ruling Class: the Nomenklatura   *18*
   Industrial Feudalism   *22*
   The Central Committee and the Council of Ministers   *24*
   The Top Leadership   *28*
   The General Secretary   *32*

2:   The Soviet Union Today: Domestic Problems and
Contradictions   *39*

   The Problems of Industry, Planning, and Technological
   Innovation   *40*
   The Crisis of Soviet Agriculture   *45*
   The Nationality Problem   *50*
   The Decline of Ideology   *55*

The Increasing Importance of Social Problems *59*
The Degeneration of the System *64*

3: Characteristic Features of Soviet Foreign Policy *71*

From Ivan I to the Present: Continuity in Russian Foreign
Policy? *72*
How Important Is World Revolution? *76*
The "International Correlation of Forces" *79*
Economic Interests and Risk-Consciousness *81*
Decision Making in Soviet Foreign Policy *82*
How the Soviets Negotiate *86*
Language as an Instrument of Politics *91*
Diplomacy and Mass Appeal *95*

4: The Foreign Policy Objectives of the
Nomenklatura *102*

I. The Socialist Camp *102*

Economic Coordination *104*
Political-Ideological Cooperation *106*
Military Cooperation *110*
Deviations from the Soviet Model *116*
Two "Outsiders": China and Yugoslavia *118*

II. The Soviet Union and the Third World *120*

Noncapitalist Development *121*
Countries of "Socialist Orientation" *123*
Soviet Policy in Developing Countries *124*
Successes and Failures *126*

III. The Soviet Union and Western Democracies *130*

The Soviet Doctrine of Coexistence *130*
Soviet Policy in the Decade of Détente *132*
The Deployment of American Medium-Range
Missiles in Europe *135*
The Peace Movement *137*
Soviet Policies after the Deployment (1983–86) *138*

IV. Present Soviet Foreign Policy Aims *141*

5: Can the Soviet System Change?   *145*

Internal Repression and External Expansionism *145*
Changes in Communist Systems *147*
Reforms in the Soviet Bloc: Conditions and Forces *150*
Dissensions in the Nomenklatura *154*
Economic Modernization *156*
The "Commercialization" of the System *159*
Liberalization: Hope or Illusion? *163*
Toward a Russian-Authoritarian State? *167*
The Danger of Neo-Stalinism *171*
How Likely Is a Military Dictatorship? *176*
Consequences for the West *179*

6: How Can the West Support Liberalizing
Tendencies?   *181*

The Struggle for Human Rights *181*
East-West Trade *189*
The Importance of Western Radio Broadcasts *195*

7: Proposals for a New Western Approach to the Soviet
Union   *200*

Leadership and Population *201*
Our Realistic Aim: Businesslike Relations *202*
Differentiation Between Eastern Europe and the Soviet
Union *203*
Negotiations with Communist Leaders *204*
Military Aspects: Arms Control and Disarmament *206*
Economic Relations *207*
Building Bridges to the Population *209*
Greater Emphasis on Long-Term Objectives *210*
Solidarity with the Reform Movements *211*

NOTES *215*
INDEX *219*

Author's Note

I was fourteen years old when my mother and I arrived in Moscow as refugees from Nazi Germany. I was then a committed young Communist, always trying to defend all aspects of Soviet life, even if at times I had personal misgivings. My first shock came one year after my arrival, in 1936, when the Great Purges began: My mother, a loyal Communist, was arrested and would spend twelve years in Stalinist camps. In 1939, my father, who was Jewish, was arrested in France and spent the war years in a Nazi prison.

I became more critical after the Hitler-Stalin Pact of 1939, but when German troops invaded the Soviet Union on June 22, 1941, all critical thought receded into the background: the defeat of Nazism was now my main concern. I did not even waver when I was deported to Northern Kazakhstan in the autumn of 1941.

For me the decisive turning point came when, in 1942, I was selected to study at the Comintern School in Ufa, the most important school for the political education of foreign Communists in the USSR. From 1943 until the end of the war, in 1945, I worked in Moscow for the radio station of the "Free Germany National Committee," a Communist-led organization of exiled anti-Nazi Germans.

On April 30, 1945, a week before Germany's capitulation, I was flown to Berlin as a member of the "Ulbricht Group." It was only after my arrival that I learned that our group had been assigned the task of setting up a Communist state in what would become the German Democratic Republic. As a privileged member of the new elite, I had a successful life as a Communist official ahead of me. However, it was in those years that my doubts about Stalinism crystallized into outright opposition, and when Tito in Yugoslavia dared to challenge the Soviet dictator, I took the opportunity to flee to Yugoslavia, where I remained for two years. In 1950, I came to the conclusion that as a German-language author, my place was in a German-speaking country, and consequently I moved to West Germany.

Life was very difficult at first in the West, as everything seemed alien—from the vast choice of consumer goods to the style of political discourse. I was eager to compare my personal itinerary with the experiences of those who had broken with Stalinism before me, and eagerly started reading the memoirs and reminiscences of former Communist officials. I was disappointed to find that some of them had espoused an extreme form of anticommunism soon after their break. Their kind of hate-inspired settling of accounts I found distasteful, and in reaction began advocating an objective analysis of events and developments in the Communist world.

With this in mind, I started writing my first book, *Child of the Revolution,* which came out in German in 1955 and has been translated into nine languages. My aim was to use the story of my life to give an account of the contradictions and transformations in Communist states, and to recount my own experiences, hopes, and doubts without the benefit of hindsight.

This book led to an invitation to go to Oxford and spend some time at St. Antony's College. The serene atmosphere at Oxford, and the quality of intellectual exchange that I found there, made a deep impression on me. It was during two years at St. Antony's (1956–58) that I succeeded in ridding myself of many ideological preconceptions and overcoming many prejudices, without, however, forgetting or negating my fourteen years in the Soviet bloc.

My stay at Oxford confirmed for me the view that those of us who have a firsthand experience as Communist officials have at times a decisive advantage when it comes to analyzing the Communist world: a knowledge of the inner mechanisms of the system, the ability to imagine what forms changes might take, and above all, a certain empathy for the people in Communist-ruled states—including Party members, Party officials, and even Party leaders. The arcane ideological jargon that puzzles those who are not used to it is an open book to one who grew up and was educated within the system.

Whatever the object or form of my analyses, all of them are pervaded by one central motivation: I have a deep, personal, and not just academic interest in real or possible changes in the Communist world. I have never given up the hope that the existing systems in Eastern Europe might change from within, so as to replace the bureaucratic dictatorships of today with "socialism with a human face." I am often asked what my own political position is. My answer is this: I am a follower of Sakharov. Politically I support those men and women who struggle for a liberalization and democratization in the Soviet Union. Although I have been living in the West since 1950, my political thoughts, hopes, and interests focus on reform movements in the East. There are no political currents with which I identify as much as with the "Prague Spring" of 1968 or with the Solidarity movement in Poland.

My personal experience and my academic studies have convinced me that domestic developments in the Soviet Union affect not only the daily lives of the Soviet people, but also have a direct impact on East-West relations. The more repressive the regime is inside, the more aggressive its foreign policy is likely to be.

Conversely, any movement toward reforms, more freedom, and a beginning liberalization would result in a more realistic and moderate Soviet foreign policy. Thus East-West relations depend to a considerable degree on how the Soviet Union develops internally.

In the West, there are two opposing views concerning policies toward the Soviet Union. Traditional anti-Communists regard the Soviet Union as an adversary and a threat. They favor economic sanctions against the USSR and a military buildup in the West to counter the Communist menace. In contrast to this group, the adherents of détente consider the Soviet Union to be a mature superpower whose security needs the West should respect. For these people, stability in the Soviet bloc is a precondition for international peace.

Both groups project their own hopes or fears onto the Soviet Union and neglect to analyze Soviet reality in a sober manner. It is important to examine the situation in the Soviet Union today and in possible future scenarios, especially in light of Mikhail Gorbachev's nomination to the post of General Secretary in the spring of 1985. On the basis of such an analysis it is possible to propose a new policy toward that USSR. Such a policy should prevent a relapse into the Cold War and primitive anticommunism, but also help to avoid over-optimistic illusions about détente.

New Haven, March 1986   Wolfgang Leonhard

The Kremlin and the West

1

The Soviet Power Pyramid

With whom is the West really dealing? People often simply speak of "the Russians." Many people then think of wide plains and dense forests, merrymaking and vodka, but also of the music of Tchaikovski and the novels of Tolstoy and Dostoevski. All of this has very little to do with East-West relations. The foreign policy of the West is addressed not to "the Russians" but to a system that can be likened to a power pyramid whose various levels are hierarchically separated.

The population of the Soviet Union forms the base of this pyramid. One level above, we find the ruling party, the Communist Party of the Soviet Union. At the middle of the pyramid there are the four power bases of the regime: the Party apparatus, the state administration, the armed forces, and the security services. The core of political power is in the hands of the nomenklatura, the new ruling class. The Central Committee of the CPSU and the Council of Ministers of the USSR are the highest level of this pyramid, although all really important matters are decided by the top leadership, i.e., the Politburo and the Central Committee Secretariat.

The Soviet Population

At the base of this pyramid we find the Soviet population, which numbered nearly 278 million in 1985. Russians constitute only about 53 percent of the total.

It is very difficult to make empirically well-founded statements about the mood of the general population in the USSR. There are no opinion polls as we know them, and the authorities censor the few that Soviet sociologists are allowed to take. The Party's information departments and sometimes the KGB carry out opinion polls, but their results, perhaps being too informative, are kept secret. A last reason why it is very difficult to construct a global picture out of individual insights and impressions is that one has to take into account the differences between social strata, regions, and nationalities.

However, it is not farfetched to assume that for the overwhelming majority of Soviet citizens everyday problems rank highest in priority. Matters that are routine in the West take up a lot of time in the Soviet Union, as people have to stand in line to obtain basic foods, search for a long time to find the desired consumer goods, and wait for years to get an apartment.

Many people are tired of all the official promises. They may take part in mass meetings, but on the whole they are increasingly indifferent to socio-political problems. There is a widespread retreat into private life as people organize their lives around the family and small informal groups. The fact that the Soviet standard of living is well below that of comparable Western countries is generally known in the Soviet Union. There is widespread criticism of the way the regime spends huge sums of money on the arms industry and on economic "window dressing," especially in heavy industry. Soviet citizens fault these priorities for the neglect with which the consumer preferences of the population have been treated until now. Many people, even those who in principle approve of the system, are unhappy about the great difficulties associated with foreign travel. Finally, there is a great deal of dissatisfaction with the social differentiation between normal citizens and the privileged officials.

The ideology of Marxism-Leninism, an important social force in the 1920s, 1930s, and 1940s, has lost most of its influence. Its place has been taken by patriotism, nationalism, even chauvinism, sentiments that are far more common in the Soviet Union than in most Western countries. Soviet citizens are proud of their country's might and of the fact that from an economically backward country it rose to become a superpower in a matter of decades. Their pride in the Soviet Union's military strength and its achievements in space research is accompanied by a nationalism that in some respects reminds one of the Victorian era in England or the 1880s in Central Europe. Although the constant outpouring of propaganda is ineffectual in many other areas, references to the USSR's military and political might impress many Soviet citizens.

This should not be mistaken for support for the official ideology of the Communist Party. On the contrary, increasing numbers of people are looking for alternatives to the official ideology, and religious movements are finding growing support. This new religiosity is less concerned with religious dogmas. Instead, it consists of a search for a new sense of life, for new ethical bases for human relationships. The leading representative of the Soviet human rights movement, Nobel Peace Prize winner Andrei Sakharov, summarizes the general mood of the Soviet population as follows:

[P]eople are weary of endless promises and economic flowering in the very near future, and have ceased altogether to believe in fine words. The standard of living (food, clothing, housing, possibilities of leisure), social conditions (children's facilities, medical and educational institutions, pensions, labor protection, etc.)—all these lag far behind the level in advanced countries. An indifference to social problems—an attitude of consumerism and selfishness—is developing among the broad strata of the population. And among the majority, protest against the deadening official ideology has an unconscious, latent character. The religious and national movements are the broadest and most conscious. . . . Among some people the same feeling of dissatisfaction and internal protest takes on other asocial forms (drunkenness, crime).[1]

In addition to the two tendencies just mentioned—retreat into the private sphere and pride in the country's might—a third tendency is emerging, and that is a widespread yearning for reforms. There is an increasing number of people in the Soviet Union who, having grown up under the system, confront it critically, reflect independently on its shortcomings, and look for new ways. Most of them, understandably, do this on the basis of their own experience and concentrate on possible changes in the limited areas they themselves know well. They include engineers who are weary of directives coming from incompetent Party secretaries, enterprise directors who criticize the petty tutelage of the authorities, workers who are angry about the growing social differentiation and the fact that it is impossible to air their grievances, kolkhoz farmers who complain about the low prices paid for their produce (prices that are in no way proportional to the necessary labor), lawyers who dislike the general state of arbitrariness and who would like to give a more legalistic basis to many problems, writers and artists who clamor for more literary and artistic freedom, and the growing numbers of religious people who notice with dismay how the regime uses petty administrative tricks, and sometimes force, to hamper the activities of the churches and other religious communities.

There are some who go one step further. Transcending their immediate concerns, they try to integrate their personal experience into a wider vision, an effort that often leads them to advocate a real reformist overhaul of the entire system. These people are more numerous than the small circle of active and courageous civil rights activists and dissidents. Typically, this larger group has elaborated quite detailed plans for reforms in the planning system, in the economy, in agriculture, in national-ity policy, in social policy, in cultural affairs, in scientific re-search, and even in the political system of the USSR, which they would like to liberalize.

The same wide range of opinions can also be found in Soviet citizens' attitude toward foreign policy, this book's main con-cern. Among the population there is a widespread yearning for peace. *Mir i druzhba,* "peace and friendship," is by no means a propagandistic formula of the regime, but expresses the gen-eral mood of the majority of the population. It is unlikely that more than a small fraction of the population is favorably dis-posed toward the global foreign policy practiced by the Soviet leadership today. Among those people who are interested in foreign policy, one can assume that a far higher percentage is skeptical about the Soviet Union's increasing engagement in distant Arab, African, Asian, and Latin American countries and the financial burdens associated with this policy.

"What are we doing in Afghanistan and Cambodia, when here at home we have no meat?" is a question many Soviet citizens ask today. Economic officials in particular are increas-ingly voicing their doubts about the expansionist foreign policy.

The general attitude toward the Soviet Union's domination of Eastern Europe is more ambiguous. Here we find that many people deem this domination legitimate, sometimes arguing that it was, after all, the Soviet Union that liberated the countries of Eastern Europe in 1945. Others, whether due to national-Rus-sian or liberal-democratic principles, would prefer their country to give up its domination over Eastern Europe, so that it might concentrate all its energies on urgently needed domestic re-forms.

None of these tendencies and moods can be expressed pub-licly. The Soviet population enjoys no freedom of expression, no freedom of the press, no freedom of association, no right to strike, and only very slight freedom of conscience and religion. It is very important to people in the USSR that there is no right to foreign travel, except for a few privileged individuals. Even when an opportunity to travel abroad presents itself to a Soviet citizen, he has to undergo undignified procedures in order to get permission to leave the country.

The citizenry's only right consists in participating once every five years in so-called elections to the USSR's Supreme Soviet, but for each election district there is only one candidate, nominated by the regime. Even when they "vote," very few people do so in the closed polling booths, for the regime propagates open voting, under the slogan "a Soviet citizen has no need to hide his opinions from his patriotic fellow citizens."

Once every five years a Soviet citizen steps before the electoral commission in order to cast his ballot for the official candidate. Even this election concerns only the utterly insignificant Supreme Soviet, a body that meets briefly twice a year to approve unanimously the decisions of the top leadership. The official (and only) slate of candidates usually receives more than 99.8 percent of the vote, and as a rule even more than 99.9 percent.

Under these conditions, one has to exclude the Soviet population as a factor in the decision-making process of the top leadership. Only in times of growing dissatisfaction, work stoppages, and restiveness does the Soviet leadership react decisively and swiftly to pressure from below. Typically, it will make concessions, and at the same time arrest the so-called ringleaders. Aside from this, the population has no way of influencing the politics of the country.

The Ruling Party

The Communist Party of the Soviet Union constitutes the next level of the power pyramid. In the summer of 1984, the Soviet Communist Party had 18.5 million members, that is to say, a little more than 6 percent of the total population, or 9.5 percent of the adult population.

This figure of 18.5 million means that, while it is no longer an elite party, the CPSU certainly does not deserve to be called a "mass party." As a matter of fact, membership in the Party is quite restrictive even today, and it is not possible simply to join the Party. Officially, only "the more advanced, politically more conscious sectors of the working class, collective farm peasantry, and intelligentsia" are allowed to enter its ranks. A citizen who would like to join the Party needs written recommendations from three Party members who have been in it for at least five years and who have known the candidate and worked with him for at least one year. In addition, the candidate has to provide a handwritten autobiography and a statement, also handwritten, explaining why he wants to become a Party member. He gives these to a "basic (or primary) organization" of the Party, usually at his place of work. If his request is accepted by the basic organization, it still has to be approved by the next level of the Party organization, usually the district committee. According to the new Party rules established at the Twenty-Seventh Party Congress on March 7, 1986, admission to Party membership is now to take place at open meetings. At these meetings, attended by Party and non-Party members, the qualifications of the potential candidates are discussed. Even then, the candidate does not become a full member of the CPSU immediately but has to be content with being a "candidate member" for one year.

A candidate member is supposed to use this year to familiarize himself thoroughly with the CPSU's program and statutes to prepare himself for full membership. When the year is over, the primary organization decides whether to approve or to reject his membership. This long screening process guarantees that only those persons who meet the official requirements and who can be of use to the primary organization in one or the other way can gain entry into the Party.

Membership in the ruling Party of the USSR entails both duties and privileges for the member. The basic duties were formulated when the Bolshevik Party was founded and by now they are taken for granted: members have to work in one of the Party organizations, carry out Party decisions, and pay their membership dues regularly (usually between 1 percent and 3 percent of their monthly income). More interesting are those duties that were added later and that are spelled out in the detailed Article 2 of the Party rules. Their importance becomes obvious if one divides them thematically into ideological duties, duties that serve to strengthen the Party, and duties that members take on as model citizens.

In this article, ideological duties receive the smallest space. Party members have to master Marxist-Leninist theory, contribute to the education of people in the direction of communism, place public interests (which always means the interests of the state) above personal interests, and combat vigorously all manifestations of bourgeois ideology, remnants of a private-property psychology, religious prejudices, and other survivals of the past. In the new changed version of March 1986, the "remnants" and "vestiges of the past" have been deleted and replaced by such evils as "private enterprise mentality" and "customs alien to the socialist way of life."

The Party duties are formulated with greater detail. Among other things, a member has to carry out firmly and steadfastly all Party decisions, explain the Party's policies to the masses (i.e., the population), strengthen the ideological and organizational unity of the Party, be truthful and honest with the Party, be vigilant, guard Party secrets, safeguard the Party against the infiltration of people unworthy of the lofty name of Communist, resist all damaging actions to the Party, and give information of such actions to the higher Party authorities, up to and including the Central Committee. These Party duties serve the purpose of increasing its prestige, strengthening its internal cohesion, maintaining discipline, and increasing its influence on the population so that it may exercise its "leading role."

Finally, we have to mention those duties that have relatively little to do with Communist ideology or with the Communist Party and might well be called the tasks of a "model citizen." These are very detailed, and therefore quite revealing.

Party members are told to work for the Soviet Union's industrial might ("the creation of the material and technological basis for communism," to use the official terminology), to be hard working in their profession ("to serve as an example of the communist attitude toward labor") and to increase productivity, to support all modernization efforts of the leadership ("to display initiative in all that is new and progressive"), to master new technologies, to increase their professional qualifications, to protect and increase state ("socialist") property, to participate actively in political and administrative matters, to expose shortcomings boldly and to endeavor to overcome them, to combat ostentation, conceit, complacency, and localism, to maintain state discipline, and "to help in every possible way to strengthen the defense potential of the USSR."

The fact that the citizen's duties of Party members are given more weight than Party duties or ideological demands clearly shows the real importance and function of the CPSU. The regime wants it to be an association of the most loyal, most reliable, most obedient, and most disciplined citizens. They must not only approve of official policies but also actively support them. The Party comprises all those citizens on which the top leadership of Party and state can rely. This has hardly anything to do with the original role of the Communist Party, for instance during the revolutionary period under Lenin. It is therefore not surprising that Party members endure their obligatory ideological evening courses without showing much genuine interest. These activities have nothing to do with Party members' lives, their functions, and their duties in the CPSU of today. It would be more appropriate to call today's CPSU "The Union of Soviet Patriots," or "The Fatherland Party."

It is the Party's task to socialize its members into the ways of the regime; one could say that it is a school for adaptation to the system. Party meetings serve to familiarize members with the regime's terminology, and members learn how to make politically "correct" statements, how to exaggerate small successes, how to find seemingly convincing excuses for inadequacies, and how to find the appropriate formulations for praising the leadership and condemning its enemies.

As they master this "Party language" with all its nuances, Party members increasingly lose touch with everyday life. If this process does not meet with complete success, they typically develop a split personality: on official occasions they play a certain role, and when they are at home or among friends they become their old selves again.

Such sudden personality changes occur all the time in the 415,000 primary organizations that the Party maintains in enterprises, commercial offices, schools, universities, cultural and scientific institutions, and army units. Even if it is difficult in the beginning, Party members gradually learn to master the "Party language," and assume their functions in the regime.

As compensation for their services and troubles Party members enjoy three advantages at their workplaces. First, they have access to so-called closed Party meetings, during which they receive additional information about the internal affairs of their enterprise that is not available to nonmembers. Second, they have some influence (in some cases, even control) over management (as spelled out in Article 60 of the "Rules of the CPSU"), which means that Party members have a limited degree of power within their workplaces. Finally, and this is, of course, not mentioned in the official Party rules, they have far better opportunities for upward mobility.

Since all important jobs in the Soviet Union—even on the local level in administration, the economy, education, and justice—are open primarily to Party members, Party membership is indispensable for moving up in the world. Most of the time this means joining the bureaucracy, which is why the Party is sometimes referred to as an "armchair party." To sum up, the members of the CPSU constitute a pool of candidates out of which the regime can coopt those whom it considers most loyal and competent. But, of course, only very few make it that far.

The Four Power Bases of the Regime

After the general population and the members of the CPSU, the four power bases of the regime constitute the third level of the pyramid. These are the Party, the State, the Army, and the Secret Police. These four "power bases" are not abstract constructions of Western sovietologists but a clearly discernable reality of the Soviet system; even an attentive and politically interested tourist can verify that.

If one visits the administrative center of a Soviet *raion* (sometimes translated as district, this is a territorial unit inhabited by, on an average, 80,000 people), one will notice at the center of the locality a large square, very often named after Lenin. Overlooking the square, or at least very close to it, there are likely to be two large buildings that house the district committee of the Party and the district soviet. The latter is usually smaller than the former, so as to leave no doubts as to the "leading role of the Party." The army building (known as *Raivoyenkomat,* district military committee) is usually not far away. The local headquarters of the fourth power base is not indicated by a sign, but even a tourist could quite easily find it after a few conversations with local residents.

This pattern is repeated on all higher territorial levels: in each region or province (*oblast,* in Russian), each with, on average, 1.7 million inhabitants, in the fifteen Union Republics, and ultimately at the central headquarters of all four power bases in Moscow.

The functionaries of all four power bases have many common characteristics. They are usually referred to as "responsible workers" or "cadres." As such, they represent the regime and have power, influence, and privileges. They stand far above the ordinary population and are totally independent of it, as there are no elections. Although they share these and some other features, there are subtle differences between them, as all four power bases pursue their own specific interests.

The Party apparatus is undoubtedly still the decisive pillar of the Soviet system, although there are some indications that its influence has begun to wane somewhat. Nowadays it is only very rarely referred to as "the light of our life" or "heart and brain of our epoch," designations that were frequent in the 1950s and 1960s. On the other hand, Article 6 of the 1977 Constitution defines the role of the Party in the broadest terms: it is the leading and guiding force not only of all state institutions but also of all "public organizations," such as the official trade unions, with their 100 million members, and the Communist Youth Organization, with more than 42 million members.

The offices of the Party cannot be compared to those of a political party in a Western country, but rather resemble a government with all its departments. The CPSU maintains a variety of departments for industry, several departments for agriculture, and departments for transportation, health, supply, commerce, handicrafts, culture, education, security, and military affairs. These Party departments have a greater number of and more qualified employees at their disposal than the corresponding state organizations.

The Party's relations with the government apparatus are somewhat peculiar. The Party gives "directives," to use official Party language. It plans and directs certain projects and exercises some control over their final outcome. Yet it is not supposed to interfere with their implementation. Ideological textbooks give an analogy to explain the Party's role: the Party is like a conductor who leads the orchestra but does not try to play every single instrument. This may sound clear enough in theory, but it is very difficult to carry out in practice.

The state apparatus, the second power base, consists of the numerous employees of the central state administration in Moscow, the administrations of the Union Republics, the regional and district soviets, and the state enterprise directors in industry, agriculture, and commerce. Of course, all state officials are also Party members, but given their function they primarily identify with their own power base, rather than with the Party.

In some respects, the state officials act as a link between the economic managers (the enterprise directors) and the Party apparatus. They have to fulfill both political and economic tasks, and are therefore subject to the influence of both the economic managers and the Party. However, in some cases they are also able to exert some influence on the latter. The state apparatus and the Party apparatus have to fulfill the same tasks and carry out the same directives, but there is frequent friction between the two, as their respective turfs are not clearly delineated.

With very few exceptions, the officers of the Soviet Army are also Party members, but they often consider themselves to be a separate force and an independent institution. Some officers are weary of the constant meddling of the Party and and the secret service, but they only rarely dare say so openly.

The Soviet regime pampers its armed forces. Officers, generals, and marshals enjoy many material privileges and therefore show little propensity to risk their lives in a military coup. The officer corps's authority has never come under attack, as it bears no responsibility for the difficult domestic situation and the endemic economic crisis. During the Brezhnev years the regime tried to enhance this authority by introducing what was called "military-patriotic education" and by building memorials to World War II, officially called "The Great Patriotic War" in the Soviet Union. Nevertheless, the regime has never ceased to keep a watchful eye on its armed forces: officers are politically controlled by the Central Political Administration of the Soviet Armed Forces, an organization that is not part of the Ministry of Defense but is a department of the Central Committee. In addition, the *zampolits,* or deputies for political affairs, represent the Party within the army.

The fourth power base, the state security system (called the KGB after 1954), is the one most closely identified with Stalinist terror. As a result of this historical burden, it was stripped of some of its powers and lost a great deal of authority during the de-Stalinization of the Khrushchev era (1953–64). After Khrushchev's downfall, however, Brezhnev proceeded to upgrade the KGB, and it was greatly expanded during the fifteen years that

it was led by Yuri Andropov (1967–82). Andropov's rise to full
membership in the Politburo (April 1973) was an important step
in this process. Many KGB officials secretly consider themselves the true elite not only of the country but also of the Party.
In the present Politburo, the KGB Chief, Victor Chebrikov, plays
a very important role and must be considered one of the top five
leaders of the USSR.

Unlike the Western democracies, where the activities of the
security agencies are treated with benign neglect by some and
are openly criticized by others, the KGB is publicly praised in
the Soviet Union. Every December the regime celebrates with
solemn pomp the founding of the Cheka, as the Soviet security
agency was first called. The names of successful and well-
known Soviet spies are immortalized in films, novels, and
poems, and streets and schools are named after them. In the
early 1970s, the KGB managed to dislodge the "corrupt" first
Party secretary of Azerbaijan and to replace him with the local
KGB chief, Geidar Aliev. Aliev is now a Politburo member and
First Deputy Prime Minister.

Who Are the Soviet Officials?

What is the social background of Soviet officials? What conditions are decisive for their rise? What special abilities must
they have? What kinds of problems do they have to confront,
and how do they try to solve them?

In the past, the officials' family background played an important role in their selection and promotion; those coming from the
working class received preferential treatment. Nowadays, however, family background—and professional qualification—take
second place to a person's absolute loyalty to the regime ("political reliability") and his belonging to one of the many informally
constituted groups of functionaries that will help the ambitious
official on his way up. It is most important to have a high-
ranking mentor who will take one along with him at each promotion and who will provide his protégés with opportunities for
upward mobility.

As a rule, Soviet officials have studied at Soviet universities, most often at specialized technical colleges. As students they have already been "socially" active in the Communist youth organization Komsomol or in Party organizations. A close link between higher education and "socio-political activity" usually facilitates an aspiring official's rise. "Socio-political activity" does not mean that one has to know Marxism-Leninism in great detail. Rather, it means that one has to master the official Party jargon, recognize subtle changes in the Party line, and thereby contribute to the concrete application of the new line in his field of activity.

In addition to being energetic, hard working, and tenacious, it is essential that an aspiring official develop a certain flair for detecting possible changes in the official Party line before they occur, whether they are policy shifts or personnel changes at a higher level. He needs excellent nerves and must be tough, decisive, and without compassion. Although he has to know how to use his elbows on occasion, he must also have diplomatic skills, so that under changing conditions he may still discern what his tasks are, in order that he may then carry them out, whether by using persuasion or by applying pressure.

Often this is more difficult than it sounds. One of the major difficulties facing Soviet functionaries is that their tasks are generally defined in unrealistic terms, reflecting the congenital optimism of the leadership. Since he cannot question the wisdom of the official directives, the functionary has to try to maneuver between the unrealistic demands placed on him by his superiors and his real possibilities. When he cannot fulfill these demands, he either has to hide this fact by a careful wording of his reports to his superiors, or he has to blame others for his failure.

The methods of covering up for failures have become a highly developed art. But when even they no longer work, the official has no choice but to prepare a highly embellished report. This method is so widespread that the official Party press keeps writing about what it calls *ochkovtiratelsvo,* "eye rubbing." For fifty years the regime has been trying to stamp it out, but it cannot be done, for it is part of the system. Another method consists in "covering one's back." When given directives that are clearly unfulfillable, the hapless official will send his superiors a pointed warning. This will, of course, not change the directives, but it can become useful later on, when he can justify his failure to carry out the directives in full by pointing to his earlier report and saying "we told you about it."

Of course, it is very difficult for a single functionary to deal with all these problems. He needs the support of a group of friends, functionaries like him, who will give each other mutually beneficial assistance. In recent years, these groups have grown in size and have often become large fiefdoms grouped around one high official. The latter protects those below him, but they in turn constitute his power base.

The New Ruling Class: the Nomenklatura

It would be a gross simplification to infer from what has been said so far that the Soviet system is essentially a kind of civil service hierarchy; that is only one side of the coin. Within Soviet officialdom one can distinguish a dichotomy between those functionaries who carry out policies and who could therefore be likened to civil servants in Western countries, and those who really wield power, the members of the nomenklatura.[2]

The term nomenklatura refers to a list of all leading positions in the different power bases on various levels of the hierarchy, whose holders are appointed not by the departmental heads but by higher authorities. It also refers to a list of all the persons who occupy the positions or who might be called upon to fill vacancies. Since all important power positions in the Soviet Union are filled within the nomenklatura system, it represents the sole executive authority in all walks of life: governmental, economic, political, social, cultural, and ideological. All information on nomenklatura positions and nomenklatura functionaries is kept secret, and only a very limited number of people receive full lists of the leading functionaries.

The nomenklatura is the true power elite in the bureaucratic-dictatorial regime of the Soviet Union. Ironically, it displays all the characteristics of a ruling class as defined by Lenin: it wields total power over all means of production, and its members have the power to organize these means of production in their own interest. Since the entire production of all Soviet enterprises is collected centrally, the nomenklatura has the possibility to gain material benefits out of the total value produced, a process that is akin to the dividends paid to capitalists in the West. As Mikhail Voslenski argued in his book,[3] the nomenklatura is the sole recipient of the surplus value and can dispose of it as it wishes. It alone decides what part of it is reinvested in the economy and what portion is used to maintain or enhance its privileges.

The main goal of the nomenklatura is to secure and extend its own power. Economic priorities are defined with this end in mind: the privileged status of the arms industry and heavy industry in general can be explained by the nomenklatura's desire to strengthen the army, the KGB, and the police both qualitatively and quantitatively. In addition, it has set up a strong propaganda apparatus in order to justify and legitimate its continued rule. All other areas of the economy, from consumer industries to the population's food supply, have lower priorities. Only at times when the nomenklatura senses the threat of increasing protests and possible uprisings does it attach more importance to these usually neglected aspects of Soviet life.

The absolute merging of economic, political, military, and intellectual-ideological power is the decisive hallmark of the Soviet Union's ruling class. Its material and social privileges are very impressive, but they are only a tiny fraction of a nomenklatura official's monetary income. This is done on purpose, so that an individual holder of a nomenklatura position may not develop too much independence. Although a nomenklatura functionary's salary is four or five times that of an ordinary worker, the real gap between the two is much wider, given the former's material benefits.

These begin with their living conditions. The houses in which officials live are quite luxurious by Soviet standards, and their (free) apartments are far roomier than the best apartments an ordinary citizen can hope for. Most nomenklatura officials have a dacha, a country house, at their disposal. Usually these dachas are within easy reach of the cities and are shielded by high fences. They are grouped in closed communities that are accessible only to the happy few and that include excellent restaurants, clubs, cinemas, libraries, and athletic facilities.

Nomenklatura officials enjoy their own "closed" shopping and eating facilities. In restaurants, they not only receive meals of a quality and variety that normal citizens can only dream of, but they pay less for them than others do. As for medical care, the members of the nomenklatura are serviced by a network of medical establishments, including sanatoriums, clinics, and hospitals, that spans from Moscow down to every provincial nomenklatura neighborhood. All these establishments are under the jurisdiction of the "Fourth Department" of the Ministry of Health and are equipped much better than normal clinics.

Nomenklatura members are also privileged during their vacations. Unlike other working people, who as a rule receive only two weeks' vacation, they get a whole month. They spend their holidays in specially reserved sanatoriums and resort areas that are free of charge for them, and much cheaper than usual for their family members. Also, a nomenklatura official pays only a minimum amount of taxes. Whatever his earnings, the highest tax rate is only 13 percent, which is very low, considering that he receives much of his income not in monetary form but in material benefits.

The nomenklatura official is not only privileged during his lifetime; there are even special cemeteries for him. A tomb in the Kremlin Wall, however, is a privilege granted only to the highest members.

Since money plays only a minor role among the privileges of the nomenklatura, external marks of distinction receive great attention: the size and equipment of the offices, the number of telephones, and the size of the secretarial and technical staff.

Another revealing aspect of the nomenklatura's psychological makeup is the carefully structured system of titles and the awarding of medals and decorations. Gone are the times of Lenin when there were only two orders, the Order of the Red Banner (1917) and the Order of the Red Banner of Labor (1920). In the meantime, seventeen new medals or titles have been added to these two, including the Order of Lenin (1930), the Order of the Red Star, as well as the titles Hero of the Soviet Union (1934) and Hero of the Socialist Labor. The military, or, to be more exact, the nomenklatura officials in the armed forces, have their own medals: the Order of the Patriotic War, other orders named after such Russian military heroes as Suvorov, Kutusov, and Alexander Nevski, the Order of Honor, and for the Soviet Navy, the Order of Ushakov and the Order of Nakhimov. To all these, Brezhnev added the Order of the October Revolution (1967), the Order of International Friendship (1972), and the Order of Work Merit (1974).

Of course, it does occasionally happen that these medals are given to model workers or successful milkmaids, but generally speaking they are reserved for the most loyal members of the nomenklatura. And unlike the practice of most Western countries, the Soviet Union can confer the same medal on a person several times.

Although the nomenklatura is a privileged class in comparison with the general population, it is not a homogeneous class, as there are sharply defined distinctions between the various hierarchically structured levels. This internal differentiation and the total isolation from the ordinary citizenry are closely linked with the fact that nomenklatura officials have relatively little personal income to spend: they receive all privileges directly from above. All the furnishings in their houses—the expensive furniture, the oil paintings on the walls, and the crystal —are state property. A nomenklatura official owns nothing personally, but receives everything, from teaspoons to pianos, from the state.

Although a nomenklatura functionary has to pass repeated tests and exams before he is admitted to the ruling elite, he is still subject to official controls once he has arrived. Each member of the nomenklatura is constantly surrounded by KGB people, whose official task it is to protect him but who also have to keep him under observation. Not even a member of the ruling class enjoys personal freedom.

Industrial Feudalism

The rule of the nomenklatura, as outlined above, has, of course, very little in common with the original ideas of the Revolution of 1917, and most of the Soviet Union's more thoughtful citizens, including Party members and officials, are aware of this.

But what kind of system is this? Often the nomenklatura is likened to a kind of bourgeoisie; some people speak of a "Soviet-bourgeoisie" and define the ruling system as "state monopoly capitalism." This comparison is insufficient. Under capitalism, the means of production are privately owned, production follows demand as determined by the market, companies compete with each other, and prices are set by supply and demand. None of these conditions obtain in the Soviet Union.

It would be equally wrong to liken the nomenklatura official to a capitalist entrepreneur. To be successful, a capitalist entrepreneur needs, above all, such character traits as initiative, independence, decisiveness, the willingness to take risk, and flexibility. His main concern is the productivity of his company, not how many medals he has. For him, success is the measure of things, not bureaucratic adaptation—all characteristics and values that have nothing to do with the nomenklatura system.

The difference between the two social classes becomes even clearer if we recall Marx's definition of the bourgeoisie in the Communist Manifesto:

The bourgeoisie cannot exist without constantly revolutionizing the instruments of production, and thereby the relations of production, and with them the whole relations of society. ... Constant revolutionizing of production, uninterrupted disturbance of all social conditions, everlasting uncertainty, and agitation distinguish the bourgeois epoch from all earlier ones. All fixed, fast-frozen relations, with their train of ancient and venerable prejudices and opinions are swept away, all new formed ones become antiquated before they can ossify.[4]

These lines sum up why the nomenklatura is not a bourgeoisie. To understand it, we need to turn to another system.

A functionary's admission into the nomenklatura is a difficult and, above all, secret process: does this not remind one of admission into the knightly orders of feudal times? Stalin once called the Communist Party "a sort of Order of Knights of the Sword within the Soviet state, directing the organs of the latter and inspiring their activities."[5] The feudal connotations of this term are revealing. What is more, the promotion of a nomenklatura official depends less on his own activities than on the goodwill of his superiors—is this not closer in spirit to feudalism than to capitalism? The fact that a nomenklatura official receives only part of his total income in cash, while all the privileges that he enjoys are allocated not to him as a person but to the function he occupies, also points to the feudal system. The same can be said about the strict hierarchical order that prevails in the Soviet elite.

What distinguishes a nomenklatura official are not his professional qualifications or his sense of initiative, but his absolute loyalty to the regime, which he has to express time and again, just like the bond of personal loyalty between a vassal and his suzerain. The official has the duty to defend the interests of the nomenklatura and the leadership at all times, but the nomenklatura in turn takes good care of all his needs. The relationship is reciprocal and again reminds one of feudalism.

In view of all this, it seems more appropriate to characterize the Soviet system as a kind of industrial feudalism.

The Central Committee
and the Council of Ministers

Until 1961, Soviet Party congresses took place once every four years. Since 1966, they have occurred only once every five years. These congresses determine the general line for long-term policies. In between these events, usually two or three times a year, the Party's Central Committee (CC) convenes to discuss and enact short-term policies or policies regarding particular issues. The meetings of the Central Committee are therefore of utmost importance for Soviet domestic and foreign policy.

The curious thing is that the Central Committee is not mentioned in the Soviet constitution. Even the Party rules (Article 34) mention only in passing that in between Party congresses the Central Committee directs the Party's activities. The CC is responsible for selecting and appointing officials (i.e., trade unions, the Komsomol, and other organizations), directs the work of central government bodies and the public organizations (i.e., trade unions, women's organizations, etc.), and represents the CPSU in its relations with foreign parties. Officially, the CC is obligated by its statute to inform the Party organizations regularly about its deliberations. This, however, happens very rarely. In the Khrushchev era, full protocols of CC meetings were published for a while, but since his downfall in 1964 only individual speeches and final resolutions are made public, and these rarely provide any insights into discussions and controversies between among CC members.

Since the Twenty-seventh Party Congress, in March 1986, the Central Committee has had 309 full members and 170 nonvoting candidate members. These people are the only Soviet citizens who have the right—within limits—to discuss draft resolutions of the Soviet leadership.

Although it is the leading organ of the CPSU, the Central Committee is, strictly speaking, not a pure Party organ. The two most important power bases of the regime are most widely represented in it. The Party apparatus as a whole is represented by 137 members on the Central Committee, among whom thirty-two come from the central bureaucracy in Moscow and eighteen are delegated by the nomenklatura of the Union Republics. Of these 137, the eighty-two regional Party secretaries constitute the single biggest bloc, while mass organizations such as the trade unions and the Komsomol (the Communist Youth Organization) together have only five members.

The State apparatus is represented by ninety-five officials. These include the chairman of the Council of Ministers and his main deputies, forty-two cabinet ministers, representatives of the State Committees, government officials from the Union Republics, and the chairmen of the City Soviets of Moscow and Leningrad. Unlike the previous Central Committee, which included six enterprise directors, the current Central Committee has only one: the Director General of the Gorki Automobile Plant.

From the foreign service, naturally the foreign minister and his first deputies are members of the Central Committee. Also included are a number of ambassadors: those to the European bloc countries (East Germany, Poland, Czechoslovakia, Hungary, Romania, and Bulgaria), and the Soviet ambassadors to Cuba, Afghanistan, India, Algeria, and France. In addition, the current Central Committee includes the chairman of the U.S.S.R. State Committee for Foreign Tourism, the chairman of the Union of Soviet Societies of Friendship and Cultural Relations with Foreign Countries, the chairman of the Soviet Committee for European Security and Cooperation, and the director of the Institute for the Study of the U.S.A. and Canada.

Twenty-three Central Committee members represent the Soviet armed forces. These comprise the minister of defense, the chief of the general staff, the commanders-in-chief of the naval forces, the air forces, the ground forces, the air defense forces, the missile forces, the Warsaw Pact forces, the Soviet forces in East Germany, and the Far-Eastern forces, as well as the head of the Main Political Administration and the commander of the Moscow military district.

Curiously enough, the powerful KGB is represented in the

Central Committee by only four officials. The entire judiciary system of the Soviet Union is represented only by the chairman of the Supreme Court and the Procurator General, while the ministry of the interior fares worst, with only one member.

The mass media, which the new leadership under Gorbachev obviously intends to play a greater role, are represented by the chairman of the State Committee for Radio and Television, and the chief editors of *Pravda,* the Party journal *Kommunist,* and the literary journal *Literaturnaya Gazeta.*

Among the representatives of science and culture are the president of the Academy of Science (who is simultaneously director of the Institute for Atomic Energy), the vice-president of the Academy and rector of Moscow State University, and a few other scientists, mainly from the natural sciences. The Central Committee also includes the secretary of the Union of Soviet Writers, and the director of the Institute of Marxism-Leninism. Finally, there are twenty-five representatives of the "working people": eighteen industrial workers and seven collective farmers.

Membership in the Central Committee represents a privilege that is often more important than the member's governmental function. This fact has practical implications for the visits of Western politicians in the Soviet Union. It is important to have a clear idea not only of one's host's position in the government but also of his status in the Central Committee. At times, it happens that a regional Party secretary who is a CC member plays a more important role than a government minister who is not.

Except for the twenty-five working people, the 309 full members of the Central Committee thus constitute a kind of Estates General of the nomenklatura, and evidently a certain effort is made to maintain an equilibrium between the center, the Union Republics, and the regions, so that regional officials may feel that they receive adequate representation too.

Looking at the national composition of the CC, one is struck by the overrepresentation of Russians. The age structure clearly shows the preponderance of older members, although since Gorbachev a certain rejuvenation has taken place. Officials over fifty make up 240 or 78 percent of the 309 full members of the CC (in the previous CC, of 1981, in Brezhnev's last year, 91 percent of the CC members were over fifty!) The average age of the CC members is now sixty (as opposed to 62.2 years of the previous CC, in 1981).

The Central Committee is therefore characterized by an over-representation of Party officials compared to government and economic officials, by a preference of Russians over non-Russians, and by only token representation for workers and women. Under these conditions, the Central Committee cannot function as an integrative force in society. Moreover, since its deliberations are not published, there can be no genuine public discussion about its decisions. Nor can the CC function as a brain trust; for that it would have to have a strong representation of experts and scientists.

More important than the 309 full members and 170 nonvoting candidate members is the apparatus of the Central Committee. This consists of full-time nomenklatura officials who, without usually being CC members themselves, prepare the work of the Party leadership. These officials are also responsible for the implementation of the decisions taken, and in this context it should be emphasized that a CC department is far more powerful than a corresponding government ministry, just as a regional Party secretary stands above the chairman of the regional soviet.

The number of the CC departments varies. At present, there are twenty-four of them in this "super-government." Of these, seven deal with industry and planning, two with agriculture, four with organization, ideology, and culture, one (and a very important one) with the political control of the army, and four with international affairs, including one department that oversees the international Communist movement. Other departments deal with transportation and communications, letters and petitions, management, and administrative matters. Of particular importance is the "general department": it has to coordinate the activities of all other departments.

The Soviet government, the Council of Ministers of the Soviet Union, is not a government in the Western sense of the term but rather that country's highest administrative organ. It has between 125 and 130 members—the total number varies, as frequently new ministries are created and others are dissolved or amalgamated and then established anew. At the head of this government we find the chairman of the Council of Ministers, who is surrounded by two "first deputy chairmen" and around ten ordinary "deputy chairmen." The ministers number between sixty and sixty-five (there were sixty-four as of January 1986) and are mostly responsible for different branches in industry, agriculture, and commerce. Often a ministry is not much more than the administration of a single branch of industry. To these ministers one must add between twenty and twenty-five (twenty-two, in January 1986) heads of the state committees and the chairmen of the Council of Ministers of each of the fifteen Union Republics.

Only three members of this government play a really important political role: the minister of defense, the head of the KGB, and the foreign minister. But their influence stems from the fact that most of the time they belong to the top leadership of the Soviet Union: the Politburo.

The Top Leadership

Together, the Politburo and the Central Committee Secretariat constitute the real government of the Soviet Union. The Council of Ministers is the highest administrative authority in the country, but not a government in the political sense of the term. Even less important is the Supreme Soviet (with 1500 deputies), constitutionally the highest body of the Soviet Union. It meets only twice a year for very short periods of time and takes all decisions by a unanimous vote.

Neither the Soviet constitution nor the Party statutes define the powers and the functions of the Politburo and the CC Secretariat. There are no written rules governing how the two bodies' members are chosen, what their functions are, and how they can be relieved of their posts. The two leading organs of the Soviet Union operate without any constitutional or legal legitimation.

The Politburo is the only body whose decisions affect all walks of life, as it deals with domestic and foreign policy, economic matters, military affairs, culture, and ideology. Its decisions concern not only "big-time politics" but also contain pronouncements on such relatively minor matters as opera, novels, or poetry. As a rule, the Politburo issues its decisions not in its own name but in the form of Central Committee resolutions, decrees of the Council of Ministers, or common resolutions of the Politburo and the Council of Ministers. Until very recently there had never been any communiqués about Politburo meetings. Only in 1983 did the regime begin to publish such communiqués in the press, but these are worded in such general terms that they do not convey any meaningful picture of the Politburo activities.

Usually the Politburo has between nine and thirteen members. In March 1986 there were twelve. In addition, there are between five and nine nonvoting candidate members (at this point, seven). Of the current candidate members, Vladimir Dolgikh at the same time belongs to the CC Secretariat, Boris Yeltsin is head of the Moscow Party organization, and Sergei Sokolov is Defense Minister. Some of the candidate members are active outside Moscow and go to the capital only to take part in the discussions.

Although the Politburo is not mentioned in the constitution, its members act in public as the true leadership of the Soviet Union. One can often see portraits of the country's top leaders, in parks or on official buildings, but contrary to what many tourists think, these portraits show not the members of the government but the members and candidate members of the Politburo. The press, too, accords them a lot of attention: first the General Secretary, followed by the other Politburo members in alphabetical order.

The Secretariat of the CC (with eleven members), headed by the General Secretary, collaborates very closely with the Politburo. The General Secretary alone is not responsible for any specific area. All the other officials have specialized tasks such as Party organization, cadres, heavy industries, armaments, consumer and construction industries, agriculture, and the international Communist movement. Its most important members are also members of the Politburo. At present, besides Gorbachev, this applies to Yegor Ligachev (the second-in command at the Kremlin) and to the newly appointed Lev Zaikov, who is in the Secretariat and who is responsible for the military industrial complex.

The CC Secretariat prepares the work of the Politburo and is, as a rule, responsible for the implementation of Politburo decisions. It transmits individual decisions to the relevant authorities, which means that every organization knows only about those Politburo decisions that affect it directly. Finally, the CC Secretariat plays a major role in the appointment and demotion of important officials in the power apparatuses.

Until Konstantin Chernenko's death in March 1985, the average age of Politburo members had constantly gone up, as it took officials longer and longer to rise in the strictly hierarchical bureaucratic-centralist system. In 1919, in the time of Lenin, the average age of Politburo members was forty years. In 1934, it had risen to forty-eight years, in 1957 to fifty-eight years. In the last years of the Brezhnev era and during the short Andropov and Chernenko interludes, the average age of Soviet Politburo members was between sixty-nine and seventy years; the top leaders were as a rule older still.

Only the nomination of fifty-four-year-old Mikhail Gorbachev in March 1985 changed matters. The new General Secretary lost no time bringing into the Politburo younger people such as fifty-seven-year-old Nikolai Ryzhkov, who became Prime Minister in October 1985, and fifty-eight-year-old Eduard Shevardnadze, the new Foreign Minister.

With two exceptions, all current Politburo members joined

the CPSU during the Stalin era, 1931–53. Even Mikhail Gorbachev became a member in 1952, Stalin's last year. Only Nikolai
Ryzhkov and Lev Zaikov joined the Party in 1956 and 1957,
respectively, the years of de-Stalinization under Khrushchev.

All Politburo members have had higher education. With the
exceptions of First Deputy Prime Minister Geidar Aliev and
Foreign Minister Eduard Shevardnadze, both of whom studied
history, and Gorbachev himself, who graduated from Moscow's
Faculty of Law and then took a degree in agronomy, most have
studied engineering, the dominant discipline in the Soviet
Union.

The typical itinerary of a Politburo member begins at an engineering school. After graduation, he works as an engineer, is
promoted to chief engineer, and finally rises to become director
of a major state enterprise. At this point, he joins the Party
apparatus. Serving many years as regional secretary or sometimes as Party secretary of a Union Republic is a precondition
for acceding to the highest positions in Moscow.

The last two to three years have witnessed a kind of generational change, as those leaders who made their careers under
Stalin have been pushed into the background or replaced by
men who have been formed by the post-Stalin era. Men like
Gorbachev, Shevardnadze, and Vitaly Vorotnikov, Prime Minister of the Russian Republic, are basically products of the
Khrushchev and Brezhnev eras. But even they represent, above
all, the nomenklatura and have its interests in mind.

The extreme assumption that the top leaders of the Soviet
Union are "ideological fanatics of world revolution" is as far
from reality as the idea that they are pragmatic practitioners of
realpolitik. These people's thoughts and actions are mostly
guided by considerations of power politics, and their main concern is to maintain, consolidate, and extend the powers of the
nomenklatura. They oppose everything that might limit its privileges. This does not mean that ideology has become totally
irrelevant, but it acts less as an inspiration and more as a legitimation. Although Khrushchev was the last really believing

Communist in the top leadership, there are still many others who, having spent many decades in the Party, take its ideology for granted and continue using a language rooted in that ideology.

The fact that the Soviet Union's top leadership represents, above all, the interests of the nomenklatura, and that it can even be thought of as its executive organ, does not mean that there are no differences of opinion within the leadership. Admittedly, the top Soviet leaders have less scope to disagree in public than do politicians in parliamentary systems. Most of the time they try to reach decisions by unanimity, but every now and then it may happen that they differ on specific issues, e.g., the allocation of investments in the next five-year plan (among heavy industry, consumer indusries, or agriculture, or among various geographical areas); the question whether serious thought ought to be given to limited economic reforms; the attitude toward the scientific-technical and artistic intelligentsia; the suppression of dissidents; nuances in Soviet policy toward the United States, Western Europe, the Middle East, Afghanistan, and China; the attitude toward arms-control negotiations, and how best to reestablish the bureaucratic dictatorship in Poland.

When such differences of opinion occur, what matters most is on what power base the contending leaders can count. Personal sympathies and antipathies, power positions, and considerations of prestige also play a role in Politburo decisions. Of course, on these matters very little information leaks out, and details about serious differences of opinion within the Politburo usually come to light only long after the defeated side has been ousted.

The General Secretary

At the top of the Soviet power pyramid we find the General Secretary, who is the main force within both the Politburo and the Central Committee Secretariat. In the first sixty-five years of Soviet history, there were only four leaders: Lenin (1917–24),

Stalin (1924–53), Khrushchev (1953–64), and Brezhnev (1964–82). Each of them represented a historically well-defined period of Soviet history, and each succession has led to important changes in the regime.

Generally these changes would not occur immediately after the accession of a new ruler, but only a few years later, after he had had the time to consolidate his power. After Khrushchev's downfall in 1964 and Brezhnev's death in 1982, many people expected quick changes or at least some new emphases in Soviet politics, but this is not how the system works.

One of the reasons for this is that the gradual extension of the nomenklatura system has increasingly narrowed the General Secretary's scope of action. In addition, every new leader inherits a Politburo and a CC Secretariat whose composition was determined in large measure by his predecessor. He therefore has to act carefully in the beginning, so as not to antagonize the other members of the two supreme bodies. His main aim has been to replace leaders of the preceding period with his own supporters.

Thus Joseph Stalin, who had become General Secretary in April 1922, needed five years after Lenin's death in 1924 before he succeeded in eliminating Lenin's close companions— Trotsky, Zinoviev, Kamenev, Bukharin, Rykov, and Tomsky— and call himself *vozhd* (leader). It took Nikita Khrushchev from 1953 to 1957 before he could oust Molotov, Malenkov, Kaganovich, and later Bulganin and Voroshilov from the top bodies and replace them with his supporters. Leonid Brezhnev, First Secretary as of 1964 and General Secretary after the Twenty-third Party Congress, in March 1966, needed several years to get rid of Shelepin, Voronov, Shelest, Podgorny, and a few others.

Mikhail Gorbachev, who became General Secretary of the CPSU on March 11, 1985, faces similar problems. After three elderly top leaders had died in office in rapid succession, the nomenklatura needed a younger, more energetic leader in order to infuse some dynamism into the country. At the same time, the nomenklatura feared that a younger leader might start reforms and encourage those forces which favor a liberalization of the system.

Thus official photos and television in March and April 1985 showed the new General Secretary surrounded by eighty-year-old Prime Minister Nikolai Tikhonov, seventy-six-year-old Foreign Minister Andrei Gromyko, and seventy-year-old Victor Grishin, the Party chief of Moscow. The message was clear: fifty-four-year-old Gorbachev was to act in close collaboration with his older Politburo colleagues, who were to safeguard continuity and make sure that the new General Secretary would not go too far in his innovations. Despite these precautions, Gorbachev's nomination had not gone smoothly. Official statements spoke of the Politburo having chosen him *edinodushno,* "moved by the same spirit," rather than *edinoglasno,* "unanimously," as is customary in the Soviet Union. The hard-liner Party bosses of Leningrad and Moscow, Romanov and Grishin respectively, probably voted against him. But Gorbachev received the decisive backing of Gromyko.

By recent Soviet standards, Gorbachev was an unusual choice. He is the first lawyer in the top leadership since Lenin, and is also an agronomist. He made his career in the post-Stalin era, and is the first Soviet leader not to have participated in World War II: he was fourteen when the war ended.

Gorbachev's rise to the top has been particularly rapid. Until 1978, he was active in the Stavropol region of the Northern Caucasus. In the summer of that year, he was called to Moscow and joined the CC Secretariat, where he took charge of agriculture. In November 1979, he joined the Politburo as a candidate member, and by October 1979, he had become the youngest full member of that body. In the summer of 1983, during Andropov's short rule, Gorbachev took over responsibility for cadres, ideology, and consumer industries. In April 1984, he extended his influence by becoming chairman of the Committee on Foreign Relations of the Supreme Soviet, after which it took him less than a year to accede to the top post. Past top leaders had needed three decades to accomplish what Gorbachev had done in eight years. His quick rise nurtured the hope that his resoluteness, independence, and sense of initiative had not been broken by decades of bureaucratic routine work.

The older Politburo members' early attempts to "rein in" Gorbachev failed. It took the new General Secretary only seven weeks to change the balance of power in his favor. In April 1985, two of his supporters joined the Politburo as full members without having gone through the candidate stage: these were fifty-eight-year-old Nikolai Ryzhkov, who had been director of the giant "Uralmash" machine industry enterprise, and sixty-four-year-old Yegor Ligachev, who had been active in Siberia for a long time. Ryzhkov was put in charge of the economy, while Ligachev took over responsibility for personnel and administrative matters. In addition to these two, sixty-one-year-old KGB chief Victor Chebrikov, a candidate member of the Politburo, rose to full membership.

Two months later, at the end of June 1985, Gorbachev further consolidated his hold on the country by eliminating his longtime rival Nikolai Romanov and naming the fifty-seven-year-old Georgia Party secretary Eduard Shevardnadze first Politburo member and later Foreign Minister. Andrei Gromyko, who had held that post since 1957, became head of state (officially, Chairman of the Presidium of the Supreme Soviet). In September 1985, Gorbachev succeeded in replacing Tikhonov, who opposed all change and innovation: the new Prime Minister was Nikolai Ryzhkov. Shortly thereafter, the chairman of the State Planning Committee, Nikolai Baibakov, was demoted. In December 1985, Viktor Grishin had to yield his post as Moscow Party chief, but, strangely enough, remained a Politburo member for the time being. It took Gorbachev another two months to eliminate him from that post. This was an obvious indication that the resistance of Brezhnevite bureaucrats was stiffening. Despite harsh attacks against the leading Brezhnevites (Vladimir Shcherbitzky in the Ukraine, and Dinmukhamed Kunayev in Kazakhstan), the Party apparatchiks remained firm and the two retained their positions on the Politburo.

At the Twenty-seventh Party Congress (February 25–March 6, 1986) the struggle continued. Gorbachev's plea for a "radical reform of the economy" and for a "turning point" was supported by the new Moscow Party chief, Boris Yeltsin. But there were also prominent voices of caution, particularly Yegor Ligachev, the number two man in the Kremlin, and State President Gromyko. The congress showed that the tug of war continues between the new technocrats who follow Gorbachev, and those elements one might call "bureaucratic traditionalists."

This ambivalent situation was reflected in the changes in the composition of the Politburo, which were fewer than many had expected. Lev Zaikov, a highly qualified engineer from Leningrad, was elevated to full membership, responsible for the military-industrial complex. Among other changes, one should mention the elevation of two officials with long experience in the West to membership in the CC Secretariat: Aleksander Yakovlev, former ambassador to Canada, who took charge of propaganda, and Anatoly Dobrynin, former ambassador to the United States. For the first time since 1961 a woman joined the top leadership: Aleksandra Biryukova became a member of the CC Secretariat.

There will probably be more changes in the course of the next few months, as Gorbachev will continue trying to put his own men on the Politburo. Opposition to Gorbachev is likely to be strongest in the State Planning Committee, in many economic ministries, and in parts of the armed forces, especially since the defense minister, seventy-three-year-old Marshal Sokolov, is only a candidate member of the Politburo, unlike his predecessors, who were full members.

By the spring of 1986, there had not been any substantive changes in Soviet policy, although the style of government has changed. In official speeches, articles, and Party meetings, one can observe a turning away from bureaucratic style and empty rhetoric; there is now open discussion of concrete problems. Some of the most incompetent officials have been fired, and there are timid attempts to fight corruption. There has been a campaign against alcoholism, but the most important problems, i.e., economic reform, the nationality question, and growing social contradictions, have received no attention so far. Gorbachev has hinted at the necessity of economic reforms a number of times, but he has not specified the details of the "reform," and always qualifies his statements by stressing that central planning of the economy has to stay. His promise "to give the enterprises more independence and to increase their interest in the final products within the framework of the planned economy" has so far remained a declaration of intent. The regime's increased struggle against violations of labor discipline is an expression of Gorbachev's intention to couple possible future reforms with harsher disciplinary measures.

Gorbachev's record to date seems to indicate that he wants to improve the productivity and the efficiency of the Soviet system without truly transforming it. Reactivation, mobilization, and modernization—these are the main objectives of the new leadership. So far, there has not been the slightest relaxation in relations with either dissidents or religious communities; only in the mass media and in the cultural sphere has there been a bit more critical "openness" than before. Pressure on the Soviet Union's East European allies has even increased.

To judge him by his performance so far, Gorbachev is neither a neo-Stalinist nor a reformer, but what one might call a "hard-line modernizer" who wants to combine administrative pressure with economic modernization. In the long run, this would appear to be a self-defeating objective.

The personnel changes at the top of the Soviet hierarchy have attracted a lot of attention, but one should not overestimate their significance. Developments in the Soviet Union are less and less determined by the top leadership, and more and more by the nomenklatura. The Soviet ruling class has become almost a closed caste, as the bureaucratic system has ossified. It has become ever more difficult to introduce innovations or reforms, even if they are urgently needed.

This brings us back to the central problem: the Soviet Union's bureaucratic-centralist system. At first sight, it might seem as if an awareness of the Soviet power pyramid's internal workings might be useful only for an evaluation of domestic developments in the Communist superpower. But even this brief overview has shown that Western foreign policy vis-à-vis the USSR has to confront a qualitatively very different system, namely a bureaucratic-centralist dictatorship that deprives its citizens of elementary civil rights. The West is therefore dealing with neither "the Russians" nor "the Soviets," but with a hierarchically structured nomenklatura that concentrates all power in its hands, that enjoys enormous privileges, that is completely isolated from the population, and that is only committed to maintaining and extending its power.

Contrary to a widespread assumption, the difficulties that are inherent in Western relations with the Soviet Union and its allies do not stem from the two opposing economic systems—"socialist" versus "capitalist" countries—but from the deep antagonism between dictatorship and democracy.

The Western democracies therefore have a difficult task. It is essential that they negotiate with the dictatorial governments of these countries about such vital problems as arms limitation and, if possible, disarmament, but they should never forget about these countries' populations, which means that the West should do everything it can to forge direct contacts with the populations of Communist-ruled countries.

2

The Soviet Union Today: Domestic Problems and Contradictions

The Soviet system of the 1980s still bears considerable resemblance to the system Stalin created in the early 1930s in order to harness all available forces to industrialize the then economically backward Soviet Union. Almost six decades have passed since then. The goals of industrialization have been largely achieved, and yet the Soviet Union is still led and controled by a top-heavy, centralist bureaucracy.

The contradictions between the socio-economic demands of an industrial society and the obsolete power structures that govern that society are becoming more apparent as the years pass. The obsolete, centralized, and bureaucratized power structures act as a break on the economic, technological, and cultural development of Soviet society. The dominant bureaucracy opposes urgently needed reforms for fear that it might lose its power and privileges.

The Problems of Industry, Planning, and Technological Innovation

In its early years, the Soviet Union achieved important economic successes. In the 1920s and 1930s, the main aim was to transform an economically backward country into into a mighty industrial power; that has been achieved. Production in the conventional sectors of industry, such as coal, oil, iron, steel, and cement, has increased tremendously. This rapid industrialization was carried out at the price of inflicting great hardship on the population and using the forced labor of millions of prisoners. The absolute concentration of all power in the hands of a bureaucratic-centralist system had a certain justification in the first period of industrialization.

However, the structures Stalin created still exist today. Thus, instead of having a single Ministry of the Economy, as is customary in Western democracies, the Soviet Union still has forty-seven different economic ministries, each overseeing production in one sector of the economy. Many of these ministries exist not only on the Union level, but also in the Union Republics. In addition, the Central Committee of the Communist Party maintains its own industrial departments. There are eleven State Committees that also deal with economic and industrial matters. Finally, all 155 regional Party committees have different economic departments that are responsible for the enterprises of their region.

This centralist administrative apparatus of the Soviet economy is structured vertically, with all orders coming from the top. It is complemented by a large number of officials who are responsible for propagating the official ideology ("agitation," or "agitprop") and organizational activities, and who are supposed to implement "socialist emulation." This administrative apparatus is not only cumbersome, but is also often paralyzed by internal disputes over jurisdiction, a process the Soviet press calls *dublirovanie,* "parallelism." What is more, local, republican, and all-Union bureaucracies often set different (and, at times, mutually incompatible) priorities.

The directors of enterprises are ill-equipped to deal with all the different demands of the various levels of bureaucracy. They enjoy almost no independence; they cannot make the slightest structural changes, or transfer somebody from one department to another without first seeking permission from the authorities. According to official Soviet sources, an enterprise director each year receives an average of 3,000 orders from the economic bureaucracy, and that figure does not include Party orders. In the span of one year, he is supposed to prepare 11,000 reports for his superiors. It is obvious that his available time hardly allows him to read all that is demanded of him and to write all the reports.

To fulfill the plan is what matters most in the Soviet economic system. As a rule, a Soviet factory director gets sixteen quite detailed yearly plans. Their targets are often so high that it is impossible for the factories to fulfill them. Since nonfulfillment of the plans would result in considerable difficulties for the directors, one of their first goals is to obtain fulfillable plans. Most of the time, this "struggle for an easy plan" is not possible without intermediaries: colloquially, these are called *tolkachi* ("pushers"). They are in the service of the factories and travel to Moscow on their behalf in order to convince the authorities to grant "easy" plans to their enterprises. For this task they use all means at their disposal: pleading, begging, threatening, and bribing. Because the *tolkachi* have no legal existence, their expenses cannot appear on official accounts. To pay for their indispensable services, directors have no choice but to falsify the balance sheets of their enterprises.

When it is in difficulty, a Soviet enterprise has two ways of getting out of trouble. First, the management tries as far as possible to produce expensive goods. In this way, at least the financial plan will be fulfilled. Failing this, it will attempt to produce heavy goods (a common process chided as "tonnage ideology" by Soviet officialdom), since another of the sixteen plans is calculated on the basis of weight. If neither alternative proves possible, the director has no choice but to formulate his reports in as positive a way as he can and to present his work as successful after all.

Because in Soviet enterprises the quantitative fulfillment of plans has top priority, quality suffers most of the time, which has led to the proverbial bad quality of Soviet consumer goods. Of course, there are official standards of quality, called "state norms," and most plants have a special "department for technical control." The people who work in these departments, however, are also employees of the plant itself, and therefore it is not in their interest to jeopardize the fulfillment of the plans by exerting effective quality control.

Since most factories depend for their own production on the products of other factories, and since they cannot count on receiving all necessary deliveries on time, directors constantly try to hoard all the machines, tools, and spare parts that they can find, whether they need them for their own production or not. This, too, is widely known and is officially derided as "warehouse ideology." But the directors know what they are doing: even if certain goods cannot be used within the firm, they can still be exchanged for other urgently needed products.

Reenter the *tolkachi.* They are not only Soviet-style lobbyists trying to procure "easy plans," but also act as brokers between individual enterprises. When a firm urgently needs some tools, machines, or spare parts that have not been allotted by the planning authorities or that have not been delivered by other factories, the *tolkach* will travel from one enterprise to another until he finds one that happens to have a stock of the sought-after goods and that in turn needs something the first firm can provide. The *tolkach* arranges for the barter without the knowledge of the economic bureaucracy.

Although operating on the borders of legality, these intermediaries have a very important function: they establish horizontal links between enterprises, links that are not provided for in the vertically organized state planning system.

One of the grotesque features of the Soviet planned economy is that the bonus system of the directors and other leading employees is calculated on the basis of the enterprises' wage funds: the higher the number of employees, the greater the benefits. This means that Soviet factory directors have a personal interest in employing a lot of people. As a rule, Soviet enterprises have far more workers at their disposal than necessary for fulfilling their production goals.

As far as the workers are concerned, the low level of material incentives, and the lack of any possibility of having a word to say in the running of the enterprise, have led to very low working morale. The workers are above all else interested in discovering the easiest way to fulfill the norms, or at least to give the impression that they have been fulfilled. This is how the workers take their revenge for the low wages paid by the state. It also explains why productivity is far lower than in the West, for Soviet workers have lost all sense of responsibility and all incentives to take risks.

How is it, under these conditions, that the USSR has been able to achieve its well-known successes in the arms industry? It has done so by clearly favoring those industries and workers that are involved with it. The process starts during the final examinations at technical universities. Representatives of the armed forces, the Ministry of Defense, and the defense industry are present during these examinations, and have the right to "offer" employment to the best graduates. Thus the factories and research institutes producing and developing armaments get top priority in selecting manpower.

These enterprises are not allowed to publicize their addresses; they are known only by a post office box. Those who work "in the post office box" are paid the highest salaries and enjoy other privileges as well.

Finally, the arms industry is bound to much more serious

standards of quality. Its products are not inspected by internal "departments of technical control," as is the case in civilian enterprises, but by representatives of the Ministry of Defense. These inspectors are independent of the enterprise and represent the interests of the "consumers," namely the army. By favoring the arms industry in all sorts of ways, by effectively controlling the quality of its products, and by making huge sums of money available to the armed forces, the Soviet Union can achieve its impressive successes in the armaments sector, albeit at the expense of the overall economy.

The leadership of the Soviet Union is well aware of the importance of technological innovation. Time and again it has stressed the necessity of introducing new technology into the production process. In practice, however, innovation is slow to come, as industrial managers are reluctant to endanger the fulfillment of their plans. Most of the time the introduction of new technologies and the manufacture of new products necessitates a reorganization of the firm, which might entail temporary losses and jeopardize production schedules. It is therefore far simpler for the management to keep producing the same goods and fulfill the plan.

Whole new administrations have been created to implement technological innovations. There is a State Committee for Inventions and Discoveries and one for Science and Technology. All areas of research have their own research institutes with a plethora of scientific directors, projects, and engineers. Under these conditions, a decision can come about only as a result of a long process of coordination; often the final documents need so many signatures that in the end it becomes very difficult to know who is responsible for what.

Frequently, the Soviet press complains that many research institutes and laboratories have no connection with the production process, and that scientific and technological planning is totally separate from industrial planning. But all these complaints are in vain, for this state of affairs is a logical outcome of the bureaucratic-centralist economic system.

For at least two decades, there have been a number of proposals for overcoming these difficulties. They generally aim at putting an end to the petty tutelage of the authorities over the enterprises, transferring production decisions to lower levels, replacing the current rigid planning of the economy by a more flexible system, and abolishing the cumbersome bureaucratic system of allocating goods and replacing it by a trade system. Plants should be allowed to maintain horizontal links with each other, and the activities of the *tolkachi* should be legalized. The hierarchical structures of Soviet enterprises should be replaced by a creative association among engineers, technicians, and workers in which employees partake in the direction of enterprises.

All of these proposals are formulated by Soviet economic reformers, but the bureaucratic power elite opposes them. It is feared that such innovations might render parts of the bureaucratic power apparatus superfluous. Moreover, the leadership is afraid that a reform of the planning system might have a contagious effect on other areas of Soviet society and thus lead to a liberalization of the system.

The Crisis of Soviet Agriculture

Since 1972, the Soviet Union has been obliged to import millions of tons of grain from abroad in order to prevent a serious food crisis. Even Party officials no longer deny that agriculture has become the biggest problem, the "Achilles heel," of the Soviet Union. The roots of the shortcomings of Soviet agriculture lie in the overblown bureaucracy that has to administer it. In addition to the Ministry of Agriculture, there are the ministries of Meat and Dairy Industries, of Fish Industry, of Food Industry, of Rural Construction, of Land Reclamation and Water Resources, of Tractor and Agricultural Machine Building, and of Machine Building for Cattle Raising and Fodder Products. Within the central Party apparatus, there are Central Committee Secretariats for agriculture, agricultural machinery, light in-

dustry, and food industry. In addition, there are state committees for agricultural machinery and for forestry. Regional Party
committees, as well as regional and district soviets all maintain
various departments in charge of different branches of agriculture, resulting in the usual overlapping of authority and responsibility.

All these authorities are busy promoting Soviet agriculture
and "supervising" the kolkhozi and the sovkhozi, the collective
and the state-owned farms. They give orders, threaten, promise,
inspect, praise, reprimand, administer long questionnaires, organize competitions, distribute medals, direct, and control.
Their only "success" is to keep those active in agriculture from
doing their work.

The 27,000 kolkhozi and 21,000 gigantic sovkhozi are organized in a way that hampers agricultural production. As in industry, the collective and state farms are bound to a system of
norms set, sometimes quite arbitrarily, by the bureaucrats.
There are different norms governing all aspects of work, and the
wages of the farmers depend on their fulfillment. That is why
they, too, are only interested in nominally fulfilling the norms:
quantity is more important than quality.

The wages on the collective and state farms, paid partly in
kind and partly in money, are so low that one cannot speak of
any material incentives for the farmers. And there are no possibilities for developing personal initiatives.

Theoretically, the chairmen of the kolkhozi are elected by a
general assembly of all members, but in practice this is not so.
In reality, the chairmen of the collective farms are appointed
from above, and often they come from other parts of the country,
and at times lack any relevant expertise. These kolkhoz chairmen and their small group of friends are totally independent of
the kolkhoz members and not controlled by anyone. Even the
official Soviet press admits that this state of affairs leads to an
inefficient administration by unproductive bureaucrats. It is natural that under these conditions the kolkhoz members find it
difficult to identify with their collective farms. Productivity is

correspondingly low, and the grain harvest per hectare is only about 60 percent of that achieved in West Germany.

In the Soviet press one can also find other examples of this lack of interest in work. The handling of agricultural machinery is publicly called "barbaric," chaos and fraud reign supreme in the repair shops, and it is widely admitted that the quality of agricultural machines is often so bad that some tractors "literally fall apart." Many collective farms cannot start sowing on time because the necessary machines stand around idle for want of spare parts.

Long distances are another big problem. The Hungarian journal *World Economy* calculated in May 1981 that a large part of the produce is spoilt as a result of long transportation routes and delays. The yearly loss for Soviet agriculture is more than four billion rubles. The long transportation routes have negative effects on animal husbandry, too. Officially, cattle should not be slaughtered more than 150 kilometers from where they were raised. But as the then Central Committee Secretary for Agriculture, Mikhail Gorbachev, once admitted, in some parts of the Soviet Union cattle are transported more than 2,000 kilometers.[6] In the eleventh five-year plan (1981–85), 40 percent of all investments in agriculture were allocated to the construction of grain silos and other storage facilities.

In order to overcome these problems, farm work is often treated like a military campaign: the regime speaks of "harvest battles," "mobilizations," and "breakthroughs." Again and again, large numbers of city dwellers, in the last few years between five and seven million, have to go to the countryside and help out with the harvest. Their departure from the cities results in considerable difficulty for urban enterprises, whose production suffers at harvest time. To this, one has to add the cost of transporting large numbers of people over long distances. The productivity of these urban auxiliaries is very low, as they are unfamiliar with agricultural work.

When the harvest has finally been brought in, and, after the usual losses, has been transported to the cities, manpower is needed to unload the cargo trains. These "transportation campaigns" may lead to more losses. The Soviet writer Lev Kopelev, who participated in a number of them, remembers:

> Workers and professors, lecturers and engineers are mobilized, organized into brigades, and sent to the railway station to unload mostly rotten potatoes . . . as others just stamped around, trampling the potatoes into the dirt. This is how they then reach the shops.[7]

There is nothing inevitable about this sorry state of Soviet agriculture, as the miracle of the "private plots" shows. These are limited to half a hectare per family, but yield bountiful harvests. On these plots the farmers can usually keep one cow with its offspring till the age of one year, one beef cow (up to two years old), one sow, and up to ten sheep and goats. According to the constitution, only a formal decision by a Republic's Council of Ministers can allow these numbers to be exceeded; instead, local authorities often make work on the private plots more difficult. The chairmen of kolkhozi and directors of sovkhozi often prohibit the private sale of meat, potatoes, vegetables, and fruits, arguing that they endanger the production of the public sector. In order to borrow a tractor or a truck for a short time, a collective farmer has to get permission from the chairman of the kolkhoz, the section leader, the brigade leader, and the tractor driver—and often he will not succeed. Sometimes local authorities will bring out the police to stop the sale of the produce from the private plots, occasionally they even go so far as to confiscate it, a practice that has been openly castigated in the Soviet press lately.

The Soviet leadership's attitude toward the private plots varies. When it feels safely entrenched and the harvests are relatively good, it intensifies the struggle against private plots. But when agricultural difficulties and supply problems mount, it becomes more liberal and conciliatory.

Since the spring of 1982, there has been evidence of more

flexibility. At that time, the Russian journal *Economy of Agriculture* approvingly noted that 34.8 million families worked private plots covering a total area of 8.4 million hectares. There were 13.2 million cows, 14 million pigs, 30.2 million sheep and goats, and 387 million fowl.[8]

There are interesting statistics about the "miracle" of the private plots. For instance, they produce 25 percent of all potatoes, vegetables, fruits, eggs, and milk although they constitute only 1.7 percent of all agriculturally usable land.

Soviet officials are well aware of the catastrophic state of agriculture, and there are proposals to remedy the situation. The gist of these proposals is to increase the independence of the collective farms by reducing the numbers of authorities above them, by limiting the state planning schedules, and by giving the kolkhoz members the right to elect their chairmen and most important officials freely. Collective farms and other smaller units such as the agricultural brigades should obtain the right to manage their own affairs independently and to deliver their production at the end of the year. They would be paid according to a fixed scale and would have the right freely to market the greater part of their production. The influence of official agricultural authorities should be limited to encouraging the producing of desired crops by providing material incentives, and to assisting the kolkhozi and sovkhozi by sending them agricultural experts.

Other proposals for reform suggest that the private plots be extended, that all administrative limitations on private agriculture be eliminated, and that the collective and state farms help the farmers by generously providing machinery and transportation, in order that they may freely market their produce.

There could even be a certain amount of cooperation between the collective farms and the private sector. The collective farms, for instance, could sign agreements with the farmers to "lease" them cattle for their private plots and provide fodder and technical assistance. Because the animals would be privately raised and readied for slaughtering, the collective farms would buy them back for a price reflecting the farmers' expenses. In a similar way, other agricultural tasks could be given out to the farmers.

The supporters of these reforms like to point out that their proposals would benefit everybody: the state would save money by limiting its investments in cattle raising, farmers would receive help for their private plots, the collective farms would increase their meat production, and the public would enjoy an improved food supply.

There have been timid attempts to implement such reforms on a limited local basis. Although these reforms were very successful, they were interrupted for fear that they might undermine the bureaucratic apparatus, creating a breathing space in agriculture that might affect other areas of Soviet society.

The Nationality Problem

The importance of the nationality problem is obvious in a country inhabited by more than ninety different nationalities and ethnic groups.

Of the 276 million Soviet citizens, 140 million, or 52 percent, are Russians; almost half the citizens of the USSR are, therefore, non-Russians. Closely related to the Russians are the 45 million Ukrainians and the 10 million Belorussians, both Slavic peoples. The nationalities of the Baltic Republics (Lithuanians, Latvians, and Estonians) number about 5 million, while the various Muslim nationalities (Uzbeks, Kazakhs, Azerbaijanis, Tajiks, Kirgiz, and Tatars) total more than 40 million. In the Caucasus, the Georgians, Armenians, and other smaller nationalities number about 10 million. The other nationalities, including 1.9 million Jews and almost 2 million Germans, can be found all over the vast country.

The vast majority of the Soviet Union's non-Russians did not join the Russian state voluntarily but were forcibly integrated into the tsarist empire by conquest. This was the case of the Baltic provinces, of great parts of Poland, of what is now the

Moldavian Republic (whose inhabitants are Romanians), and of the Central Asian peoples. These areas were therefore de facto colonies, a fact Lenin liked to stress.

With the exception of Finland and Poland, all of the areas conquered by the tsars still belong to the Soviet Union today, even the Baltic states that enjoyed independence in the interwar period. In the 1920s, as a result of Lenin's relatively liberal attitude toward the nationality problem, the Soviet regime promoted the non-Russian peoples' languages and cultures, struggled against Great-Russian chauvinism, encouraged the non-Russians to increase their participation in Party and state affairs, and helped the backward nationalities to develop their own written languages and cultures. All these positive efforts came to an end in the late 1920s with the rise of Stalinism and were increasingly replaced by Russification policies.

Russification denotes all those measures taken by the Party and the state, as well as the cultural and economic bureaucracies, that aim at increasing the influence of Russians and curbing that of non-Russians. To this end, the regime increases the role of the Russian language in the educational establishments of the non-Russian areas at the expense of the local languages, extols Russian traditions in official historiography, and generally increases the proportion of Russian publications. There is more and more talk of a "Soviet People," and the "bourgeois nationalism" of the non-Russian peoples is castigated, while nothing is said about Great-Russian chauvinism. Key positions in the Party and state apparatus, in the army and in the secret police are filled primarily with Russians. Economic activities are increasingly centralized, and the new Soviet constitution of 1977 even mentions the possibility of large economic regions that would take no account of the existing Union Republics.

People in the Soviet Union all have an internal passport that mentions not only their citizenship but also their nationality. When a Soviet citizen applies for a job, he has to hand over his passport to a personnel office, and it is no secret that often Russian applicants get preference over non-Russians.

One of the most important aspects of the nationality problem in the Soviet Union is the varying birthrates among the different nationalities. Since the end of World War II, the birth rate of the Slavic and Baltic peoples has tended to fall, while that of the Muslim peoples has been rising rapidly. Such a disequilibrium can have important political, economic, and psychological consequences in a multinational state such as the Soviet Union. According to some forecasts, by the end of the century the proportion of Russians in the total population will have fallen to 44.3 percent, while all other European nationalities—Ukrainians, Belorussians, Moldavians, Lithuanians, Latvians, and Estonians—will constitute 20.5 percent of the population. The eight major nationalities of the Caucasus and Central Asia, by contrast, will then number about 80 million and rise to 25 percent of the total population.

In the context of Soviet nationality problems one has to mention the case of the "deported nationalities." It all started in September 1941, when all Soviet citizens of German nationality, most of whom had settled in the Volga area in the eighteenth century, were deported to Siberia and Kazakhstan under a policy officially called "enforced resettlement." I myself witnessed this. I was then a student in the English department of the State Pedagogical Institute for Foreign Languages in Moscow. Together with all other Germans, whether they were Soviets or anti-Nazi activists who had sought refuge in the Soviet Union, I was rounded up and had to spend eighteen days on freight trains before we reached our destination in northern Kazakhstan. We were left in the freezing steppe, without shelter, and many did not survive the first winter.[9]

Two years later, from the end of 1943 to March 1944, Stalin deported seven other nationalities who had allegedly collaborated with the enemy: the Crimean Tatars, the Kalmucks, Chechens, Ingushs, Karachai, Balkars, and Meskhetians. They were deported under unspeakable conditions to distant parts of the Soviet Union. Although these peoples were all rehabilitated by Khrushchev in the course of his de-Stalinization policies, and were, with the exception of three of them, allowed to return to their homelands, they have not forgotten the difficult period of their exile. The problem is still a burning one for those nationalities that have still not been allowed to go back to their ancestral regions, namely the Volga Germans, the Crimean Tatars, and the Meskhetians of Georgia.

Also, it is not possible to ignore growing anti-Semitic tendencies in the Soviet Union. Of course, the regime always pretends that there is no anti-Semitism and even points out that it is forbidden in the Soviet Union. Officially, only "Zionism" is struggled against, but this means that those Soviet citizens of Jewish background who want to emigrate to Israel are also harassed. What is more, the official anti-Zionist campaign in the mass media is carried out in such a way that large parts of the Soviet population interpret it as a campaign against Jews as such. Soviet Jews are often harassed and sometimes actually beaten. Jewish members of institutions and government bureaucracies are sometimes demoted or even fired. Lev Kopelev recently noted:

> There are institutes which not only refuse to accept Jews, but even take no half-Jews. Some institutions have even started inquiring after grand-parents, for such a person might get an invitation to go to Israel.[10]

The Russification policies of the Soviet regime have tended to strengthen the national consciousness of the non-Russian peoples. The striving for national identity and more autonomy is especially noticeable in the Ukraine, in Catholic Lithuania, in Protestant Estonia, in Georgia, and in Armenia. In Estonia, demonstrations have occurred in which people carried the old outlawed flag of independent Estonia. Demonstrators in Lithuania have demanded national independence. After it became known in 1978 that the new draft constitution of Georgia omitted any reference to Georgian as the official language of the republic, between thirty thousand and forty thousand people demonstrated in the streets of Tbilisi, the capital. The regime caved in and restored the official status of Georgian. In the Muslim republics of Central Asia, active opposition against Russification has been weak so far, because the standard of living of the local populations, very low before the revolution, has risen considerably in recent times.

Even official Soviet statements have begun to admit the existence of a nationality problem. In contrast to previous claims that the Soviet Union had "solved" the national question and was a "model" for the equality among all nations and peoples, Yuri Andropov declared in his speech on December 21, 1982 commemorating the sixtieth anniversary of the founding of the USSR that in the area of nationality policies "not all problems had been solved," which was not surprising, given that national distinctions would "persist for a long time."

In reality, the situation is even more serious. It is undeniable that Russification has exacerbated national differences in the Soviet Union. The non-Russian peoples are increasingly likely to react against this policy, and their dissatisfaction will affect future developments in the USSR. Here, too, early reforms are urgently needed. Soviet dissidents have formulated a number of proposals: All peoples of the Soviet Union should obtain cultural and economic autonomy, and the regime should end all discrimination against non-Russians in society, in the economy, and in the Party and state apparatuses. Passports and questionnaires should no longer have a space for nationality. The choice of candidates for leading positions should no longer depend on their nationality but be a function only of their professional qualifications and their character. All Party, state, and economic officials in the non-Russian republics should be chosen from each republic's dominant nationality, and those officials who do not belong to the dominant nationality should learn the local language. The deported Volga Germans and Crimean Tatars should be allowed to go back to their traditional homelands. Soviet citizens of Jewish origin should be free to decide whether they want to live in the Soviet Union and enjoy the same rights and duties as all other citizens, or whether they want to emigrate to Israel. The same applies to Soviet citizens of German nationality. Those who want to stay in the Soviet Union should receive as wide a cultural autonomy as possible, like all other peoples.

These and other similar measures would undoubtedly contribute toward an easing of the current tensions. But so far nothing has been done in that direction.

The Decline of Ideology

Marxism-Leninism, the official ideology of the Soviet state, played a very important role in the early years of the Soviet Union. Many people sincerely believed in it and were inspired by it, not only in the revolutionary years under Lenin, but even during Stalin's rule. I remember that during my ten-year stay in the Soviet Union most of my friends and acquaintances believed in it and were ready to make sacrifices and bear severe hardships in order that it might triumph. My own impressions of those years have since been corroborated by the accounts of other people who came to the West after I did.

The ideology of Marxism-Leninism seemed to offer certainty. It seemed to provide infallible methods to explain all phenomena in nature and society and to analyze the historical developments of all nations and the problems of the present time. What impressed many people, especially among the young generation, was the idea that they could attach themselves to a "scientific" theory and belong to a historical movement that was founded on scientific principles.

The main ideas of Marxist dialectics, the emphasis on the inner connections between apparently unrelated phenomena, the principle that all developments and changes result from contradictions, the transition from quantitative to qualitative changes, were all concepts that many found fascinating at the time.

Historical materialism, with its detailed accounts of the interrelations between the economic base and the ideological super-structure, and the analysis of man's history as a development of different socio-economic formations (from primitive commu-nism to a slave-holding society, and then via feudalism to a capitalism that was now reaching its end) seemed for many people in the Soviet Union to be a good analytical account of history so far. Moreover, it provided the basis for understanding the present and for anticipating the transition from capitalism to socialism and eventually communism. They had the cer-tainty, no matter what their difficulties and no matter how many events they found incomprehensible, that what they were going through was the realization of a lawful, albeit painful, transition from capitalism to a new classless society. Reaching the class-less society was an aim that corresponded to the objective laws of history and was morally justified. With the establishment of communism, i.e., a society in which there was no state, no op-pression, no exploitation, and no social classes, poverty and need would disappear forever, and the principle "from each according to his abilities, to each according to his needs" would reign supreme. People would enjoy a totally new type of rela-tionship with each other and the individual would be truly liber-ated. Freedom would triumph at last.

Little of this idealism remains in the Soviet society of today. The decline of ideology has been noticeable since the death of Stalin in 1953. Stalin's successor, Khrushchev, was probably the last top Soviet leader to be thoroughly inspired by Marxism-Leninism. During the period of de-Stalinization (1953–64), he tried to blow new life into the ideology by criticizing the Stalin era and emphasizing the promises that Marxism-Leninism had in store for the future. He did not succeed. Since his downfall, in 1964, the erosion of ideology has been so palpable that one can speak of an ideological vacuum in the Soviet Union.

Many factors have contributed to this most important change of attitude. First, there is the growing discrepancy between the claims of the ideology and the reality of Soviet life. Second, and this applies particularly to those who were initially attracted to

Marxism-Leninism, there are the clearly observable contradictions between the original ideas of Marx and Engels (and, partly, even Lenin) on the one hand, and on the other hand the official ideological textbooks, whose contents are diverging more and more from the original canon.

Other Soviet citizens, especially members of the scientific-technological intelligentsia, turned away from Marxism-Leninism because its Soviet variety seemed incapable of explaining the many novel problems of a modern industrial society. Still others found that Marxism-Leninism was unable to provide convincing answers to humanity's existential problems, to satisfy people's ethical concerns, and to explain, let alone remedy, the moral crisis of Soviet society—the increase in theft, corruption, bribery, and hypocrisy.

The fact that Marxism-Leninism is an obligatory subject in all Soviet institutions of higher education (440 hours of lectures and seminars are devoted to it) did not not stop the erosion of ideology; it actually contributed to it. Courses are one-sided, schematic, and boring, and irrelevant to everyday concerns. Students have to memorize the supposedly infallible theses and concepts of the official ideology and are not allowed to take an active interest in independent varieties of Marxism: the study of Trotsky and Bukharin, of Chinese and Yugoslav communism, of the Frankfurt School and Eurocommunism is still forbidden. All of this led most people in the Soviet Union to the conclusion that Marxism-Leninism is little more than a means for the regime to legitimize its continued rule and to justify its policies. Thus Marxism-Leninism has degenerated so much that most people pay only lip-service to it. Andrei Sakharov has summed up the situation as follows:

Communist ideology, with its promises of a socially harmonious society in which everybody works and enjoys prosperity and freedom, has been transformed into an ideology of bureaucratic totalitarianism in those countries that call themselves socialist.[11]

The ideological vacuum in the Soviet Union has led to a growing sense of resignation among the people, which has resulted in an alarming increase of alcoholism. The losses suffered by the Soviet economy as a result of the absenteeism or shoddy work of drunken workers are enormous. Increasingly, high school students are beginning to drink. Even the armed forces are not immune to drunkenness, and the subject is constantly mentioned in army journals. The problem has reached such dimensions that the Party has begun to react. Since Gorbachev became General Secretary, stern measures have been taken to bring alcoholism under control. The misuse of alcohol on the streets and on public transportation, and attempts by adults to make young people drink alcoholic beverages, are now punished by two years in jail or a minimum fine of 300 rubles. The authorities have begun a "temperance campaign," and in some cities "temperance clubs" have sprung up with official encouragement. Unofficial sources speak of 40 million alcoholics in the Soviet Union (out of a total adult population of 175 million), and the total damage caused by alcohol-related problems is estimated at 180 billion rubles—one-third of the country's GNP. By initiating a serious antialcohol campaign, the new leadership around Gorbachev has demonstrated that it is willing to tackle some of the intractable problems in Soviet society. However, the basic causes of the problem, i.e., the dullness of everyday life, insufficient entertainment, and the loss of ideological convictions, remain unmentioned.

Many Soviet citizens are seeking an ideological alternative to Marxism-Leninism, and of those many are finding it in Christianity. Gone are the times when religious believers could be found mainly among the rural old. More and more young people, among them even sons and daughters of Party officials, profess their faith openly—much to the chagrin of the Party. Another alternative consists in seeking one's historical roots and national traditions. In some intellectual circles one finds a renewed interest in such political alternatives as liberalism, social democracy, democratic socialism, and, increasingly, conservatism. But such ideological reflection remains limited to narrow groups of intellectuals.

Under these conditions it is understandable that the Party's repeated demands for an intensification of ideological work should meet only with disinterest, even rejection. The ideology of Marxism-Leninism, once both a source of inspiration and an instrument for the legitimation of the regime, is no longer a vital force in Soviet society. There can be no doubt that the Soviet regime has lost its ideological legitimation for most people.

The Increasing Importance of Social Problems

The low standard of living and food shortages are the most pressing social problems in the Soviet Union. To be sure, the Soviet standard of living has improved in the last two decades, but it still lags behind that of the Western democracies; in the last two or three years the situation has even partially deteriorated. The average monthly salary is 180 rubles, far less than in the West. Soviet citizens are painfully aware of this gap.

Often no meat, vegetables, or fruits can be found in the state-owned stores, and what food there is, is often of bad quality. The supply of produce is much better at the kolkhoz markets in the cities, but prices are such that the average wage earner can only rarely afford them. Long queues in front of shops are part of everyday life. Even in Moscow, which is relatively well supplied, people have to spend many hours a day hunting for basic necessities. In provincial towns, the situations at times becomes so bad that the authorities have no choice but to introduce a rationing system with coupons. That is why many Soviet citizens from outside Moscow try to do their shopping in the capital.

In the Soviet Union, industry is divided into five categories: the arms industry comes first, food industry last. A worker who is employed in food or consumer industries earns less than one doing equivalent work in the arms industry. Admittedly, the production of some household appliances—refrigerators, radios, and TV sets—has risen significantly in recent years. However, their quality is often inferior, and relative to the earnings of the average citizen they are so expensive that many Soviet consumers cannot afford them. The same is true for textiles and shoes. As soon as good quality textiles, shoes, furniture, or household appliances (often of Yugoslav or Western provenance) arrive on the market, there is such a rush for them that many people have to leave empty-handed.

A severe housing shortage is another big problem for Soviet citizens. As Soviet publications are right to point out, rents are quite low. But these low rents also mean that necessary repair work is often done badly and only after years of waiting. Officially, every Soviet citizen is entitled to nine square meters of pure living space, but this norm is often not attained in big cities such as Moscow, Leningrad, or Kiev. Many people still have to live in so-called communal apartments, where families occupy one room each and share bathroom and kitchen facilities.

Compared to the situation in the Stalin era, housing construction has expanded significantly. Each year, seventy-three new flats per 10,000 inhabitants are built, which still leaves the Soviet Union only in fourteenth place internationally—and behind almost all other Soviet bloc countries. The apartments built during the five-year plan 1976–80 had an average size of fifty-two square meters, half the average size of all those built in West Germany during the same period. There is not enough new housing to satisfy the demand, and newlyweds often have to wait for years before they can set up their own home. Of course, if one is able and willing to pay a big bribe it is quite easy to get a nice place to live.

Public health in the Soviet Union has always been praised as one of the most impressive success stories of Soviet socialism. Medical care is free for all citizens, and nobody would deny the USSR's accomplishments in the building of hospitals and the training of physicians and nurses. But even the Central Committee of the Party recognizes that there are shortcomings. A report published in August 1982 confirmed that in rural areas there are

serious shortages of hospitals, medical instruments, and first aid
stations. Even in the big cities, hospitals are overcrowded and
do not have enough personnel at their disposal. Seriously ill
patients often have to lie on plank beds in hospital corridors for
days before they are operated on. Many hospitals have a serious shortage of bedding. The meals in the hospitals are so bad
that people often have to provide extra food for their hospital-
ized relatives and friends. The report goes on to complain that
the Soviet Union does not produce enough baby food, special
diet food, and eyeglasses. The numbers of maternity centers
were so insufficient that the Soviet leadership, given its interest
in higher birth rates (especially in the Russian areas), decided
to allocate more funds for the establishment of such facilities.

What irks many Soviet citizens most about these difficulties
is that they do not affect everybody equally. Party and state
officials eat in their own dining halls, shop at special department
stores that stock a variety of goods, even imported, and have
luxurious hospitals to cater to their medical needs. Thus the
everyday difficulties I mentioned earlier affect, above all, the
man in the street.

For an evaluation of the social situation in the Soviet Union
it is also indispensable to look at the working and living conditions in the factories, a subject Western publications all too
often neglect. Many arrangements that have become standard
practice in the West and that are taken for granted by workers
are still lacking in the Soviet Union. If, for some reason, production lines have to be stopped, workers are not paid, even if the
stoppage was not their fault. It happens not infrequently that
workers are called upon to work during weekends without receiving overtime pay. Only exceptionally will they get a bonus
for long years of service to the same enterprise. Wages are often
paid with considerable delay, and workers often have to stand
in line for two or three hours to get them.

Workers who want to protest against embezzlement, bribery,
or the nonobservance of occupational safety standards in their
work place have no rights whatsoever, a particularly depressing

feature of the system. If they dare disclose such incidents, they expose themselves to reprisals by the management or the local authorities. Sometimes they are even fired, in which case an official note is made of their dismissal, which makes it more difficult for them to find another job. They might even have their retirement benefits cancelled. That is why workers who have been unsuccessful in claiming their rights at the local level often travel to Moscow in the hope that they might get a chance to air their grievances in the capital. Most of the time, however, they are treated in the same way as they were in their hometowns. Their requests and complaints are rejected, they are sometimes accused of "disturbing the peace," and some of them have even been sent to psychiatric hospitals.

These experiences have led to two attempts to form independent trade unions in the Soviet Union. The term "independent trade union" usually brings to mind the Polish Solidarity movement, which, led by Lech Walesa, spread over all of Poland in the summer and fall of 1980. Unfortunately, it is less well known that as early as 1978 a miner from the Donets Basin, Vladimir Klebanov (born in 1932), founded an "Association of Free Trade Unions of Soviet Toilers" in Moscow. Its forty-three founding members were Soviet workers who had lost their jobs because they had uncovered various cases of abuse of power and had protested against embezzlement of raw materials, bribery cases, and the cover-up of industrial accidents. They invoked article 23, point four, of the United Nations' Universal Declaration of Human Rights, according to which "everyone has the right to form and to join trade unions for the protection of his interests." The association issued a statement pointing out that the official Soviet trade unions no longer fulfilled their original functions and that there were no organizations that represented the interests of the workers. The existing trade unions had their leaders appointed by the Party and were, in fact, mere tools in the hands of management. Elections were only formal exercises, as officials at every level were chosen and "coopted" by those on the next level.

In addition to the defense of workers' social rights, these activists resolved to fight against bureaucratism, bad management, waste, and the irresponsible handling of public property. Only a little later the regime crushed the movement by arresting many of the forty-three founding members and the roughly 100 workers who had shown an interest in joining. Some were sent to psychiatric hospitals, and a few have disappeared without a trace.

It took the opposition only a few months to raise its head again. On October 28, 1978 a meeting was held at the house of M. Morosov in Moscow, during which Western correspondents were informed about the founding of a "Free Interprofessional Association of Toilers," known by its Russian acronym SMOT. Its initiator, forty-five-year-old Alexei Nikitin, had worked for many years as a miner, had joined first the communist youth organization Komsomol and then the Communist Party, and had then worked his way up to study at a polytechnical institute, where he was trained as an electromechanical engineer. Time and again he protested against violations of the labor code, insufficient safety measures, and high-level corruption in the enterprises. As a result, he was excluded from the Party and lost his job in February 1970. His attempts to present his grievances to the leading organs of Party, state, and the Supreme Court only led to more reprisals. He was arrested a number of times and sent to psychiatric hospitals. After his liberation he became one of the founders of SMOT.

In its first declaration, SMOT stated that it was open to workers of all political persuasions. Independently of Party and state, it aimed at defending the economic, social, cultural, and political rights of workers and would endeavor to work on behalf of workers who suffered political persecution. SMOT was necessary because workers had insufficient knowledge of their legal rights, did not enjoy the support of public opinion, were afraid of the possible legal consequences of their actions, and therefore could not enforce their rights. SMOT promised to respect the Soviet constitution and all international agreements signed by the USSR. It planned to provide legal aid to workers who wanted to lodge complaints, and would ask to join the International Confederation of Free Trade Unions in Brussels.

Again, the regime quickly tried to crush these activities, but this time the authorities were not able to bring the activities of SMOT to a complete halt. For a while the underground *SMOT Information Bulletin* appeared at regular intervals.

These attempts at forming independent trade unions are indications of the growing self-confidence of the Soviet Union's industrial labor force, a development also borne out by the increasing number of strikes in a variety of enterprises and regions.

The majority of today's industrial workers are the grandchildren of those peasants who left their villages in the mid-1920s to work in the new industries of the first Five-Year Plan. They are therefore third-generation workers, and history has shown that it is often this generation that has a heightened sense of its worth and that wants to become an independent social force.

Admittedly, many strikes have been put down in the Soviet Union, but in a few cases the authorities have had to make concessions to the workers. Until now, the regime has crushed all attempts at creating independent trade unions. But there are some thoughtful officials who realize that in the long run a modern industrial state cannot solve its labor problems by arresting all independent labor activists. Sooner or later the Soviet regime will have to legalize free trade unions. It is very likely that industrial workers will play an increasingly influential role in the future.

The Degeneration of the System

One of the Soviet Union's most serious domestic problems is the growing practice of corruption and bribery on all levels. In the last ten to fifteen years it has reached such proportions that it now pervades most areas of public life. Let us begin with the lowest level: The shortage of food and consumer goods means that so-called *defitsitni* goods, i.e., goods that are not offered in sufficient quantities and that one can get only by standing in line, are sold secretly to customers willing to pay a higher price. This method is so widespread that it already bears a name: one gets the desired goods *na levo,* which roughly translates as "from the left side." The extra amount of money that the customer pays to the salesperson is sometimes referred to as *podarki,* meaning "gifts." This practice also has to be understood in the light of the low wages paid to salespeople.

Podarki are common not only in stores but also in the public health system. The salaries of physicians and other medical personnel are quite low: a nurse, for instance, can often count on not more than 100 rubles a month, while a pair of ladies' winter boots costs about 150 rubels on the black market. The average salary of a physician is 180 rubles, and only a specialist or hospital director can earn as much as 300 rubles. Under these conditions, doctors and nurses are dependent on their patients' *podarki.* Although medical care is officially free in the Soviet Union, Soviet citizens know that in order to get really good service they have to pay 20 rubles for a consultation, 150 rubles for the delivery of a child, and 300 rubles or more for an operation. And given the shortage of medicine, a Soviet hospital patient is well advised to pay *podarki* to the hospital, too.

Somewhat more has to be spent in order to get repair jobs done in one's apartment or to send one's son or daughter to a particular university. In the Soviet Union, students have to pass a very difficult entrance exam to enter a university, but even this can be avoided. All the parents have to do is to pay a certain sum of money, which is divided among the members of the examination committee, the school director, and other participating officials.

It is still more expensive to obtain a graduation diploma from a university or to be allocated an apartment without having to wait for the usual period of time. To carry out such transactions, it is not only necessary to have large sums of money, but it is also important to have detailed knowledge about who is in charge of what and how much each transaction costs. Needless to say, one also has to observe a certain code of behavior.

The question arises as to how Soviet citizens manage to obtain the rubles to pay for their bribes. The answer lies in what is called the "second," or "parallel," economy. By this we mean all those economic transactions that take place outside the official state economy of the USSR. Official Soviet publications call those active in it "black marketeers" or "speculators." Thus they want to give the impression that their activities are isolated phenomena stemming from the moral deficiencies of individual Soviet citizens. In reality, however, these practices have reached such proportions that a whole new system of socioeconomic relationships has emerged; to me it therefore seems more accurate to use the neutral term "representatives of the second economy."

The apparent inability of the state to produce enough food and consumer goods has led to the emergence of the "second economy." It all started in trade. The perpetual bottlenecks in the state supply system enabled enterprising citizens to set up a parallel, illegal, black market. Private trading groups illegally transport vast quantities of fruit, vegetables, and fresh flowers from the Caucasus and Central Asia to the industrial cities of the north. In the beginning, these entrepreneurs used to book additional seats on domestic flights and personally carried their merchandise. But as trade flourished, they began hiring truck drivers or taxi drivers to convey the goods. In recent times, it has even become possible to bribe railroad officials and thus use state freight trains.

This type of supply is both in the interest of consumers, who get what they want, and in the interest of private businessmen, who make huge profits. Their income enables these businessmen to extend their operations to the production of goods. For this they obviously need labor in addition to capital, but that has become available, too. There are workers, called *shabash-niki,* who have either managed to elude the state employment services or who hold an official daytime job in the state sector. They try to expend as little energy as possible and then spend their evenings working in private enterprises, which pay six or seven times the wages offered by the state. This explains why the *shabashniki* are known to be diligent workers.

Real "underground factories" have thus come into existence. As in the early stages of capitalism, an entrepreneur accumulates his initial capital through trade, then engages a few free workers, gets hold of raw materials and other necessary products, finds a well-hidden site to set up his factory, organizes production, and finally sells his goods through salesmen who are also in his pay.

These private enterprises produce much-needed consumer goods of much better quality than those produced by the state factories; products like shoes, household articles, fashionable clothing, cosmetics, leather goods, electrical appliances, knitware, blue jeans, and radio equipment that facilitates the reception of Western broadcasts. At one point there was a very successful, privately owned car repair shop that easily outperformed its state-owned competitors. Still more surprising was the case of a Caucasian village that privately produced fashionable woollens and put out a catalogue to enable people all over the Soviet Union to order their products through the mail. A shoe manufacturer with ten to fifteen workers and about sixty private salespersons managed to earn over a million rubles per year. The employees kept the secret well and it took the authorities a year and a half to uncover the enterprise.

Private enterprise is so successful in the Soviet Union that even state organizations have begun occasionally to use their illegal services. Kolkhoz or sovkhoz directors and other local authorities turn more and more to private enterprises to get important repairs done, all attempts to get things done through the normal channels having failed. The most recent development is that private businessmen in different parts of the country have begun to establish networks, which enables them to offer their services on a nationwide scale.

Profits are very high, but so are the risks involved. Private economic activity is not only strictly forbidden in the Soviet Union, but is actively combatted by specially created authorities. The most important of these is the Department for the Struggle Against Theft of Socialist Property, known under its Russian acronym OBKSS. When the authorities uncover some kind of private economic activity, all those involved are arrested and are liable to be condemned to death for "economic crime."

To avoid these dangers, private businessmen spend large parts of their profits bribing officials, especially those of the OBKSS. These bribes, sometimes called *prinoshenie* ("tribute"), are paid at regular intervals, either to get the authorities to leave the enterprise alone, or to reach specific agreements with Party or state officials. These officials, having witnessed the extraordinary success of the "second economy," are themselves increasingly turning toward capital accumulation. One of these "underground millionaires" of the Party and state apparatus was a certain Firidun Kadyrov, who used his position as Minister for Social Affairs of the Azerbaijan Republic to rent out cars that were meant for invalids, to healthy people who were unable to rent a car in any other way. In the course of his long activity he made enough money to be able to afford two apartments in Baku, the capital, and a dacha with a swimming pool and an orangery. As a hobby he kept black swans. When he was arrested, the police found a valuable collection of paintings, porcelain, silver, and jewelry, and more than seventy pounds of gold.

A director of a technical school in Uzbekistan managed to become rich by selling graduation diplomas. When he was arrested, it turned out that he owned three cars, forty carpets, and gold, jewelry, and cash worth about 1.2 million rubles—the equivalent of 600 average yearly salaries.

Each of these examples stands for dozens of similar cases reported at length in the Soviet press, particularly during Andropov's anticorruption campaign in the spring of 1983. There are probably hundreds of other cases that are either not uncovered or that the Party leadership prefers not to talk about. Primarily this is because in recent years more and more officials (in the West, we would say "civil servants") of the central ministries in Moscow have turned to such underground activities, sometimes involving smuggling with the West. Their connections reach into the highest levels of the Soviet leadership.

The growing willingness of many Soviet officials to partake in illegal activities can no longer be explained in terms of some individuals' moral failures. Rather, it reflects a serious change within the system. The Party and state apparatuses and their officials, who fulfilled a socially necessary and useful role in the early years of Soviet history (for instance, during the first five-year plan or World War II), have long since ceased to be the engine of development and have instead come to act as a brake on it. The less these officials are driven and inspired by the official ideology, to which most of them pay lip-service anyway, the more they are likely to cater to their own personal interests, and that leads to corruption, favoritism, careerism, egoism, and cynicism.

Here, too, we should not overlook the other side of the coin: The same Party and state apparatuses also contain honest and thoughtful officials who are aware of the problems, who give their origins and consequences serious and critical thought, and who are sympathetic to reforms.

The problems and contradictions that I have tried to sketch out above concern a variety of aspects of contemporary Soviet communism: the economy, technological innovation, agriculture, the national question, the loss of ideological motivation, social problems, and the increasing degeneration of the power apparatus itself. What is more, the Soviet system as it exists now contains no mechanisms to improve matters and to apply the necessary solutions to the problems. There is not even the slightest possibility to discuss them publicly.

All of this is relevant not only to the citizens of the Soviet Union but also to East-West relations. There is an obvious contradiction between the mighty Soviet Union that is willing and capable of exerting its influence in remote corners of the world, and a country that is domestically plagued by serious problems, contradictions, and weaknesses.

When looking at today's Soviet Union, one should therefore not pay exclusive attention to its military might, but also consider the system's internal problems. The Soviet Union of the 1980s is more than just a territorial base for SS-20 missiles.

3

Characteristic Features of Soviet Foreign Policy

Many analyses of East-West relations do not take into account the special characteristics of Soviet foreign policy. Sometimes it is assumed that the Soviet Union respects customary practice on the international level. According to this view, there can be no "characteristic features" of Soviet foreign policy, and some go so far as to suggest that East-West relations boil down to relations between two similar superpowers, the USSR and the United States.

This is not so. Soviet foreign policy is different in a number of ways. Its special features seem to me to be the following:

• the interaction of Soviet state interests (often continuing those of tsarist Russia) with certain aspects of international communism;

• the importance of the Soviet principle of "international correlation of force";

• the expansionist tendencies of the nomenklatura, limited by its reluctance to take unnecessary risks;

• the special way of Soviet decision making in foreign policy;

• the special Soviet negotiating strategy;

- the use of political language to further Soviet interests;
- the direct appeal to the people of other countries, hoping that "pressure from below" will induce those countries' leaders to do what the Soviets would like them to do;
- their control over a plethora of nongovernmental international organizations, such as the World Peace Council, that support Soviet foreign policy objectives.

It seems to me that the special characteristics of the Soviet Union's foreign policy are of great importance to any evaluation of East-West relations. Moreover, only these special features explain why it is that the Soviet Union can successfully exert its influence as a superpower everywhere in spite of its economic, political, and social weaknesses.

From Ivan I to the Present: Continuity in Russian Foreign Policy?

This question has preoccupied experts for decades: is Soviet foreign policy merely a continuation of traditional Russian great power politics, or is the USSR the center of an ideologically based world revolution?

At first sight, geographic factors alone would seem to militate in favor of the first thesis. The Soviet Union has almost unlimited space, almost no natural borders, and no warm water ports. Its gigantic Eurasian territory contains almost all necessary mineral resources. These are the preconditions for a relatively autarchic economy and a strong military potential.

Russia's rise to the status of a great power was continuous, although occasionally interrupted by setbacks. A comparison between the small Muscovite principality of Ivan Kalita (1325–40) and the empire of Tsar Nicholas II is indeed impressive: no other existing state can claim such a continuous expansion, although one should add that this expansion was achieved only through hard-fought struggles and conquests. George Kennan, who has been studying Russian history and Soviet problems for decades, concluded that:

Their history has known many armistices between hostile forces; but it has never known an example of the permanent peaceful coexistence of two neighboring states with established borders accepted without question by both peoples. The Russians therefore have no conception of permanent friendly relations between states. For them, all foreigners are potential enemies.[12]

According to Kennan, a typical tactic of Russian foreign policy consisted of intimidating the enemy with the terrifying might of Russia, while leaving it unclear to what extent this might would actually be used. In this way, the Russians could make sure that all their desires and goals would be taken into account and accorded special respect.

Messianism is another component of Russian tradition. Let us not forget that Moscow was proclaimed the "third Rome," that Russia claimed to be the leading force of Christianity, and that the tsars often used the term "people's liberation" to justify their attempts to increase Russian influence in Eastern and Southeastern Europe.

The suspicion of foreigners that characterizes today's nomenklatura system also has roots in Russian history; many foreign travelers of past centuries have insisted time and again on Russian xenophobia. The close connection between internal repression and external expansion has also been emphasized by many West European observers, including Marx and Engels.

The strong influence of the army on tsarist Russia's domestic politics and foreign policy and the highly developed militarization of society this influence entailed, the extremely hierarchic power structure of tsarism, the brutal repression of critical thought and the at times panic fear of libertarian ideas that might endanger the dictatorial system: all these elements are believed by historians and observers to have conditioned the later development of Soviet communism.

A similar continuity can be observed in the directions of Russian and Soviet foreign policy: the striving to increase Soviet influence in Finland, the Baltic states, Poland, the Balkans, Iran,

Afghanistan, Manchuria, and Korea are all rooted in Russian foreign policy. The crushing of the Hungarian revolution of 1848 by tsarist troops and the cruel suppression of a number of uprisings and revolutions in nineteenth-century Poland also have astonishing parallels in recent Soviet history.

Soviet leaders tend to confirm this continuity in their attitude toward Russian history. Soviet textbooks and films glorify Ivan the Terrible and Peter the Great almost without reservation, and this is also true for the tsarist generals Suvorov and Kutusov and to the admiral of the Russian fleet, Nakhimov. Not a few contemporary Soviet officers proudly wear Suvorov, Kutusov, and Nakhimov medals. The Soviet regime makes increasing reference to Russian historical traditions and celebrates victories of tsarist generals. Even the subordination of non-Russian peoples is cause for celebration in today's Soviet Union, although this subordination is reinterpreted as having been "peaceful."

The Soviet leadership has clearly been aware of this continuity. This is evinced by the fact that Stalin personally intervened to prohibit the publication in the Soviet Union of Friedrich Engels' 1890 essay "The Foreign Policy of Russian Czarism." On the occasion of the twentieth anniversary of the start of the First World War the publishers of *Bolshevik*—the then official journal of the Party and predecessor of today's *Kommunist*—wanted to print it in a special issue of July/August 1934. However, Stalin, in a letter to the Politburo dated June 19, 1934, wrote that Engels' essay had a number of shortcomings and was therefore unsuited for publication.

Nobody in the Soviet Union got wind of the matter. Only seven years later, in May 1941, did things suddenly change. I was then a student in Moscow and remember that day as if it were yesterday. A few friends came to visit me and put the latest issue of *Bolshevik* on the table. There it was in the May 1941 issue: an article by Stalin! That was quite an event, for Stalin had not written an article since 1934, confining himself to speeches. We read the article with great excitement. Stalin explained all the points that Engels had got wrong in "The Foreign

Policy of Russian Czarism"—but unfortunately we could not read a single line of the original Engels article. Even then I hoped that one day I would be able to get my hands on it.

This proved to be very easy when I arrived in the West in late autumn 1950. The article had been published in the May 1890 issue of *Neue Zeit,* a social democratic monthly edited by Karl Kautsky; since then it has been reissued a number of times in the West.[13] In this essay, Engels provided an account of tsarist Russia's foreign policy that was both informative and powerful. A number of times he emphasized the close link between expansion without and oppression within, which probably was what moved the Soviet dictator to prevent its publication, for Engels' analysis applied equally to the Soviet Union under Stalin. Here are a few key sentences from this important text:

So far as internal politics is concerned . . . the impotence of the Czarist regime lies exposed to the light of day. However, it is necessary not only to know the weaknesses of the enemy, but also his elements of strength. And foreign policy is unquestionably the side on which Czarism is strong, very strong . . .

[The Russian diplomatic corps is a] secret society which has raised the Russian empire to its present plenitude of power. With iron perseverence, eyes set fixedly on the goal, not shrinking from any breach of faith, any treason, any assassination, any servility, distributing bribes lavishly, never overconfident following victory, never discouraged by defeat, over the dead bodies of millions of soldiers and at least one Czar, it is this gang . . . which has made Russia great, powerful, and feared, and has opened up for it the way to world domination.

Russia is becoming daily more Westernized; . . . But the incompatibility of absolute Czarism with this newly evolving society grows in the same proportion. Constitutional and revolutionary oppositional parties are being formed and the regime can dominate them only through increased brutality. And the Russian diplomatic corps sees with consternation approach the day when the Russian people will take part in the debate . . .

The entire danger of a world war will vanish on the day when the situation in Russia permits the Russian people to draw a thick line under the traditional policy of conquests of the Czars, and to attend to their own vital interests at home —interests which are threatened in the extreme—instead of phantasies of world conquest.

As if on an inclined plane, Europe is sliding with increasing speed into the abyss of a world war, a war of as yet unheard-of extent and violence. Only one thing can now halt it: a change of the regime in Russia.[14]

It was only many years later, during Khrushchev's de-Stalini-zation, that the taboo around this text was broken. The new complete edition of the works of Marx and Engels that appeared in the 1960s both in Moscow and in East Berlin finally included Engels' article of 1890. But for obvious reasons it is never quoted in the Soviet bloc.

How Important Is World Revolution?

Contemporary Soviet foreign policy transcends Russian-tsarist great power politics; it aims at worldwide change. The USSR acts as a global power.

To be sure, at present, world revolution is a far less important goal of Soviet foreign policy than it was in Lenin's time or even in the early years of Stalin. Important pronouncements of Lenin concerning world revolution are no longer mentioned in the Soviet Union, particularly those in which he had said that the destiny of the Soviet Union depended on the success of revolutions worldwide. Withal, the ultimate goal of world revolution is still a significant component of Soviet foreign policy, one that has both ideological and practical-political aspects.

The ideological aspect consists in the fact that the official concept of the "world revolutionary process" is an important component of the official ideology, above all in the political conceptions of Marxism-Leninism known as "scientific communism." According to this concept, the world is now in a revolutionary transitional period in which capitalism is being replaced by a new socio-economic formation: socialism and eventually communism.

This transition is the core element of the "world-revolutionary process." The latter is driven by three main forces. First, the ruling Communist parties of the Soviet bloc, to which accrues the task of strengthening the "socialist world system" and which have "actively and decisively to support all forms of struggle for liberation against imperialism." Second, the Communist parties of capitalist countries, whose main task, according to official formulations, consists in "toppling the capitalist order by socialist revolution." Third, the liberation movements of the Third World, whose goals are defined as breaking the dominance of foreign, i.e., Western, capital in their countries, creating centrally planned economies, bringing about agrarian reform, and entering an alliance with the socialist camp.

The practical and political aspects of this world-revolutionary component consist above all in the strengthening of the international Communist movement with its total of ninety-four Communist parties, the overwhelming majority of which still toe the Moscow line and are subsidized and guided by the Soviets. Soviet leaders hold regular official meetings with representatives of Western Communist parties, and the resulting communiqués stress the solidarity and agreement between them.

The semi-official journal of international communism, *Problems of Peace and Socialism* (the English and North American edition is called *World Marxist Review*), dates back to 1958 and appears in forty languages. It is distributed in 145 countries and has a total circulation of over half a million, half of it outside the Soviet bloc. Representatives of sixty-three Communist parties belong to its editorial council, while the narrower editorial board includes members of fifteen Communist parties. The chief editor is a nomenklatura functionary. Leading representatives of the CPSU, of other Communist countries, and of Western Communist parties publish articles in this journal so as to stress their common interests. The journal also organizes regular conferences for Communist parties of various countries around such themes as the class struggle in capitalist countries, national liberation struggles in Africa and Asia, the special role of liberation movements in Latin America, and the problems of the peace movement.[15]

To cement the close ties between the Soviet Union and foreign Communist parties, the Soviet Union provides one- and two-year courses of political and ideological training for foreign Communist officials at the international section of the Soviet Party Academy.

The International Department of the CPSU Central Committee oversees the activities of all pro-Soviet Communist parties. It has been headed for more than a decade by a candidate member of the Politburo and employs more than 200 full-time officials. The International Department maintains contact with Communist parties in the West and is also responsible for the guidance and support of Communist and liberation movements in the Third World, provided they serve the interests of Soviet foreign policy.

Most people in the West have become so accustomed to the activities of the international Communist movement that they no longer perceive its importance; let us therefore imagine a Western equivalent of it. There would be regular receptions by the U.S. president, the British prime minister, and the German chancellor for dissident groups of Soviet bloc countries, followed by communiqués expressing total agreement. There would be official or at least semi-official international conferences at which leading Western statesmen as well as representatives of Soviet and East European dissident and opposition groups would take part. There would be a common journal of all democratic countries, perhaps called *World Democratic Review*, which would appear in forty languages and have a circulation of over half a million. It would publish articles by leading representatives of NATO countries and of oppositional dissident and human rights groups from the East. Western countries would have an official textbook for students in all NATO countries that would argue in great detail why the current regimes of the Soviet bloc countries have to be toppled and that would also present all the forces, forms, and methods whereby this change could be achieved. This comparison alone throws light on the importance of international communism in Soviet foreign policy.

Soviet foreign policy thus has a dual nature, as traditional Russian great power politics work hand in hand with Communist aims of world revolution. Thus it is only natural that the Soviet regime should indiscriminately celebrate the anniversaries of battles successfully fought by tsarist generals as well as the birthdays of Marx and Engels, the anniversary of the Paris Commune of 1871 as well as the founding of the Communist International.

The interaction of these two components creates the dynamic of Soviet foreign policy and enables Soviet leaders to stress alternatively national-Russian or international-Communist aspects in their legitimation of their foreign policy moves, depending on what population groups they try to address.

The "International Correlation of Forces"

The nomenklatura also pursues its main objective, the consolidation and extension of its power, in foreign policy. For this it tries to transfer to other Soviet bloc countries all the main characteristics of the Soviet system: unrestrained rule of the Party apparatus, total control from above, and central planning of the economy.

In East-West relations, the nomenklatura strives to strengthen the Soviet Union's military might and to extend its sphere of influence to more countries. The nomenklatura is by its very nature expansionist. It knows that it can keep and consolidate its power inside the Soviet Union only if it can point to foreign policy successes:

> For the vulgar patriotic public the glory of victory, the series of conquests, the power and glitter of Czarism fully outbalances all its sins, its despotism, all its injustices and arbitrary actions; the boastfulness of chauvinism fully compensates for all kicks received.[16]

This formulation of Engels' 1890 essay, too, has kept its validity for the Soviet Union of the 1980s.

In this context, the Soviet conception of the "international correlation of forces" plays an important role. Contrary to the West, where the balance of power is conceived of mainly in military terms, in Soviet terminology it also includes the economic, political, and moral-ideological forces of both systems, as well as the capacity of the two systems' leaders to make use of these forces in a politically fruitful manner. Needless to say, in all these areas the nomenklatura strives to change the balance of power in its favor.

According to official Soviet publications, a long-term shift of the "international correlation of forces in favor of the socialist camp" is contingent on four factors. First, the Soviet Union, the main power of the socialist camp, must continue to become stronger. Second, the role of the "socialist world system" has to be expanded. Third, the unity of the "three main revolutionary currents"—the Communist Parties of the Soviet bloc and the capitalist countries, and Third World national liberation movements—must be enhanced. Finally, the increasing likelihood of crisis situations in Western capitalist societies is closely intertwined with the economic, political, military, and ideological strengthening of the Soviet bloc.

Economic Interests and Risk-Consciousness

The expansionist tendencies of the nomenklatura and its consistent efforts to shift the balance of power in its own favor do not mean that Soviet leaders would be willing unnecessarily to risk armed conflict. As already noted, the Soviet nomenklatura always keeps in mind all aspects of the balance of power, not only its military side. Therefore, it knows that it cannot afford to let East-West tensions build up beyond a certain point, as that would endanger economic and technological cooperation with the West. The nomenklatura depends so much on this cooperation that it accepts a certain degree of moderation in its foreign policy.

Moreover, since the ruling stratum does not want to jeopardize its position of power, it has become very risk-conscious. It is an important principle of Soviet foreign policy that all power relationships be observed carefully and that all uncalculable risks be avoided. If one looks closely, one will note that most aggressive actions of Soviet leaders have been directed against weak countries that had no powerful allies at the time of the aggression. The occupation of Poland in September 1939 (when the country had already been defeated by Hitler Germany); the "Winter War" against Finland (November 1939–March 1940); the occupation of Estonia, Latvia, and Lithuania in the summer of 1940 (after the Hitler-Stalin Pact had put these three nations in the Soviet sphere of influence); and, finally, the suppression of the emancipatory movements in Hungary (November 1956) and Czechoslovakia (August 1968, the "Prague Spring"), two countries that belong to the Soviet sphere of power, are all cases in point.

In conflicts with a higher risk potential, such as the Berlin blockade in 1948–49, the Korean War in 1950, the Berlin ultimatum of 1958, and the Cuban missile crisis of 1962, Soviet leaders realized after a while that they had moved forward too boldly and therefore tried to find a way out of the dangerous situations they had created. The unwillingness of the Soviet leadership to take great risks can also be seen by their reluctance to get militarily involved in distant parts of the world. In such areas, they prefer to leave military involvements to their allies, such as the Cubans, so as to avoid a direct military confrontation.

In addition, Soviet leaders fear that their country might not be able to bear the economic burden of an escalating arms race. This in itself acts as a moderating influence on their foreign policy. Admittedly, with a national income half that of the United States, the Soviet Union has reached near strategic parity with their rival. Nevertheless, there are clear limits to how much longer it can sustain an unrestrained arms race. The Kremlin leaders are aware that they cannot indefinitely increase the military budget and expect the population to go on tightening their belts; this could lead to growing discontent, and even unrest, and would thus endanger the power position of the nomenklatura. And this is precisely what they want to avoid at all costs.

Decision Making in Soviet Foreign Policy

Soviet leaders can make foreign policy decisions without having to take account of public opinion, without having to face parliamentary debates, and without having to deal with journalists asking troublesome questions in interviews or at press conferences. Secrecy is always maintained, and they need not worry about "leaks" to the press. All this means that Soviet leaders have an extraordinary freedom to formulate long-term foreign policy objectives and to realize them.

Foreign policy decisions are taken jointly by the Ministry of Foreign Affairs and by the Central Committee of the Party. The latter's Department for Relations with the Communist Parties of Socialist Countries is responsible for harmonizing the policies of the various Communist Parties of the Soviet bloc. Although the Ministry of Foreign Affairs is also responsible for relations with Communist countries at the governmental level, its main task is to attend to relations with capitalist and Third World countries. It is important to note the continuity in the Ministry of Foreign Affairs. Of the six foreign ministers that the Soviet Union has had in its sixty-seven-year history, four (Chicherin, Litvinov, Molotov, and Gromyko) have served for more than a decade. Andrei Gromyko occupied his post for twenty-eight years (1957–85) before he was replaced by Eduard Shevardnadze, erstwhile First Party Secretary of Georgia.

All major foreign policy decisions are taken by a small group of top leaders. Five of these—the General Secretary, the Foreign Minister, the Defense Minister, the head of the KGB, and the Prime Minister—are usually also full members of the Politburo. When economic questions are to be discussed, the Minister for Foreign Trade and at times leading representatives from the State Committee for Science and Technology and the State Committee for Foreign Trade join the other top leaders. When relations with other Communist countries are on the agenda, leading officials of the Central Committee's department for relations with the ruling parties of the Soviet bloc countries may also be invited to take part in the discussions. Increasingly, high army officers play a role in the foreign policy decision-making process. This is especially true for security and defense policy; for military actions inside the Soviet bloc, such as the invasion of Hungary in 1956, of Czechoslovakia in 1968, and the proclamation of martial law in Poland in December 1981; and lastly for foreign policy actions with important military aspects, such as the invasion of Afghanistan in December 1979. The security apparatus, too, has a certain influence on foreign policy. The most powerful leaders of the KGB, Beria during the Stalin era and Andropov during Brezhnev's rule, were both full members of the Politburo and had their word to say regarding foreign policy.

The concentration of all foreign policy decisions in the hands of such a small group of leaders has both advantages and disadvantages. On the one hand, it guarantees resoluteness, continuity, and the coordination of all foreign policy activities according to a coherent plan. On the other hand, however, the inevitable lack of public and open discussion and the absence of any independent fact-finding means that the top leaders are more likely to miscalculate. This danger is heightened by the fact that they base many of their decisions on information provided by the secret services. But this information is not chosen according to objective criteria, since Soviet leaders are accustomed to seeing the world through the filters of the dogmas with which they have been brought up. This often leads them to overestimate Soviet capabilities and to underestimate the potential force of their adversaries, all according to the principle of "Leninist Optimism," which is considered to be an important virtue for all party officials. For Soviet policymakers there can be no doubt about the inevitable and unstoppable advance of socialism and communism on a world scale, since this advance is prescribed by the objective laws of history. Soviet leaders are by no means oblivious to the dangers inherent in such an attitude: they even criticize it ideologically by disparaging it as "adventurism" and "subjectivism." However, this does not mean that they always succeed in overcoming it.

In addition, Soviet leaders are wont to misinterpret the politics and social structures of Western countries. They are, of course, not alone in falling victim to this fallacy, for it is natural to evaluate other countries by applying to them the standards and criteria of one's own system. In the case of Soviet decision-makers, it means that they often tend to overestimate the influence of economic interest groups on the policies of Western governments, having been taught to consider Western systems as "state monopoly capitalism" in which the monopolies are the true centers of power and the official governments are mere tools in their hands. Soviet officials also vastly overestimate the West's capacity for overall planning and coordination, both regarding individual countries and NATO. They have been brought up with the notion that there is an "imperialist global strategy" elaborated by some central organization somewhere in the West. It prepares detailed plans for the economic, political, and military confrontation with the Soviet Union, plans that are binding on all NATO-member countries.

The highest officials probably do not take these theses very seriously, but over the years they have internalized the type of argumentation inherent in them to such a degree that they do not challenge its underlying assumptions. Their own experience teaches them to pay great attention to the planning and coordination of policies; hence they tend to assume that this is the case in the West, too. Soviet officials have great trouble comprehending the confusion and the frequent accidents in the political life of Western democracies. Consequently, individual actions or declarations of Western governments are often interpreted as "steps" or "building blocs" of a "master plan," and Western politicians' frequently casual remarks are closely scrutinized for clues to such a grand strategy.

Just as they overestimate the role of central and coordinated planning in Western political systems, Soviet officials tend to underestimate the importance of Western parliaments, mass media, and public opinion. Of course, the higher-level officials know full well that in Western democracies parliamentary committees and the mass media are not mere "transmission belts" for the political leaders. Nevertheless, they often misjudge the extent to which these institutions are free to criticize governmental action. As a result, when articles critical of Western or Soviet politicians, or of certain aspects of East-West relations, appear in the Western press, this is often believed by Soviet officials to be inspired by Western governments themselves. Similarly, when Western parliaments engage in open criticism of the Soviet Union or, as happened in the United States, go so far as to refuse to ratify a treaty negotiated by their own government, this is seen by some Soviet officials as a skillful maneuver to sabotage already concluded treaties.

With the exception of specialists in international law, Soviet officials often have a tendency to belittle the constitutional and legal constraints under which Western negotiators are bound to operate. They tend to brush aside any reference to these constraints and consider them "excuses." This underestimation of the mass media, public opinion, and parliaments, of laws and constitutions, has little to do with ideology. Rather, it reflects the Soviet officials' own life experience. A Soviet official is accustomed to a state of affairs where Party resolutions are far more important than laws and the constitution, where the Supreme Soviet always confirms Party decisions unanimously. No Party official would ever dream of taking into account the constitution and the law in carrying out a particular action. As for the mass media, they can be counted on unfailingly to support and popularize all Party decisions. For a Soviet official, it is therefore difficult to imagine that in the West there are people who take constitutions and laws seriously and who respect and take into consideration the independence of the media and parliamentary committees—not necessarily because they want to, but because they have to.

How the Soviets Negotiate

Many Western diplomats have given us first-hand accounts of how the Soviets conduct negotiations. In preparing such negotiations, the Soviets pursue definite objectives that go beyond the diplomatic talks per se. In all countries of the world it is customary that visiting foreign diplomats, politicians, and journalists are taken to places that have a special historical or cultural significance. In the Soviet Union, however, visitors are only rarely taken to places that played a major role in the history and culture of the Russians or the non-Russian peoples. Instead, every attempt is made to show such visitors places, houses, and memorials from recent Soviet history: the battleship *Aurora,* which played a big role in the Bolshevik coup in 1917; the Smolny Institute, where the Bolsheviks prepared their seizure of power; Lenin's study and the Museum of the Revolution; the Lenin Mausoleum; and the various monuments commemorating the "Great Patriotic War" of 1941–45. Needless to say, these places of worship do not so much commemorate the suffering, deprivations, and sacrifices of the Soviet population as to glorify military heroism and give central importance to that period in Soviet history when the regime had to fight off foreign interference and thus defended the national interest.

To emphasize the specifically Communist dimension of the Soviet Union even further, Soviet hosts often attempt to hold negotiating sessions, not at the seat of the government, but at that of the Party Central Committee. Unfortunately, many foreign dignitaries unthinkingly accept this. At times, even communiqués and international agreements are signed by the Soviet side in the name of the Communist Party, rather than in the name of the government. This point may seem trivial to a pragmatic Western observer, who may find it only natural that those in the USSR who wield real power should also be the hosts and negotiating partners of Western leaders. Not so the Soviet leaders themselves. Let us not forget that it is *governments,* not ruling parties, that maintain diplomatic relations, negotiate treaties, and sign agreements. By accepting to deal with Soviet leaders *qua* CPSU officials, Western visitors implicitly sanction one-party rule in the Soviet Union and let themselves be used by their hosts to enhance the prestige of the Soviet regime. This, it is hoped, will legitimize the nomenklatura in the eyes of the population.

In their reports and memoirs, foreign statesmen and diplomats have stressed the following points about Soviet negotiating strategy:

Opening Speeches

Soviet negotiators like to begin proceedings with long-winded and quite ceremonial speeches that Westerners tend to find tiresome and boring. This practise results from a long-standing, ideologically induced habit to go from the general to the particular. The "international correlation of forces" is evoked first to provide a general background, then the field is narrowed to the particular part of the world that is to be discussed, and finally attention is focused on the subject of the negotiations.

Quite often the opening speeches are used to make accusations against the foreign country whose representatives are at the negotiating table. The latter are thus put in an awkward position: should they deny the accusations and thereby further delay the start of the real talks? It often happens that the foreign dignitaries do not bother to do so, which gives the Soviets a psychological advantage right from the outset.

The Leninist "Principle of Initiative"

This consists in always trying to keep the initiative. Concretely, it means that Soviet negotiators try never to respond to proposals made by their partners in the course of the talks, but rather confront them with long series of detailed proposals of their own. In the West, public opinion is often divided in its evaluation of such proposals, and the question is often debated whether they are "sincere" and "realistic," or whether they merely serve Soviet propaganda. The sad result is that this debate often extends into the Western delegations themselves, giving yet another advantage to the more monolithic Soviet negotiating teams. There can be no clear-cut answer to this question, for it is wrong to phrase it in terms of either-or: as a rule, Soviet proposals to the West contain *both* pragmatic *and* propagandistic components.

Purposefulness and Coherence

Once they have set themselves a goal, Soviet leaders never give it up without a compelling reason; even occasional defeats and setbacks cannot deter them from pursuing it. They stick to their demands and proposals until public opinion in the West gets used to these and begins to regard accommodation with the Soviets on their own terms as the most "realistic" alternative. Furthermore, Western negotiators are under constant pressure from their own public opinion to come up with "concrete results," and to be "realistic," which often means that they have to give up positions they had taken at the outset of the talks and thereby adapt to Soviet proposals.

In the West, there is a certain readiness to abandon objectives if after a while there is no progress in attaining them. The Soviets, by contrast, steadfastly stick to their long-term objectives. If they cannot attain them immediately, they are patient, accept temporary setbacks and defeats, and later try to get what they want by other means of political strategy.

Agreements "in Principle"

After long and tiresome talks, often fraught with suspicion, accusations, and reproaches, Western diplomats and politicians often consider it a relief to come up with some document, vague as it may be, as public opinion at home regards almost any agreement as a "success." At this point, Soviet negotiators often propose that the two sides reach agreements "in principle." The Soviets use these for their own purposes, in order either to circumvent their implementation or to reinterpret them so drastically that they end up serving only Soviet objectives. Usually these agreements contain no provision for verification.

A classic example for this strategy is the Declaration on Liberated Europe, which was issued at the Yalta Conference on February 11, 1945. It was considered a great success at the time and guaranteed all nations the right "to create democratic institutions of their own choice," and "to form interim governmental authorities broadly representative of all democratic elements in the population and pledged to the earliest possible establishment through free elections of governments responsible to the will of the people."

In the countries of Eastern and Southeastern Europe, especially in Poland, Romania, and Bulgaria, the leaders of the Soviet Union interpreted such malleable concepts as "democratic institutions of their own choice" and "democratic elements" in a very one-sided way and managed to delay elections long enough to consolidate their own position of power. In spite of this experience, Western countries have signed many agreements "in principle" in the years since Yalta—with similar results.

No Time Pressure

Since they control all mass media and need not heed public opinion, Soviet negotiators do not operate under time pressure and are under no obligation to come up with quick, tangible results. The small group of men who make all final decisions is free to decide for how long talks should go on and at what level of intensity they should be held, and they instruct Soviet delegates accordingly. The Soviet side uses this freedom to wrest concessions from the West, knowing very well that Western delegates are under pressure to get "results."

Compromise and Concessions

One of the biggest differences between Soviet and Western negotiating strategies consists in the two divergent attitudes toward small preliminary concessions. A Western diplomat tends to think that an occasional concession improves the general atmosphere of the talks and thereby makes it easier for both sides to reach their common goal. They assume that at some later stage the Soviets will remember the gesture and reciprocate in kind. Time and again this has proved to be wishful thinking. Soviet negotiators interpret small concessions as a sign of weakness on the part of the West and as a result become even more insistent. George Kennan writes:

> Few of us have any idea how much perplexity and suspicion has been caused in the Soviet mind by gestures and concessions granted by well-meaning Americans with a view to convincing the Russians of their friendly sentiments. Such

acts upset all their calculations and throw them way off balance. They immediately begin to expect that they have overestimated our strength, that they have been remiss in their obligations to the Soviet state, that they should have been demanding more from us all along. Frequently, this has exactly the opposite effect from that which we are seeking.[17]

Conversely, those Western negotiators who clearly and decisively formulate their own views and never tire of repeating them earn a surprising amount of genuine respect from their Soviet counterparts. When the two sides' differing positions are clearly recognizable throughout the talks, agreements can be reached under far better conditions, and with better results. The West should avoid unilateral concessions, show a readiness to resist time pressure and "agreements in principle," and work out precise and verifiable agreements that will be durable.

Language as an Instrument of Politics

In order to differentiate their foreign policy from that of "capitalist" states, the Soviets have carefully redefined the major terms in international relations and use them accordingly and consistently. Everywhere, in articles and commentaries, in all books and lectures and at all conferences, writers and speakers are bound to use the terms only as defined in official dictionaries. This is an important precondition for the uniformity of rhetoric that one encounters in all walks of official life in the Soviet Union and its allies.

This manipulation of language, and therefore of political content, takes four forms. The first method consists in defining those terms that have negative connotations in such a way that they apply only to "capitalism," i.e., to the Western democracies; thus the West is always responsible for negative actions. Here are a few examples: an *annexation,* a forcible incorporation of foreign territory, is, according to the Soviets, characteristic of the foreign policy of exploiting countries, especially those that are imperialist. And that, by definition, means the West, since in Soviet ideology imperialism is the highest form of capitalism. A *sphere of influence* always connotes an area over which imperialist states or capitalist monopolies exert a decisive economic, political, or military influence. *Expansion,* to the Soviet Union, means an enlargement of the sphere of influence or direct rule of states whose socio-economic formation is based on exploitation and oppression. *Cold War* is the policy of the most reactionary and aggressive circles of the upper bourgeoisie and aims at exacerbating international tensions. And *militarism* consists of the military measures taken by reactionary political systems and their ruling class of exploiters to oppress the "popular masses" of their own country and widen their sphere of influence abroad. It is stated explicitly that the tendency toward economic and political expansion is part and parcel of capitalism.

The second method is a reversal of the first: positive actions and developments always take place in the Soviet bloc. *Disarmament* is defined as a limitation (or even abolition) of armaments and military expenditures, but it is always immediately added that the socialist countries are the strongest advocates of disarmament and that the governments of the Soviet bloc, especially the Soviet Union, have repeatedly made concrete proposals to attain full or partial disarmament. According to Soviet use of language, *freedom* is severely limited, if not altogether impossible, in countries whose social order is based on exploitation and oppression. Therefore, it is only under socialism (as defined by the Soviets) that "true" freedom can be attained. Finally, the struggle for *progress* in our time has to be equated with the struggle for socialist and Communist social systems, as only these make it possible to develop the forces of production in the interest of all working people.

Occasionally it happens that a negative phenomenon in the Soviet bloc cannot be explained away; one example is the Berlin Wall, which, after all, is meant to prevent citizens of East Germany from fleeing their own country. In such cases, Communist leaders introduce positive-sounding euphemisms: the construction of the Berlin Wall is described by the East German regime as "safeguarding its frontiers to save peace." Lastly, the suppression of all libertarian reform movements in the Soviet bloc is, in Soviet parlance, called *normalization,* a usage that unfortunately has sneaked into some Western reports and comments as well.

The third method consists of using the same words, but giving them different meanings according to the context in which they are used. Again, a few examples: In Soviet interpretation, *democracy* is a form of government whose content and functions are always preconditioned by the social system and class character of a particular state. On the basis of this class character, one has to distinguish between "bourgeois democracy" and "socialist democracy." The former is, independently of its outward forms, by its very nature a dictatorship of the bourgeoisie. Since the means of production are appropriated by capitalists, democracy remains an illusion for the majority of the people. *Socialist democracy,* on the other hand, is characterized by the rule of the toiling masses, led by the working class and its Marxist-Leninist party. It is distinguished from "formal" *bourgeois democracy* primarily by the working classes' concrete ability to defend their interests and give real content to all constitutional rights and freedoms.

The expression *military coalition* is likewise used in two different ways. In general, it signifies a pact between states for the attainment of common political goals. But what counts is the member states' class character: For imperialist nations, "aggressive military coalitions," i.e., NATO, are a means to prepare raids and conquests aimed at beating back, or destroying altogether, the forces of peace, democracy, and socialism in the world, i.e., the Soviet Union and its allies. By contrast, a "socialist military coalition," i.e., the Warsaw Pact, is based on internationalism and is a voluntary association of sovereign states aimed at preserving peace and curbing the aggressivity of the imperialists.

It is perhaps less well known that the term *national consciousness* is similarly "split" in two. In Soviet usage, national consciousness always has a clear class character, defined by the relationship between a particular class and the nation in question. With the transformation of the bourgeoisie into a reactionary class, "bourgeois national consciousness" has grown into reactionary nationalism, of which chauvinism is the highest form. The working class, by contrast, has produced its own "proletarian national consciousness," which, after the victory of the socialist revolution, developed into "socialist national consciousness." The latter combines the awareness of belonging to a particular nation with an awareness of the individual's ties with the entire community of socialist nations.

Finally, there is a fourth method. For the same type of activity, two different terms are used, depending on whether one is talking about the West or the Soviet bloc. Thus all official publications distinguish between a *spy,* a buyable subject of imperialist power holders, and a *scout,* who is a morally superior patriotic fighter struggling for the goals of the socialist community of nations. Western capitalist states engage in *psychological warfare,* which means they plan, prepare, organize, and implement various subversive actions to weaken the economic, political, military, and ideological bases of the socialist states. The Soviet Union and its allies engage in only an *ideological struggle,* which is, needless to say, a very positive thing to do.

A less important, but rather amusing detail of the semantic confusion is the differentiation between capitalist enterprises of the Western world according to their attitude toward the Soviet Union. As a rule, Western entrepreneurs are *capitalists,* that is, owners of the means of production who appropriate the surplus value created by the workers and who perpetuate their oppressive and exploitative rule by means of the bourgeois state. However, as soon as the same entrepreneurs are willing to do business with the Soviet Union, to travel to Moscow and sign economic agreements with the Soviets, they cease being exploiters and become negotiating partners. They are then officially called *dyeloyie krugi,* "business representatives."

Of course, the governments of Western democracies are not above using euphemisms either, and here, too, different terms are often used to signify similar realities in various countries, depending on whether they are pro-Western or not. But one should always remember that in the Soviet Union the regime has a monopoly on the definition of terms, whereas in the West there is a free press that can demystify tendentious usage on the part of governments.

Diplomacy and Mass Appeal

Unlike Western governments, which in their relations with the Soviet bloc limit themselves, as a rule, to official contacts with the governments of those countries, the Soviet Union always attempts to influence the West's foreign policy by appealing directly or indirectly to Western public opinion. Over the decades, the Soviets have slowly but patiently expanded their capacity to exert influence on all levels so as to help them pursue their foreign policy objectives. The main idea is to study carefully all possible rifts, controversies, and differences of opinion in Western democracies, and then use this knowledge to gain a wide variety of allies in the West for the realization of Soviet foreign policy goals. This method goes back to an important declaration of Lenin's in the spring of 1920, when he wrote in a famous book destined for foreign Communists:

The more powerful enemy can be vanquished only by exerting the utmost effort, and by the most thorough, careful, attentive, skillful, and obligatory use of any, even the smallest, rift between the enemies, any conflict of interests among the bourgeoisie of the various countries, and also by taking advantage of any, even the smallest, opportunity of winning a mass ally, even though this ally is temporary, vacillating, un-

stable, unreliable and conditional. Those who do not understand this reveal a failure to understand even the smallest
grain of Marxism, of scientific, modern socialism.[18]

Lenin's declaration can now be found in all textbooks for Soviet
foreign policy officials.

Since Western Communist parties are insignificant in not a
few cases, the Soviets establish regular contact with representatives of all political parties, regardless of their ideology. It
is hoped that this will create a climate of confidence that will
allow the Soviets to influence the attitude of the Western politicians on issues that are dear to the Soviets. Beyond political
parties, they attempt to have regular contacts with other important organizations such as trade unions, churches, cultural
groups, and business associations. In general, officials special-
ize in one type of Western organization and have no contact
with others.

Besides these personal contacts, Soviet representatives, who
in most cases speak the language of their host country fluently,
also try to use public forums to propagate their views. They
participate in seminars, symposiums, and round-table discussions on radio and television; they give lectures in schools,
universities, and institutions of adult education; and they try to
publish articles or "letters to the editor" in the most important
newspapers and journals. All these activities are presented as
representing the "personal opinion" of the Soviet citizens in
question.

Delegations of the Supreme Soviet exchange regular visits
with members of Western parliaments. This is done partly to
maintain contacts on that particular level as well, but mainly so
as to legitimize the rubber stamp legislature of the USSR and
confer on it the prestige of a real parliament.

Finally, there are the regular contacts with "Friendship Societies" and "Solidarity Organizations." In these organizations,
the representatives of Western countries are independent of
their respective governments, whereas those of the Soviet

Union are officials named by the party apparatus, to which they are answerable.

Two aspects of such now much-discussed nongovernmental contacts must be emphasized here. First, Western representatives belong to a wide variety of parties, groups, and associations. They represent a wide range of viewpoints that very often differ considerably from those of their governments. They speak in their own name, mostly without informing their governments of the contents of the talks. On the Soviet side, the situation is very different. Whomever it is they are pretending to represent, Soviet delegates remain officials who are obliged to inform their party and government departments about their talks, and, what is more, they receive detailed instructions about what it is that they have to achieve in the course of the contacts.

The second aspect illustrates the profound difference between pluralist societies on the one hand, and a bureaucratic dictatorship on the other. Soviet representatives have the possibility of using a wide variety of organizations, institutions, associations, and media in the West for the propagation of their goals, whereas their Western counterparts have no independent, nongovernmental organizations or mass media inside the USSR at their disposal.

In the context of Soviet attempts to exert their influence from "below," that is, on the grass roots level, the "mass organizations" play a very important role. These "front organizations," as they are sometimes called in the West, operate in many countries, both in the West and in the Third World. They are by no means Communist associations in the ideological sense; many even count prominent non-Communists among their members. They are, however, directed and controlled by the Soviet nomenklatura and have the task of popularizing Soviet foreign policy aims, win broad public support for them in the West, and ultimately use this support to influence the foreign policy of Western states.

Since the front organizations are less active in the United States, it is understandable that Americans sometimes underestimate their importance. Perhaps the most important is the *World Federation of Trade Unions,* which has its headquarters in Prague and has ninety affiliates in eighty-one countries. The affiliates represent more than 200 million workers. In second place, one must mention the *Women's International Democratic Federation,* which has a membership of more than 200 million women, organized in 113 affiliates in 116 countries. The WIDF has its headquarters in East Berlin. The youth of the world is of particular importance to the Soviets. The *World Federation of Democratic Youth,* centered in Budapest, has more than 270 affiliates in 123 countries and a total membership of about 150 million young people, while the *International Union of Students,* which has its central office in Prague, unites national student organizations from more than 109 countries and represents about ten million students.

A second group of Soviet-sponsored associations bring together relatively small numbers of individuals or organizations that, because of their particular activity or authority, have the actual or potential capacity to influence public opinion. Among these are the *International Organization of Journalists,* headquartered in Prague and representing about 180,000 members; and the *International Association of Democratic Lawyers,* which has its seat in Brussels and a total membership of about 25,000. Of particular importance and most well known in the West is the *World Peace Council,* which has central offices in Prague and Helsinki. Its various associations in 142 countries have become quite active in recent times.[19]

The Communists who are active in these organizations are instructed to be very careful not to act as Communists. They do not address each other as "comrade," they do not wave red flags, they do not sing the Internationale, they even avoid the term "socialism," substituting for it the more vague term "social progress." These organizations are not Communist. That would prevent them from pursuing the tasks assigned to them, which consist of supporting the *current aims* of Soviet foreign policy. On the contrary, the more a certain personality is known to be distant from Communism, the more independent he is, the more valuable he is for the organizations. Often one hears or reads that such and such an organization *cannot* be Communist because very few Communists belong to it. Such an argument is totally oblivious to reality. If there are "only a few Communists" in such organizations, this means only—and Moscow interprets it this way, too—that these few Communists have been very successful.

Inside the organizations, the tasks of the Communists are not easy, and their situation is by no means enviable. They have to win over as many independent and well-known personalities as possible, and they must try to utilize them for the aims of Soviet foreign policy. However, it can happen during meetings or conferences that these independent personalities make personal statements that are at variance with these aims. Such snags can be quite embarrassing.

The programatic statements and declarations of these organizations are consciously formulated in a way that will enable people of all nationalities, social classes, and worldviews to identify with them. All espouse peace, disarmament, democracy, national independence, and progress, and all are against imperialism, fascism, and racism, all aims that any democrat can agree with.

Besides these general aims there are, of course, the particular programs of the various organizations. The World Federation of Democratic Youth struggles for the political, social, and cultural emancipation of youth. The Women's International Democratic Federation defends women's rights, works for the defense of children, and endeavors to foster friendship among women of different countries. The International Organization of Journalists works for freedom of the press, and the International Association of Democratic Lawyers sees its main task as defending the victims of dictatorship and terror.

It is only when we look closely at the activities and publications of these organizations that their one-sidedness, and hence their true nature, becomes apparent. Criticism of economic, social, and political conditions, and the resulting demands for improvement are directed exclusively against Western countries. Moreover, all front organizations demand the "total recognition of the political and territorial realities created by the Second World War," which means the legitimation of Soviet rule over Eastern and Central Europe.

The International Organization of Journalists is opposed to the "misuse of journalism by the monopolies and the financial groupings"—without ever mentioning censorship in the East, or the simple fact that all the press is subordinated to the interests of party and government in the Soviet bloc. The International Association of Democratic Lawyers sends observers to political trials, but only in Western countries. There is no reference whatsoever to arbitrary rule, political trials, and terror in the USSR and in allied countries. The World Peace Council stresses solidarity with national liberation movements in South Africa, Namibia, Guatemala, Honduras, and Puerto Rico, but never mentions equivalent movements against Communist dictatorships such as Poland, Czechoslovakia, or Afghanistan. It favors friendship with the "progressive" regimes in Afghanistan, Ethiopia, and Nicaragua, and thereby de facto supports pro-Soviet regimes in the Third World.

All this does not mean that *all* members of these organizations are Moscow's "useful idiots," or that all approve of this bias. At important turning points in postwar history, some courageous individuals, even some national associations, have taken a position against the one-sidedness: when the organizations' leaders excluded all Yugoslav affiliates after Tito's break with Stalin (1948–50); when they showed a clear bias in favor of North Korea during the Korean War (1950–53); when they attempted to brandish the Hungarian uprising of 1956 as "fascist"; and when during the 1960s they tooks sides with the Soviets in the Sino-Soviet conflict. In recent years, voices have been raised in protest against the organizations' leaders, as they opposed only Western armament but glossed over Soviet SS-20's, and talked a lot about human rights violations in the West or in countries allied with the West, but never mentioned the oppression of the dissidents in the USSR, of the signatories of Charter 77 in Czechoslovakia, and of the members of Solidarity in Poland—or even approved and justified this oppression in carefully phrased terms. But time and again the leaders of these mass organizations are able to develop their activities, and by formulating understandable demands that are accessible to wide population strata gain wide support for Soviet foreign policy aims.

Let us summarize: the centralized direction and coordination of all activities, both on the governmental and the nongovernmental levels, enable the Soviet leadership to implement their foreign policy with much more force and consistency than democratic countries. Any analysis of Soviet foreign policy has to take this fundamental fact into account. It is only on the basis of a precise knowledge of Soviet foreign policy, of its motivations, principles, and methods of implementation, that the West can formulate adequate policies toward the Soviet Union.

We have to complement the hitherto customary comparisons of the two camps' military strength with an analysis of the economic, political, and ideological forces that are at work in the Soviet Union and its allied countries. Based on this assumption, the West should put greater emphasis on confronting the Soviet regime on the level of ideas, and should reserve a greater place for nongovernmental organizations in its foreign policy. After all, East-West relations cannot be reduced to counting rockets and holding diplomatic conferences.

4

The Foreign Policy Objectives of the Nomenklatura

Soviet foreign policy is formulated with three distinct categories of nations in mind. These are 1. states of the Soviet bloc ("the socialist world system"); 2. the less developed countries; and 3. the Western democracies ("the capitalist countries").

In the Soviet Union, the distinctions among these three groups of countries are carefully maintained, each fitting into its own conceptual framework. The differences among them are always clearly and precisely drawn in newspapers and journals, as well as at Party congresses and other major official events.

I. THE SOCIALIST CAMP

In addition to the Soviet Union, the following countries (with the population given in millions of inhabitants) are officially considered to belong to the "socialist camp": In Europe, Poland (35.9), the German Democratic Republic (16.8), Czechoslovakia (15.3), Hungary (10.7), Romania (22.4), and Bulgaria (8.9); in Asia, Mongolia (1.7) and Vietnam (55.1); and in the Americas, Cuba (9.8). All the European states are members of the Warsaw

Pact, to which Mongolia is linked de facto via a bilateral military alliance with the USSR. All the countries of the "socialist camp" also belong to the Council for Mutual Economic Assistance (Comecon). Initially a European grouping, it was later joined by Mongolia (1962), Cuba (1972), Vietnam (1978), and, as an observer, Afghanistan (1980).

The Soviets' objective is to strengthen the socialist camp's positions in the world arena. To this end, they strive to promote the economic, political, and military integration of these countries as far as possible, to consolidate and ideologically legitimate the Soviet Union's leading role in that group of nations, and to prevent any attempt on the part of the different countries to institute reforms or gain some degree of autonomy beyond the scope permitted by the Soviet leadership. Cooperation among the various secret services has high priority, and the unity of the bloc is secured by a wide-ranging system of treaties and agreements.

The Soviet leadership knows the disparity between its aims and reality. The difficulties in the Soviet Union's relations with the other bloc countries are too well known for the Kremlin rulers to be deceived by the declarations of obedience that East European leaders regularly profer, nor are they fooled by the cheering crowds that greet them on their official visits to the "fraternal nations." They know full well that, endless reaffirmations of "socialist internationalism" and "eternal friendship with the Soviet Union" notwithstanding, Soviet hegemony does meet with resistance in these countries and that nationalist feelings are rising.

The national traditions of the countries of Eastern Europe lead to demands for more independence. The important role of the Catholic Church in Poland and, to a lesser degree, in Hungary; memories of past periods of political pluralism in a country like Czechoslovakia; social-democratic traditions in East Germany, Poland, and Hungary; and, above all, the widespread feeling among the people that their countries belong to Europe and to a general European civilization—all these factors encourage attempts to move toward liberalization, democratization, and greater national independence.

So far, the peoples of Eastern Europe have made a number of attempts to emancipate themselves from Soviet rule: The popular uprising in East Germany in June 1953, the workers' rebellion in Poznan and the Hungarian revolution in 1956, the "Prague Spring" in 1968, the uprising in the Polish ports of the Baltic in December 1970, and the emergence of the powerful Solidarity movement in 1980–81. The Soviets are well aware of the significance of these events. They know that they do not represent isolated episodes but are part of a general movement for autonomy and reform in the Soviet bloc.

At this time, the reestablishment of "law and order" in Poland is the top priority for Soviet leaders. They realize that movements similar to the one that shook Poland in the early 1980s can recur not only in Poland but also in other places. This is why they are determined to maintain and, if possible, strengthen the economic, political, ideological, and military unity of all East European nations.

Economic Coordination

In the economic sphere, the Soviet nomenklatura's main objective is to increase the dependence of the Soviet bloc countries on each other and above all on the Soviet Union by promoting "socialist division of labor." Comecon, founded on January 18, 1949, is the most important instrument of this policy. This organization did not play any important role until the mid-1950s, but since then its true purpose has become increasingly apparent. The Soviet Union would like all member countries to constitute an integrated economic area, with each nation concentrating on a specific economic sector. The economic planning of member states was supposed to be coordinated, and, at least theoretically, the final aim has been to link up the national economies to form a truly regional market with a single currency, common planning of internal and external trade policies, and strong scientific and technological links. Common investments in joint projects are supposed to speed up integration.

In its efforts to realize these objectives, the headquarters of the Council for Mutual Economic Assistance in Moscow has constantly grown in size. The Council established a secretariat with forty departments employing economic, financial, and legal specialists. All member countries set up permanent representations.

Despite unrelenting efforts to implement these plans, the coordinating activities of a large number of specially created institutions notwithstanding, only a very small proportion of the initial projects have been realized so far. Economic integration of the Soviet bloc is hampered by the following sets of problems:

1. There are no real economic incentives to integrate the national economies. All trade among Comecon countries is carried out by the states, coordinated by bilateral planning commissions, and consists of barter agreements. There is some struggle over quotas and delivery deadlines, but supply and demand play no role.

2. In all Communist countries, the ruling nomenklatura's power rests on its control over state property and central economic planning. It is only natural, therefore, that each national nomenklatura should be interested in strengthening its country's economic base. To do this, they have to maintain jealously their monopoly on foreign trade. Although they pay constant lip service to "friendship with the USSR," East European nomenklatura officials refuse to do anything that might limit their nation's sovereignty. This is the decisive barrier to economic integration. Wolfgang Seiffert, an East German legal expert who between 1969 and 1978 participated in many Comecon meetings as a representative of his country, stated in his book *Can the Soviet Bloc Survive?* that it had been a surprising and sobering experience to see how openly the member states of Comecon defended their national interests at meetings.[20]

3. In the last few years it has become increasingly apparent that the Soviet Union is no longer able to provide other Come-

con nations with the raw materials (including oil) that they need. Since 1982, the Soviet Union has cut its oil deliveries to the European Comecon members by 10 percent, compelling these countries to try to find other suppliers on the world market. This diversification, in turn, has made the smaller countries more autonomous in their international trade, an autonomy that in the long run might spread to other areas.

In order to make up for shortages, the Soviets have tried to enlist the manpower and investment of the other Comecon states to develop the Soviet Union's raw materials reserves. However, they insist on maintaining exclusive control over the Soviet economy, which understandably dampens their allies' enthusiasm for these "joint ventures."

Stability, or even a general economic upswing, can only be achieved by wide-reaching economic reforms throughout Comecon. So far, however, Hungary is the only country that has done something in this respect. It remains to be seen whether the remaining Comecon nations will take the decisive steps to emulate Hungary, for only then would they be able to avert a continuing downward slide of the standard of living.

Political-Ideological Cooperation

Given the pressing socio-economic problems in the Soviet bloc, ideological and political cooperation among the Communist Parties has become increasingly important. Here, too, the Soviets wish to play the leading role and coordinate all political activity in the bloc. To this end, the CPSU (18.5 million members) works closely with the other ruling parties: the GDR's Socialist Unity Party (2.2 million members), the United Polish Workers' Party (2.1 million members), the Communist Party of Czechoslovakia (1.6 million members), the Communist Party of Romania (3.4 million members), and the Bulgarian Communist Party (825,000 members).

Outside Europe, the CPSU cooperates closely with the Communist Party of Vietnam (1.7 million members), the People's Revolutionary Party of Mongolia (80,000 members), and the Communist Party of Cuba (434,000 members).

The cooperation of all these parties has absolute priority. All other forms of interstate cooperation, economic or military, are based on the cooperation among the leaders of the ruling parties. The top Party leaders meet once a year (often on the Crimean peninsula) with the Secretary General of the CPSU, and their discussions deal not only with bilateral relations but with the problems of the Soviet bloc in general.

In addition, there are regular bilateral meetings between the individual Party leaders and the Soviet Secretary General. Finally, administrative, economic, and ideological functionaries regularly meet with their Soviet counterparts to exchange information and coordinate policies.

The ultimate aim of the close ideological cooperation among all Parties is to justify and legitimize Soviet hegemony over Eastern Europe. The Soviets have proclaimed the USSR to be the model for other Communist states and castigate all serious emancipatory moves as "antisocialist," blaming them on the activities of "imperialist agents." Consequently, they claim the right to suppress these moves by all available means, including military means.

The ideological underpinning of this position is not easy to establish. Marx, Engels, and even Lenin time and again emphasized the need for nations to pursue their own road to socialism. Lenin repeatedly stated that Soviet Russia could not claim to be a model for the future socialist states of Europe, and in March 1918 he said that Russian Bolsheviks "are confident that the European workers . . . will do what we are doing, but do it better."[21] In March 1919, he expressed the hope that Polish comrades would be "given the opportunity . . . to create a better Soviet power than ours," adding, "while foreseeing every stage of development in other countries, we must decree nothing from Moscow."[22]

Lenin also warned others not to overestimate the importance

of the October Revolution. At the Eighth Party Congress, in March 1919, he said:

> It would be absurd to set up our revolution as the ideal for all countries, to imagine that it has made a number of brilliant discoveries and has introduced a heap of socialist innovations . . . If we behave like the frog in the fable and become puffed up with conceit, we shall only make ourselves the laughing-stock of the world, we shall be mere braggarts.[23]

Later, he went even further, writing: "Soviet Republics in more developed countries, where the proletariat has greater weight and influence, have every chance of surpassing Russia once they take the path of the dictatorship of the proletariat."[24] After the victory of a socialist revolution in an advanced country, Lenin believed, there would probably be "a sharp change" in that "Russia will cease to be a model and will once again become a backward country (in the 'Soviet' and the socialist sense)."[25]

The Soviet leadership never mentions these statements by Lenin, as it attempts to prove just the opposite, namely that the Soviet Union and its historical experience are a model for all other Communist countries. The doctrinal basis of this claim is a theory called "general laws of the building of socialism," which states that after a successful revolution, politics, the economy, ideology, and culture develop according to certain general laws.

These "laws" are clearly based on the experience of the Soviet Union and contain, among other things, the following four elements: after a socialist revolution, the dictatorship of the proletariat has to be established under one form or another; the "Marxist-Leninist Party" has to play the role of a vanguard in the development toward socialism; the economy of a socialist country has to develop according to a carefully elaborated plan; and, finally, every socialist country must be ready to defend the achievements of socialism against the "plots of external and internal enemies."

These "laws" enable the Soviet Union to deny any country that is no longer ruled by the "dictatorship of the proletariat" the quality of being socialist. This applies to all Communist countries that might decide to adopt a multiparty system or gradually to introduce economic reforms favoring a decentralization of the planned economy. If these countries do not defend their socialist achievements against the "attacks of external and internal enemies," the Soviet Union claims the right to do so on their behalf and to intervene militarily.

After the Soviet occupation of Czechoslovakia in August 1968, another doctrine was added to all this, namely the doctrine of "limited sovereignty." It was first formulated by the Soviet ideologue Sergei Kovalev on September 26, 1968 in *Pravda* under the title "Sovereignty and the International Obligations of Socialist Countries." It states that the defense of the socialist system in a certain country is not just a matter for the country concerned, but primarily a matter concerning the entire "Socialist World System." The defense of "socialist achievements" is a "common internationalist duty." The socialist countries must not shirk this duty for reasons of some "abstract sovereignty" or of some "formal observance of freedom of self-determination." All law, including international law, is, according to this doctrine, subordinated to the "laws of the class struggle." It was the first time that international law was given a secondary role in comparison to political declarations.[26]

A few weeks later, in his speech to the Fifth Party Congress of the Polish Communists on December 12, 1968, the then General Secretary of the CPSU, Leonid Brezhnev, declared:

When internal and external forces hostile to socialism try to turn the development of any socialist country backward to a capitalist restoration, when a threat arises to the cause of socialism in that country, a threat to the security of the socialist community as a whole, that is no longer a problem only of the people of the country in question, but a general problem, the concern of all the socialist countries.[27]

Of course, this doctrine of "limited sovereignty" has met with resistance, even among other Communist-ruled countries. Both the then Yugoslav head of state, Marshal Tito, and the Romanian president and Party chief, Nicolae Ceauşescu, pointed out that it enabled one socialist country to force its will on another socialist country by military intervention, and that it contradicted both international law and all nations' basic right to be independent. They added that no one had a right to tell other countries how to develop socialism, since that was a matter that had to be determined by each state individually.[28]

The Chinese Communists denounced the contradiction between this doctrine and accepted principles of national sovereignty in the following terms:

According to the gangster logic of the Soviet revisionist renegades, other countries enjoy only "limited sovereignty," while the sovereignty of the Soviet revisionists knows no limits.[29]

Others, such as the Eurocommunist parties, joined in the criticism. Nevertheless, the doctrine of "limited sovereignty" still holds in Eastern Europe. Together with the doctrine of the "laws" they serve to legitimate the Soviet Union's intervention in the internal affairs of other Communist countries.

Military Cooperation

The economic and political-ideological cooperation within the "Socialist World System" is complemented by the military alliance of the Soviet bloc and by bilateral agreements that have made it possible for the Soviet Union to station a sizable proportion of its troops in the countries of Central and Eastern Europe.

The official name of the Warsaw Pact is the Treaty of Friendship, Cooperation, and Mutual Assistance, and it was signed on May 14, 1955, in Warsaw by representatives of the Soviet Union, Poland, the GDR, Czechoslovakia, Hungary, Romania, Bulgaria, and Albania. On September 13, 1968, Albania unilaterally withdrew from the treaty in protest over the invasion of Czechoslovakia, but this act has yet to be publicly acknowledged by the leadership of the Warsaw Pact.

The treaty's text is relatively short. In Article 1, "the contracting parties undertake, in accordance with the Charter of the United Nations Organization, to refrain in their international relations from the threat or use of force, and to settle their international disputes peacefully and in such a manner as will not jeopardize international peace and security." In Article 3, the member states agree to "consult with one another on all important international issues affecting their common interests," especially when "a threat of armed attack on one or more of the Parties to the Treaty has arisen."

The treaty's main point is formulated in Article 4: "In the event of armed attack in Europe on one or more of the Parties to the Treaty by any state or group of states, each of the Parties to the Treaty . . . shall immediately . . . come to the assistance of the state or states attacked with all such means as it deems necessary, including armed force."

Finally, the signatories "undertake not to participate in any coalitions or alliances . . . whose objects conflict with the . . . treaty" (Article 7), and to "adhere to the principle of respect for the independence and sovereignty of the others and non-interference in their internal affairs" (Article 8).

The treaty is therefore limited to mutual assistance against the attack of foreign countries, and concerns only interstate relations. It can therefore not legitimately be invoked in order to meddle in the internal affairs of a member state or even to suppress a popular uprising. In addition, the treaty's text makes it quite clear that its application is limited to Europe, which means that the Soviet Union may not use it to justify political or military acts outside Europe.

The Warsaw Pact spawned a number of important institutions that all have their seats in Moscow. The Political Consultative Committee is officially the pact's highest organ. It meets two or three times a year, usually in Moscow. In it, each member country is represented by its Prime Minister and its Foreign Minister, but it has happened frequently that the various member states' first Party secretaries and Defense Ministers participate in the meetings. The Political Consultative Committee is responsible for the coordination of the member states' military and, where applicable, foreign policies.

The "United Command" is responsible for strategic and operational planning, for security at the training bases in the member countries, and it prepares joint military maneuvers. The body meets once a year to decide on policies and actions for the next year. The commander-in-chief of the Warsaw Pact is always a Russian officer who is at the same time First Deputy Defense Minister of the Soviet Union and member of the Central Committee of the CPSU. The official language of the Warsaw Pact is Russian.

Since 1956, the highest executive organ of the Warsaw Pact has been the "Joint Secretariat," headed by a high Soviet official. Its most important task is to supervise cooperation with Comecon, especially in such fields as arms industry, logistics, and armaments research. In 1969, following a Soviet proposal, the member states agreed to create a "Committee of Defense Ministers" and a "Military Council" to coordinate the individual tasks of member states within the alliance and to prepare proposals for the strengthening of the Pact's military power. In addition, a "Technical Committee of the Armed Forces" has the task of standardizing existing and future weapons systems.

Although the Warsaw Pact treaty specified clearly that it was meant to protect its members against external threats, only one year after its signing the Soviet Union invoked it to suppress a liberation movement in a member country. In the course of the Hungarian Revolution (October 23 to November 11, 1956), the revolutionary councils that had sprung up all over the country demanded the withdrawal of all Soviet troops stationed in Hungary. At first it looked as if the Soviets would accede to this demand, and Soviet forces (20,000 men and 600 tanks) retreated from Budapest. But this soon proved to be a diversion designed to deceive the populace, for, simultaneously, new units crossed the border from the Soviet Union into Hungary and advanced on Budapest.

The revolutionary government under the leadership of the reform Communist Imre Nagy repeatedly protested against this violation of the Warsaw Pact. As these protests had no effect, Prime Minister Nagy handed the then Soviet ambassador, Yuri Andropov, a declaration stating that Hungary would immediately leave the Warsaw Pact, given that Soviet troops had crossed into Hungarian territory against the wishes of the legal government of Hungary.

On November 1, 1956, the Hungarian government proclaimed Hungary's neutrality. The Soviet High Command again promised to withdraw its troops—Andropov himself confirmed this to Nagy. In spite of this, Soviet troops continued their march toward Budapest. In the night of November 4, they arrested the members of the Hungarian negotiating team and attacked the capital. After one week of combat, the last Hungarian fighters surrendered their arms on November 11.

In the aftermath of this uprising, in order to forestall similar emancipatory outbursts in other countries, the Soviet Union signed bilateral treaties governing the "temporary stationing" of its troops with Poland (December 17, 1956), the GDR (March 12, 1957), and Hungary (May 27, 1957). To justify these agreements, the Soviets invoked the "international situation" and "existing international treaties." Furthermore, they pledged to respect fully the other countries' sovereignty and not to interfere in their domestic affairs. The agreements provided for the "temporary stationing of Soviet troops—but more than a quarter century has passed and the troops are still there. On the basis of these agreements, the Soviet Union maintains at the present time twenty divisions (227,000 soldiers) in East Germany, two tank divisions (20,000 men) in Poland, and four divisions (44,500 men) in Hungary.

As if these three bilateral agreements were not enough to ensure full Soviet control over Eastern Europe, the Soviets had all Communist regimes fill key military posts with absolutely reliable functionaries who were surrounded by Soviet "advisors." Entire regions were put under the direct control of the Soviet military, and Soviet units began guarding the most important railroads, airports, defense industries, and mines.

Since 1961, the armies of the various Warsaw Pact countries have periodically carried out joint military maneuvers. These maneuvers not only aim at testing and strengthening the combat readiness of the troops, but also have a political function: the demonstration of military might serves to underline the various regimes' authority and thus intimidate the populations.

The true nature of the Warsaw Pact became apparent during the military maneuvers in Czechoslovakia that coincided with the "Prague Spring." The troops (16,000 soldiers and 4,000 motor vehicles, tanks, and transport planes) arrived in that country at the end of May 1968—more than three weeks before the scheduled start of the maneuvers on June 20. Although the maneuvers had been scheduled to end on June 30, the troops withdrew only on August 11, after repeated protests by the Czechoslovak government. Ten days later, Warsaw Pact troops from all member countries (except Romania) occupied Czechoslovakia. KGB and military officers arrested the main leaders of the "Prague Spring" and deported them to Moscow. From August 23 to August 26, 1968, the Soviet leaders "negotiated" in the Kremlin with the Czechoslovak reformers, who were de facto prisoners.[30] The Czechoslovak leaders were coerced into signing a secret fifteen-point "Moscow Protocol," which stipulated, among other things, that the Soviet troops would remain in the country for the time being. Despite the promise that "the Soviet troops would not interfere in the domestic affairs of Czechoslovakia," the Prague reformists were forced to reintroduce censorship (euphemistically called "measures for the control of the

news media") and to coordinate the domestic and foreign policies of their country with those of the Soviet Union. They had
to pledge not to put the "Czechoslovak Question" on the agenda
of the United Nations, and they had to make wide-reaching
personnel changes in the Party and state apparatuses. In due
course, this led to a replacement of all reformists by pro-Soviet
nomenklatura officials. Since then, five Soviet divisions (58,270
men) have been "temporarily" stationed in Czechoslovakia.

As if to add insult to injury, Czechoslovakia had to agree in
a bilateral treaty signed with the Soviet Union on May 6, 1970,
to give military support to the USSR should the latter be attacked by any other power, even from outside Europe. This
followed a Soviet attempt to extend the Warsaw Pact to Asia
—Soviet and Chinese troops had briefly clashed on the Ussuri
River in March 1969—an attempt that had failed in the face of
the resistance of other Warsaw Pact countries, especially Romania.

The time limit of the Warsaw Pact was an additional problem
for the Soviet Union. When the pact was signed in 1955, its last
article contained a clause stipulating that the treaty would be
valid for twenty years, and that it could be renewed only *once,*
for another ten years, provided all member states agreed. Therefore, the Warsaw Pact was limited to thirty years and expired
in May 1985.

As its expiration date drew closer, there were long negotiations among Soviet officials and delegates from the other member states, in the course of which it became obvious that the
allies disagreed as to how the pact should be prolonged. A
summit conference of all Warsaw Pact countries that had been
scheduled for January 1985 in Sofia was abruptly cancelled. We
have reason to believe that the Soviets attempted to impose two
changes on their allies: first, they wanted to extend the pact to
countries outside Europe, and second, they wished to include a
new clause legitimizing the stationing of Soviet troops on the
territories of the other states, so as to justify future military
interventions against possible reform movements (officially

called "protecting socialist achievements"). But they did not succeed. When the leaders of the seven member states met on April 1985 to renew the treaty, they left its text unchanged.

Deviations from the Soviet Model

The nomenklatura regimes established on the Soviet model in the countries of Central and Eastern Europe are today supported by only a small part of the population. As in the Soviet Union itself, Marxism-Leninism is no longer a vital force in society and merely serves to legitimize the rulers' monopoly of power. What really matters to people are the shortages of food and basic products, the many privileges of the Party functionaries, repression, and bureaucratic high-handedness—not the latest Party slogans. The yearning for more freedom, human rights, democratic elections, and new values is becoming ever more apparent. Not only the population in general, but even Party members and some Party officials increasingly question the Soviet model.

East European leaders are facing a dilemma: They need the support of the Soviet Union and its armed forces, but they also know that their dependency on the USSR is detrimental to their standing at home. Proceeding gradually and very cautiously, some leaders have been trying to gain a greater measure of independence. The "satellite states" of the 1950s have become "subordinate allies." They are subordinate because they have to support all major statements of the Soviet leadership and to carry out all its major decisions. But in the last two decades they have obtained the right to decide for themselves how and at what speed to implement the policies dictated by the Soviets. Also, they can now go to Moscow, register their own interests, and try to influence Soviet policy at least a little bit.

For example, the Hungarian Communists have, as a rule, supported all Soviet foreign policy proposals, albeit sometimes in a more moderate form. But in exchange for following the Soviet line in international politics, they have gained a considerable amount of freedom in their domestic politics. They have used this leverage to carry out very important economic reforms, to liberalize cultural and artistic life, and to allow their citizens to travel abroad more easily.

Romania is a mirror image of Hungary. Internally, the Communist Party sticks to a very repressive line, but externally, it has a certain degree of independence from the Soviet Union. Unlike all other countries of the Soviet bloc, Romania never broke diplomatic relations with Israel and takes a neutral position between Israel and the Arab states. It did not participate in the invasion of Czechoslovakia in 1968 and even explicitly condemned that act. Romania has repeatedly refused to participate in Warsaw Pact maneuvers and has always remained neutral on the issue of the Sino-Soviet split; it has always insisted on maintaining friendly relations with the People's Republic of China. The Romanian leadership has also pursued more flexible policies toward the West.

In Poland, the Communist Party has always had to take into account the influence of the Catholic Church and the activities of the workers: the independent trade union Solidarity had 10 million members in 1980–81. No other development has more forcefully illustrated the weakness of a Communist regime. Even the military dictatorship of Jaruzelski, set up on December 13, 1981 but somewhat eased in the spring of 1983, has not found it easy to reestablish the bureaucratic-dictatorial regime.

The Husak regime in Czechoslovakia follows staunchly pro-Soviet policies both domestically and in its foreign relations. It faces the small but very active opposition of the Charter 77 group, but, more importantly, it meets with generalized indifference from the population.

Until very recently, the Honecker regime in the GDR and the Zhivkov regime in Bulgaria were the most consistently pro-Soviet governments in Eastern Europe. In the last decade, however, both regimes have begun to emphasize their own national traditions: they hope to find in these traditions the legitimation they cannot find through democratic means.

George Kennan summarizes the Eastern European alliance system as follows:

> It is obvious to any observer who has studied history that it could not last. It does not take sufficient account of the individual nations' sensibilities; therefore it was unnatural right from the beginning. Above all, this alliance demanded more from the Soviet leaders than they could give: wisdom, experience, and flexibility in their handling of East European peoples. All these qualities were lacking on the Soviet side, yet they were preconditions for a permanent and successful Soviet domination of Eastern Europe. Thus it was clear that the post-war situation could not last forever. Either the Soviet Union had to grant the countries of Eastern Europe more independence and freedom, or there had to be a major crisis, or a series of crises—and that is what we are witnessing today.[31]

Two "Outsiders": China and Yugoslavia

Given the problems with their East European allies, it is in the Soviet interest to improve relations with those socialist countries that are not part of the Soviet bloc: China, Yugoslavia, Albania, and North Korea. In the last three or four years the leaders of the Soviet Union have made efforts to settle their old disputes with these countries and to make a fresh start. These efforts have taken many different forms.

The Soviet Union maintains only state-to-state and economic relations with Yugoslavia, China, and North Korea, but from the Soviet point of view, party-to-party relations are far more important. The CPSU has no such links with either the Albanian Party of Labor (123,000 members), or the North Korean Workers Party (2 million members), or the Communist Party of China (40 million members). Contacts with the Yugoslav League of Communists (2.2 million adherents) have been maintained at a very low level. Yugoslav delegates have been present at the last three Soviet Party congresses, in 1976, 1981, and 1986, but used both occasions to emphasize Yugoslavia's commitment to nonalignment and self-management.

The Sino-Soviet conflict has been simmering since 1956; Soviet leaders therefore attach particular importance to their relations with China. Since the summer of 1978, two years after the Mao era ended, China's leaders have sought, above all, to promote economic development. Without abandoning their fundamental criticism of Soviet-style communism, they would like to normalize their relations with the USSR. An improvement of Sino-Soviet relations would also suit the Soviets, as it would relieve some of the pressure from the 450,000 troops they have stationed on the border between China and the USSR.

It was also in 1978, under Brezhnev, that the Soviets toned down their polemics against Chinese Communists and began referring to the People's Republic as a "socialist country" again. At the Twenty-sixth Party Congress, in 1981, Brezhnev said that his country was not interested in a "confrontation with China" and would like to "establish good neighborly relations" with it.[32]

Soviet overtures to China have continued in recent years. The two countries have expanded their economic and scientific relations and have stepped up their cultural and athletic contacts. A student exchange program has been set up, and new agreements covering economic, technological, and scientific cooperation have been signed. The total trade volume between the USSR and China has risen steadily in recent years.

The Chinese have always pointed out that a normalization of Sino-Soviet relations is contingent on the Soviets' removing a certain number of "obstacles." The Chinese demand the withdrawal of Soviet troops from Afghanistan, Mongolia, and the Sino-Soviet border. In addition, they demand that the USSR prevail on their Vietnamese allies to take their troops out of Cambodia. Since the summer of 1983, the Chinese have added that a mutual reduction of forces would have to include SS-20 missiles stationed on Soviet territory.

It will not be easy for the Soviet Union to overcome its longstanding disagreements with the four nonaligned Communist countries, especially Yugoslavia and China, and to develop normal relations with these them. The Soviets' long-term objective is probably to reintegrate them into their sphere of influence. But such a move would meet with the determined resistance of both the leaders and the populations of the concerned nations.

II. THE SOVIET UNION AND THE THIRD WORLD

The idea that the rich industrial nations of the North have a historical and moral obligation to help the poorer countries of the South never comes up in Soviet publications; the terms "North-South problem" and "North-South conflict" have no equivalents in official Soviet terminology. According to the Soviet view, it is utterly wrong to emphasize contrasts between the rich North and the poor South, since one cannot equate the capitalist former colonial powers with the socialist Soviet Union and its allies. There is no "North-South conflict": The real opposition is between the "imperialist camp" and the "socialist camp," and the developing nations of the Third World are the allies of the socialist world in their struggle against imperialism and neocolonialism.

The Soviets thus stress political problems rather than humanitarian considerations or the interests of private enterprise. They are interested, above all, in exerting influence on the national liberation movements and on the new states that emerged in the wake of decolonization. The "New World Economic Order" and development aid are treated not as humanitarian and/or economic problems, but as intrinsic elements of the political struggle against the West ("neocolonialism"). Therefore, Soviet development aid, already much smaller than that of the West, concentrates mostly on the five developing nations that are closely allied with the Soviet Union: Cuba, Afghanistan, Cambodia, Vietnam, and Laos.

More precisely, the goal of the Soviet leadership is to achieve the following ends:

1. to win over as firm allies those nonaligned developing nations that already lean toward the Soviet Union, while fostering their dependence on Moscow;

2. to strengthen systematically Soviet influence in those nations that waver between pro-Soviet and pro-Western policies in pursuit of their own interest; and

3. to accelerate the movement toward a policy of nonalignment in pro-Western developing nations.

Noncapitalist Development

At the Second Congress of the Communist International, on July 26, 1920, Lenin defined the objectives of the Communist world movement in the colonial world as enabling them to attain the Soviet order "with the aid of the proletariat of the advanced countries," and "through certain stages of development, to [achieve] communism without having to pass through the capitalist stage."[33]

Lenin's concept of reaching socialism in the colonial countries by skipping the capitalist stage altogether was soon forgotten for almost four decades. It was only at the end of the 1950s, when decolonization was making great strides in Africa and Asia and the Soviet leadership was becoming more open to new ways of looking at things in the wake of de-Stalinization, that Lenin's concept of the "noncapitalist road of development" reemerged and in due time became a central idea in Soviet foreign policy in the Third World. The first official documents to mention the concept were the Declaration of the Eighty-one Communist Parties of December 6, 1960, and Khrushchev's Party Program of October 1961.

The doctrine is still officially valid. It states that the national liberation movements in the Third World go through two phases. In the first phase, they aim at driving out the colonial powers and attaining national independence. This struggle unites all national forces, regardless of their political views or social bases. During this stage, Marxist-Leninists have to lend their unconditional support to all "antiimperialist forces."

As soon as the movement has attained its first goal, i.e., national independence, a new situation obtains, and the second phase begins. After liberation from colonialism, social contradictions grow in the newly independent nation. This leads the "national bourgeoisie" (which, for the Soviets, denotes all leading non-Communist forces in the developing countries) to come to terms with "reaction and imperialism."

Under these conditions, Communists have to strive for a noncapitalist mode of development. The countries of Africa and many Asian nations, according to official Soviet doctrine, ought to skip capitalism and reach Soviet-style socialism via a certain number of transitional stages. This "noncapitalist" path involves the nationalization of key industries, far-reaching land reform, the drastic limitation of the influence of large landowners and capitalists, the introduction of state planning of the economy, and the establishment of political conditions that will gradually create a Soviet-style system. Externally, such a Third World country should seek the friendship of the Soviet Union while simultaneously loosening its links with the West. This could be done within the framework of "nonalignment." In the official Soviet view, the young nations of the Third World cannot pursue a noncapitalist path to development in isolation from, or even in opposition to, world socialism.

According to Soviet ideologues, the noncapitalist path is characterized by deep political, economic, and social transformations and conflicts: "The noncapitalist path of development is accompanied by bitter class struggle, a struggle whose objects are power and the fundamental direction of societal development. On this road one cannot exclude the possibility of temporary setbacks." What is decisive, the ideologues continue, is that the Third World socialists build up and consolidate a revolutionary mass party that will gradually adopt Marxism-Leninism. This party then has to adopt a series of transitional measures that will gradually weaken and ultimately neutralize the forces of reaction in politics and economics. Finally, the party has to create new institutions that adequately reflect the new class configuration.

Countries of "Socialist Orientation"

Since the mid-1970s, official Soviet usage has labelled those countries which have been particularly successful in their pursuit of the noncapitalist mode of development as "countries of socialist orientation." Ethiopia, Mozambique, Angola, and the People's Democratic Republic of Yemen (South Yemen) are the most frequently mentioned states in this category, but some accounts also include Algeria, Libya, Guinea, Congo, Tanzania, and Syria. After the Soviet occupation of Afghanistan in December 1979, that nation, of course, also joined the ranks of the "countries of socialist orientation."

According to this doctrine, the most important characteristics of these countries are:

• the transfer of power into the hands of progressive forces, and the creation of a revolutionary-democratic state that is based on a new power apparatus;
• the liquidation of the economic and political rule of the monopolies, the nationalization of all foreign capital, government regulation of all economic activity, and severe limitations on all private enterprise;
• profound social and cultural transformations, including agrarian reforms, universal literacy, and equal rights for women;
• broad cooperation with the "socialist community of nations";
• struggle against imperialism, neocolonialism, and "national reformism"; and the implementation of a revolutionary and democratic ideology closely connected to the theory and the experience of "scientific socialism."

Soviet Central Asia, Mongolia, Vietnam, and Cuba are presented as models for the "countries of socialist orientation" in

Asia and Africa. The Soviet Union offers the countries of social-ist orientation preferential treatment in terms of economic and military aid, but in return expects them to support the USSR's foreign policy and to intensify not only state-to-state relations but also contacts among their ruling parties and the CPSU. The Kremlin insists that the regimes in these countries create ruling parties on the basis of "scientific socialism." If such parties already exist, the Soviets urge them to accelerate their move-ment toward a true Marxist-Leninist party of the Soviet type.

Soviet Policy in Developing Countries

The seemingly abstract conceptions of "noncapitalist path of development" and "socialist orientation" mask a very impor-tant question: Should the newly independent countries of the Third World go their own way after independence, and gradu-ally develop into modern, industrial (and, preferably, demo-cratic) states, or should they adopt the "Cuban model," which leads to a Soviet-type system?

The strong engagement of the Soviet leaders in the Third World bespeaks both fear and hope. If most of the Third World countries choose their own way, the West can maintain and perhaps strengthen its global position. However, if the Kremlin succeeds in pushing Third World developments onto the "Cuban way," the global balance of forces would shift in the Soviet Union's favor.

In its efforts to gain or extend its influence in the developing countries, the Soviets cleverly manipulate the hostility of large sectors of these nations toward their former colonial masters and depict the USSR as the main force of "anticolonialism." The Soviets deride *any* Western economic activity in the Third World as "neocolonialism," even when it is clearly benefitting the country. The support of some Western countries for corrupt and repressive dictatorships in the Third World has played into the hands of the Soviets, too.

Soviet influence in a developing nation is often greatest when that nation stands at the end of its (sometimes armed) struggle for national liberation, and faces the problems of consolidating its new state structures. But as soon as these countries are in a position to concentrate on their economic development, they often find that the West can provide more substantial assistance than can the Soviet Union and its allies.

The leaders of such countries then begin to orient their countries more toward the West. When this happens, the Soviets have an urgent interest in prolonging the national liberation revolutions as long as possible, in the hope that they can thus create a political counterweight to the West's increasing economic influence.

In order to reach these objectives, the Soviet Union uses methods that are very different from those used by the West in its relations with the Third World. The Soviets do not limit their relations with the developing countries to the intergovernmental, diplomatic, and economic spheres. Since the 1960s, they have tried to intensify the contacts between the CPSU and the various ruling parties of the Third World. The Soviets consider these parties "sympathizing" parties rather than real Communist parties, but nonetheless invite their representatives to address CPSU congresses.

Since the 1970s, the Soviet Union has also been attempting to increase its military influence, both by exporting more arms, and by sending military advisors. According to Yugoslav sources, the USSR quintupled its arms exports to the Third World between 1973 and 1978. This means that the countries receiving the arms also needed Soviet experts to train their armed forces. The drastic increase in the number of Soviet advisors, both civil and military, is an important element of Soviet policy toward the Third World.

To further this policy, the Soviet Union often enlists the help of its allies, especially Cuba and East Germany. In 1981, the Soviets maintained military and civil personnel in nineteen Third World countries. Three examples, taken from three regions of the world, may suffice: of the 9,150 advisors stationed in Angola, 8,000 were Cuban, 700 Soviet, and 450 East German; in Iraq, their total number was 10,360 (USSR: 8,000, Cuba: 2,200, and the GDR: 160); and Nicaragua was host to 3,250 advisors from the Soviet bloc (3,200 Cubans and fifty Soviets).

To anchor these military activities politically, the Soviet Union has signed "treaties of friendship and cooperation" with many developing nations, such as Egypt (1971), India (1971), Iraq (1972), Somalia (1974), Angola (1976), Mozambique (1977), Ethiopia (1978), Afghanistan (1978), South Yemen (1979), Syria (1980), and the Congo (1981). The Soviets suffered setbacks several times: in March 1976, Anwar Sadat abrogated Egypt's treaty, and Somalia followed suit in November 1977.

These treaties differ from the previously mentioned ones between the Soviet Union and its East European allies in that they do not contain an automatic mutual assistance clause. They are thus not military alliances. Nevertheless, in most cases they provide for military cooperation, the most important exception being the Indo-Soviet treaty. The military provisions of these treaties further the global interests of the Soviets, who are striving to secure bases for their expanding navy in the Persian Gulf, in East Africa, and in the Indian Ocean, and to improve their access to the raw materials of the Third World.

Successes and Failures

One cannot deny that the Soviet Union has succeeded in increasing its overall influence in the Third World. Since the end of the 1960s, a number of developing nations have adopted the noncapitalist path of development, although the ways in which this has been done vary from country to country. Many of these nations have signed far-reaching agreements with the Soviet Union, agreements that provide not only for military aid and the sending of advisors but also offer the Soviet Union military bases. The close links of the CPSU with many of the ruling parties in the Third World, especially those of the countries of "socialist orientation," are also a proof of Soviet success.

Nevertheless, there have been serious setbacks. Increased Soviet political and military activity has caused growing numbers of people in the Third World to view the Soviet Union with suspicion. Official declarations to the effect that the Soviet Union is the natural ally of the Third World stand in stark contrast to the USSR's insufficient economic assistance to the developing nations. Many Third World governments have learned to their great disappointment that the Soviets sometimes have not been able to provide the desired economic and technological assistance, and that their financial aid has often been conditional on the acquisition of Soviet arms.

It gradually became common knowledge that the Soviets generously provide propaganda, armaments, and military advisors, but that they are less forthcoming in alleviating immediate economic needs. Third World students who have studied at universities in the Soviet Union and in Eastern Europe have returned to their countries disenchanted. In many developing nations, Soviet-style socialism has lost its original "glamor." Some states have managed to free themselves from Soviet "protection": Ghana did so as early as the mid-1960s; Egypt and Somalia followed later.

After the Soviet occupation of Afghanistan in December 1979, the waning of Soviet influence in the Third World became more pronounced. At the United Nations, 104 countries voted in favor of a General Assembly resolution demanding the immediate and unconditional withdrawal of Soviet troops. Even Third World nations that had pursued relatively pro-Soviet policies until then joined the call. Among the eighteen countries that abstained were Algeria, Syria, Nicaragua, and the Congo. Only the Soviet Union's most faithful allies at that time voted against the resolution: Ethiopia, Angola, Grenada, Mozambique, and South Yemen. The Soviet Union suffered similar setbacks at the 1980 conference of Islamic states in Islamabad and at the conference of the Foreign Ministers of the nonaligned nations in 1981.

The Iran-Iraq war has created additional difficulties for the

Soviets, as it has impeded their attempts to set up an anti-Western front in the region. Nor have internal developments in Iran favored the Soviet Union. In the beginning, the Soviet Union had not only welcomed the Iranian revolution, but also had great hopes in it. But the banning of the Communist Tudeh Party and the repression of its members have led to increasing tensions between Iran and its northern neighbor. Likewise, the USSR's relations with the Palestine Liberation Organization have cooled down somewhat in recent times. So far, the Soviet Union has not come closer to participating in a "comprehensive" solution of the Middle East conflict. Soviet influence in Syria has increased to the point where that country is now the USSR's most important ally in the Middle East, but it is by no means certain whether this alliance will last. The ambiguous attitude of the Soviet leadership toward some of these (often not quite reliable) allies was also evident after the U.S. retaliatory attack on Libya in April 1986. The Soviets denounced the attack, but also made it clear that they had no intention of supporting Libya militarily to an extent that might endanger Soviet-U.S. relations. The Soviet response to the U.S. action illustrates their risk-consciousness, as mentioned earlier. Even Ethiopia, Angola, and Mozambique, the three model "countries of socialist orientation," have perhaps not yet pronounced their last word. Recent events in South Yemen also seem to indicate that the Soviet presence in that country meets with considerable resistance.

These setbacks do not mean that the Soviets have abandoned their goals in the Third World. Proceeding methodically and unrelentingly, they are trying to regain the positions they lost after the occupation of Afghanistan.

Latin America has played an increasingly important role in Soviet foreign policy considerations. This has been the case especially since Cuba abandoned its original policies and began to adopt the Soviet model. The Cuban constitution of 1976 is modeled after those of other Communist countries, and the

Cuban Communist Party is now very similar to other ruling Communist Parties in the Soviet bloc. However, contrary to a widespread opinion, the Cubans do not carry out their foreign policy, especially in Angola and Ethiopia, at the explicit command of the Soviet Union, although they coordinate it with the USSR. This is also true for Cuban policy in Nicaragua and, until the American invasion, in Grenada.

Grenada is an island covering 133 square miles. It has a population of 110,000. On March 13, 1979, the pro-Soviet New Jewel Movement, under the leadership of Maurice Bishop, staged a coup and took power. In December 1980, Bishop accepted a Cuban invitation to attend the congress of the Cuban Communist Party, and just a month later the Cubans established a regular air link between the two islands. After this, the numbers of Cuban military and civil advisors grew steadily; among other things, they were engaged in constructing a very large airport whose capacity far exceeded Grenada's needs. In late autumn 1983, dissention broke out within the ruling party about where to go next. In the course of the conflict, Maurice Bishop and some of his closest companions were killed by hard-liners, who apparently wanted an even closer alliance with Cuba and the Soviet Union. The United States responded to this threat by invading the island, so as to reestablish representative government. In the meantime, free elections have taken place and American troops have left.

In Latin America, the most important focus of Cuban and Soviet activities is Nicaragua. In the beginning, the vast majority of the population enthusiastically supported the Sandinista revolution of July 1979. Since 1981, however, the revolution has increasingly deviated from its original objective of building a pluralist society. Some of the founders and most active supporters of the Sandinista movement left public life or even emigrated, the press has been muzzled, and freedom of religion has been undermined. Closer contacts with the Soviet bloc accompanied these domestic developments. The number of Cuban advisors in the Central American nation has grown drastically since 1980, while increasing amounts of Soviet arms have found their way to Nicaragua via Cuba.

To sum up: it is undeniable that the Soviets have succeeded in extending their influence in some countries of Asia, Africa, and Latin America since the late 1960s. There are two constraints on further advances: First, the Soviets are not willing to risk a major confrontation with the United States, and, second, they have no interest in encouraging pro-Soviet developments in a Third World nation if such a move would result in an increased financial burden for them. Cuba currently receives $3 billion in Soviet aid, and Vietnam $2 billion. There is only limited interest in creating more Cubas and Vietnams; the economic burden would be too heavy for the Soviet Union.

III. THE SOVIET UNION AND WESTERN DEMOCRACIES

The Soviet Union's relations with "capitalist states," or "countries of state monopoly capitalism," to use Soviet terminology, figure last in almost all official Soviet presentations, even though relations with the West have always played a very important, sometimes even dominating, role in Soviet foreign policy. The doctrine of peaceful coexistence is the basis of Soviet policy toward the West.

The Soviet Doctrine of Coexistence

In February 1956, at the Twentieth Congress of CPSU, the meeting that heralded de-Stalinization, Khrushchev made the following statement about his country's relations with the West:

The Leninist principle of peaceful coexistence of states with different social systems has always been and remains the general line of our country's foreign policy . . .

We believe that countries with differing social systems can do more than exist side by side. It is necessary to proceed further, to improve relations, strengthen confidence between countries and co-operate.[34]

But coexistence is limited to the diplomatic realm:

Peaceful coexistence cannot extend to the sphere of ideology because it is impossible to reconcile the bourgeois and the Communist ideologies.[35]

In 1959, the Soviets added one more element to this doctrine, namely that the period of coexistence would be favorable to the "international class struggle." According to this thesis, the class struggle takes place not only between contending social classes within countries, but also on the international level between the "camp of socialism" and the "camp of imperialism."

The three elements of the doctrine, i.e., political coexistence, ideological struggle, and international class struggle, reflect the divergent interests of the ruling Soviet nomenklatura within the Soviet Union and in their sphere of influence. The thesis of "living side by side peacefully with states having different social systems" is an expression of the Soviet leadership's unwillingness to risk a major military confrontation with the West. For the USSR, it is of vital importance to maintain trade and scientific exchange with the West, and these links must not be unnecessarily jeopardized.

The second aspect of the doctrine reflects the Soviet leadership's fear of the spreading of liberal ideas. The reference to "ideological struggle" is the justification of the Soviets' attempts to prevent the spreading of liberal and democratic ideas from the industrially advanced countries to the Soviet bloc. The principle is invoked to justify the jamming of Western radio broadcasts and the stiff controls on foreign travel imposed on Soviet citizens. It is used to limit Western reporting on everyday life in the Soviet Union and to portray the West as the enemy. The concept of "ideological struggle" serves to suppress all liberal stirrings in the population and to neutralize all attempts to further human rights and reforms.

Finally, by emphasizing time and again that the "international class struggle" continues unabated during the period of coexistence, the Soviets claim the right to support, militarily if necessary, any Third World national liberation movement that suits their interests, as well as aid protest movements in the advanced countries of the West.

Soviet Policy in the Decade of Détente

In the spring of 1969, it became clear that the Soviets were interested in improving their relations with the United States and the countries of Western Europe. They offered to start new negotiations on a variety of issues, the official Soviet press toned down its polemics, and there were more contacts in general.

The Soviet Union's new attitude had to be taken seriously. However, what induced the Soviets to initiate the period of détente was not a change in the principles underlying their foreign policy, but economic considerations and political pragmatism.

Economic necessities were the most important factor. By the spring of 1969, the Soviet leadership realized that they would not be able to overtake the United States in per capita income in the foreseeable future, as had been their officially proclaimed objective since 1961. They concluded that the Soviet Union had to catch up economically and technologically with the West by intensifying economic cooperation with the industrially advanced countries. From the outset, they aimed at wresting a maximum of economic aid from the West while making as few political concessions as possible. At the same time, they intended détente to lead to East-West conferences and treaties that would legitimate their domination over Eastern Europe. Finally, the Soviets hoped that in an atmosphere of calm and decreasing international tension it would be easier for them to expand their influence in the countries of Western and Central Europe by increasing friendly visits of all kinds and signing new agreements.

During the period of détente, Western public opinion attached great importance to the spectacular summit meetings, conferences, and treaties: the German-Soviet Treaty of August 1970, the Berlin Agreements of September 1971, SALT I in May 1972, the Nixon-Brezhnev summit of June 1972 in Moscow, the Ford-Brezhnev summit in Vladivostok, and the Helsinki conference in the summer of 1975.

There is no doubt that the era of détente facilitated a number of agreements between East and West, such as the granting of exit visas to tens of thousands of Soviet Jews and Germans, that would have been unthinkable earlier. The Soviets also considerably toned down their anti-Western propaganda, although they never gave up the two themes of continuing ideological struggle and international class struggle.

What was the balance sheet of the détente era from a Soviet point of view? The Soviets' principal aim had been to increase economic cooperation with the West. What did they achieve? During the entire period they received millions of tons of grain from the West, mostly from the United States, but also from Canada, Argentina, and Australia, enabling them to avert serious supply crises that might have resulted in hunger revolts. Moreover, they managed to keep these massive imports secret —no Soviet newspaper ever mentioned that the Soviet Union was nourishing its citizens by importing grain from the West. Détente thus enabled the nomenklatura to avoid being taken to task by the citizenry for mismanaging agriculture.

The rapid expansion of economic cooperation with the West also made it possible for the leaders of the Soviet Union to import the latest technologies and to start big projects. Western nations provided the credit.

The international conferences, negotiations, and treaties consolidated and legitimized Soviet control over Eastern Europe.

Many circles in the West were reluctant openly to support reformist trends in the countries of Eastern Europe, such as the Charter 77 group in Czechoslovakia. Even Solidarity was greeted with a certain reserve in some Western circles.

The shift in Western public opinion probably went beyond the Soviet nomenklatura's expectations. In the West, many people no longer distinguished between the Western democracies and the dictatorships of the East, forgetting that there are fundamental differences between the two systems. There was increasing talk about the "two superpowers" and there was hope —also in the United States—that the Soviet Union had switched from a policy of confrontation to a policy of cooperation.

Hardly anyone in the West was interested in engaging the Soviet bloc in critical debate. Instead, more and more people came to believe that the Soviet Union was a "partner" and that one had to convince "the Russians" that the West harbored no hostility against them. The West had to cultivate Soviet trust by being flexible and understanding in negotiations. Western concessions, the argument went on, would consolidate détente. "Destabilizing developments" in the East, i.e., liberal reforms, could endanger the rapprochement between the two blocs. Therefore the West should do little to encourage them. While people in the West were content to accept Soviet hegemony in Eastern Europe, the Soviets never gave up the notion of "ideological struggle," and even edited new books that updated official Soviet conceptions of world revolution.

Optimism was great in the détente era. One often heard the thesis that the West had a genuine interest in the stability of the Soviet bloc countries, as leaders who felt secure about their positions would be more likely to cooperate with the West and pursue moderate policies within and without.

On the basis of this idea, some politicians and commentators came to the conclusion that the West should be careful about supporting human rights in the East; at most, the West should use quiet diplomacy to improve the lot of individual dissidents and help them obtain an exit visa by making generous credits available to the Communist governments. Similarly, this current of opinion wanted Western governments to discontinue or depoliticize Western broadcasts to the Soviet bloc.

The Deployment of American Medium-Range Missiles in Europe

This Western optimism occurred in a decade in which the Soviet Union vastly expanded its military might. In the beginning, it seemed as if the navy and intercontinental missiles would receive the greatest attention. But the Soviets were well aware that they could hardly win an arms race with the United States on this level: In May 1972, SALT I came close to enshrining military parity between the two nuclear powers.

Shortly thereafter, Europe became the center of attention. Here the Soviets could realistically hope to gain military supremacy and change the balance of power in their favor, especially if they managed to exploit the differences between the United States and its European allies.

This is the background to the Soviet decision in the mid-1970s to start replacing the SS-4 and SS-5 medium-range missiles with the newer and more powerful SS-20's. The differences between the older missiles and the SS-20's were enormous. The SS-4's and SS-5's had only one warhead and were immobile. They used liquid fuel, which meant that it took eight hours to refuel them and make them operational. The SS-20, by contrast, uses solid fuel and has a maximum reach of about 3,000 miles; its three warheads can be targeted on three different points. The missile can be fired from a mobile ramp and can be made operational in a matter of minutes; it takes only two hours to ready a ramp for the next launch.

At the end of 1977, Americans sighted about ten SS-20 ramps in the western parts of Russia. Even then, experts estimated that the Soviets planned to produce between 300 and 400 of the new medium-range missiles.

The deployment of the SS-20's changed the military balance

of forces between East and West. Until then, the Warsaw Pact had enjoyed conventional military superiority in Europe, but now the countries of Western Europe faced a nuclear threat that was limited to them and did not include the United States. In the event of an SS-20 attack on Western Europe, one could hardly expect the United States to respond with its intercontinental missiles, as that would provoke enemy retaliation on American cities.

In this situation the idea came up that the United States should also deploy medium-range missiles in Europe, while simultaneously trying to reach arms limitation agreements with the Soviets. But the Soviets went on deploying new SS-20's. In 1978, there were seventy of them, and by the end of 1979, their number had gone up to 140, totalling 420 warheads. Faced with the growing threat, the Foreign and Defense Ministers of the NATO countries decided on December 12, 1979 in Brussels to pursue a double-track strategy. This consisted of the firm decision to deploy 108 Pershing II missiles and 464 cruise missiles if no agreement could be reached with the Soviets in the span of four years. All Pershing II's were to be stationed in West Germany, whereas the cruise missiles, with a reach of more than 1,500 miles, would be spread throughout Europe: Great Britain would receive 160, Italy 112, West Germany ninety-six, the Netherlands and Belgium forty-eight each. The ministers also affirmed their readiness to start serious arms limitation talks with the Soviets. If these talks succeeded, the deployment of American missiles would be slowed down. At the time, this decision met with wide agreement, but it led to heated debates beginning in the autumn of 1981.

There is reason to believe that if the West had maintained its cohesion, an arms limitation agreement with the Soviets would have been reached relatively early. For that to happen, it would have been necessary that all political forces, both in the United States and in Western Europe, continued giving equal weight to the two parts of the double-track decision.

The Peace Movement

Since the NATO double-track decision of December 1979, serious differences of opinion have appeared in the Western alliance, a development that was not lost on the Soviet leadership.

Western attitudes toward the Soviet Union began to diverge after the Soviet occupation of Afghanistan in December 1979. The invasion led to a profound change in American perceptions of the Soviet Union, and President Jimmy Carter's economic sanctions met with widespread approval. When Soviet troops entered Afghanistan, most Americans saw this as the end of détente. The Soviet aggression increased American readiness to upgrade its military, led to a revival of conservative values, and played an important role in the election of Ronald Reagan in November 1980. In Western Europe, reactions were more muted. Many influential groups wished to continue détente with the East, and even expand economic relations.

The Soviets exploited these differences and responded with a harder line: Andrei Sakharov was exiled to distant Gorki in January 1980, the jamming of Western radio broadcasts resumed in August 1980, and martial law was declared in Poland on December 13, 1981 after Solidarity had rocked the very foundations of Communist power in that country.

In response, President Reagan imposed wide-reaching economic sanctions, a move that met with criticism in some West European countries. Differences of opinion within the Western alliance were exacerbated when, at the beginning of President Reagan's first term, some American politicians and military officials discussed the "winnability of limited nuclear wars" and the possibility of a "nuclear first strike." Such utterances made many West Europeans uneasy. Conversely, there was a lot of criticism in the United States when West European companies agreed to participate in the construction of the Soviet gas pipeline.

Given this lack of unity in the West, the Soviets quietly went on deploying new SS-20's. In November 1981, there were 260 ramps, and even the start of new U.S.-Soviet negotiations that month in Geneva did not slow down their deployment. By the late autumn of 1983, 350 SS-20's were targeted on Western Europe.

At the same time, the Soviets repeatedly asserted their desire for peace and made new arms control proposals. Such proposals usually did not contain any verification clauses. With these political maneuvers, they succeeded in keeping alive the hope in Western Europe that concessions could pave the way for an agreement. The Soviets were very adroit in graphically depicting the dangers of the arms race and the apocalyptic consequences of a nuclear war. In the minds of many people the term "peace" became connected with an acceptance of Soviet proposals. In the end, the Soviets even got many people in the West to believe that if a (Western) town or a district declared itself a "nuclear-free" zone, this would improve the prospects for peace.

The Soviet tactic worked. Never before have peace and security issues been so important for millions of people in Europe as since the beginning of the Geneva talks in November 1981. The longer these negotiations dragged on, the more emotional the tone of Western debates became. At the same time, the lines between hard-liners and peace activists hardened in the West. The debates between the two groups increasingly excluded the political and social dimensions of East-West relations and concentrated instead on the military side only: missiles, their reach, the number of their warheads, and how dangerous they were.

Soviet Policies after the Deployment (1983–86)

As the Geneva talks between the United States and the Soviet Union progressed, it became increasingly apparent that there would be no quick results. In November 1982, Brezhnev died, and subsequently the Kremlin sent sometimes contradictory signals to the West. At the same time, the military were gaining influence in the Soviet power elite. East-West relations deteriorated further when Soviet military aircraft shot down a Korean civilian airliner on September 1, 1983, killing its 269 passengers.

By December 1983, the Geneva talks had yielded no positive results, and as four years had passed since NATO countries took the double-track decision, Western countries began deploying the Pershing and Cruise missiles. The Soviet Union withdrew from the talks in protest, without even hinting at a future resumption of the negotiations.

Apparently the West's decision to go ahead with the deployment of its own medium-range missiles had come as a surprise for the Soviets: they had overestimated the clout of the peace movement and the disagreements within NATO, and underestimated the determination of Western governments and parliaments to implement the double-track decision after all. The Kremlin's immediate reaction was to step up drastically its verbal attacks against the West, especially the United States and Germany. Ronald Reagan was said to follow in the footsteps of Hitler, and the Federal Republic of Germany was accused of seeking revenge for Germany's defeat in World War II ("revanchism," in Soviet parlance). The Soviets boycotted the 1984 summer Olympic Games in Los Angeles and threatened to deploy new missiles in Eastern Europe. Between the end of 1983 and the summer of 1984, the Soviet leadership still hoped to prevent or slow down the implementation of the NATO double-track decision: the peace movement was still strong, and there was hope in Moscow that in the presidential elections of November 1984 the more moderate Walter Mondale might replace Reagan.

In the course of the summer of 1984, however, it became apparent that the Soviets were rethinking their policies. They were realizing that the deployment of American missiles had become a reality, that the peace movement had run out of steam, and that Ronald Reagan would probably be reelected. Finally, they realized that the Strategic Defense Initiative (SDI), which the American President had announced in March 1983, would give the United States considerable supremacy in space.

The Soviet leadership adjusted its policies accordingly. Anti-Western propaganda diminished sharply, and it was announced that the Soviet Union was ready to return to the negotiating table. The Kremlin was now trying diplomatic means to dissuade the United States from going ahead with the SDI.

In September 1984, the Soviets sent the first signals that they were seeking a rapprochement with the United States. The Soviet Chief of Staff, Marshal Nikolai Ogarkov, had to yield his position to sixty-one-year-old Marshal Sergei Akhromeyev, who gave conciliatory interviews on American television. Even the then Secretary General of the CPSU, Konstantin Chernenko, spoke of the United States in more moderate terms. On September 28, 1984, Foreign Minister Andrei Gromyko met Secretary of State George Shultz in New York, and afterwards visited President Reagan in the White House. In November, Moscow decided to resume disarmament talks with the United States. Initially, the Soviets wanted to discuss only the SDI, but after January 1985 they agreed to negotiate about all three issues: medium-range missiles, intercontinental missiles, and space weaponry. The latter, however, remained their highest priority.

When Mikhail Gorbachev succeeded Chernenko as General Secretary in March 1985, he continued the relatively conciliatory line. In early July 1985, Gromyko left his longtime position as Foreign Minister and became head of state. By replacing the experienced Gromyko with Georgian Party chief Shevardnadze, a man with relatively little diplomatic expertise, Gorbachev showed that he would take a personal interest in the conduct of Soviet foreign policy.

The new leadership maintained the basic premises of Soviet foreign policy, but changed the methods somewhat. The younger men in the Kremlin displayed great activity, reacted more promptly to international events, and proved to be very adept at making public relations work for them. Although the United States remained the main focus of Soviet foreign policy,

Gorbachev and Shevardnadze paid increasing attention to Western Europe. Occasionally, Gorbachev would emphasize the common heritage of all European nations and thereby try to draw Western Europe away from the alliance with the United States:

> Whatever aspect of the development of human civilization we take, the contribution made by the Europeans is immense. We live in the same house, though some use one entrance and others another. We need to cooperate and develop communications within that house.[36]

The Soviets' main goal remains unchanged: to analyze differences of opinion and contradictions within the Western alliance carefully, and to use these to further Soviet interests. This applies both to the differences between the United States and Western European countries, and to contradictions among political forces within individual Western nations. The Soviets try to play off the allies against each other in order to attain their most important objective of the present time: to slow down and weaken American military activities in space.

IV. PRESENT SOVIET FOREIGN POLICY AIMS

Present Soviet foreign policy is characterized by expansionist tendencies and the quest for superiority within the international correlation of forces, but it carefully takes risks into account and attempts to avoid military confrontation.

Regarding the Western democracies; the Soviet leadership is currently pursuing the following objectives:

On the *military* level, the Soviet Union seeks to establish, step by step and without undue risk, its military superiority over the West. This is to be achieved chiefly by means of a forced rate of armament. The Soviet leadership also relies to some extent on political propaganda, attempting to sway public opinion in the Western democracies and thus to delay or even limit corresponding Western efforts. Soviet support of antinuclear and peace activities in the West fall into this category.

The military superiority sought by the Soviet Union is not intended to pave the way for an armed attack on European NATO members (the Soviet leaders recognize the dangers of such an action); rather, Soviet armaments serve the following purposes:

- to solidify the authority of the power elite within the Soviet Union and especially within the Soviet bloc, ensuring Soviet dominance over the countries in Central and Eastern Europe;
- to impress upon the entire world, especially the less-developed nations, the Soviet Union's role as a superpower and its ability to support its claims and interests throughout the world;
- to secure militarily its lines of communication with the less-developed nations and thereby to ensure a sufficient level of support to specific nations and movements;
- to provide a lever with which to strengthen Soviet influence and exert pressure upon the democratic nations of Central and Western Europe;
- to divert the attention of the Soviet population from the economic and social difficulties and the increasing social contradictions of Soviet life by emphasizing the USSR's status as a world power.

The Soviet leadership, however, never sees its military policy isolated from its economic and political aims. The Soviet Union seeks to bring about far-reaching economic cooperation with the industrial nations of the West. Its *economic goals* include the following:

- to reduce and, in the long run, to overcome its economic backwardness by borrowing Western technological know-how;
- to use Western credit at low interest rates to finance large-scale construction projects designed to strengthen the Soviet

Union's economic and technological base and, through the financial success of these projects, to gain access to Western currency on a regular basis;

• to win over increasing numbers of Western business leaders and to persuade them to support policies conducive to cooperation with the Soviet Union.

On the *political* level, the Soviet Union seeks to weaken the West by adroitly exploiting differences of opinion among and controversies within the Western democracies. To achieve this end, Soviet policy endeavors the following:

• to arouse public opinion in Western Europe against the United States by representing it as a menace to Western European interests. Its main aim is to separate Western Europe from the United States and to split the Western alliance;

• to categorize and deal separately with the NATO nations according to their individual relationship with the Soviet Union and, whenever possible, to promote economic and political differences among the nations of Western Europe;

• to investigate and carefully differentiate among the diverse groups, currents, and political parties within the individual nations of Western Europe; the Soviet leadership attempts to influence and strengthen what it considers to be positive elements, labeling them "realistic," "responsible," "peace-loving," or "democratic" and bestowing upon them praise, privileges, and concessions. At the same time, it sets about defaming, isolating, and weakening what it considers to be refractory and hostile elements, calling them "adventurers," "cold warriors," "militarists," and "warmongers."

The Soviets strive to create an atmosphere in which anyone who speaks critically against the Soviet system is suspected of being a "cold warrior." Next, they try to discontinue or "tame" Russian-language radio broadcasts from the West into the Soviet Union, and to extend their influence over the mass media (including the press and publishing houses) to the point where all pronouncements contrary to the interests of the Soviet Union cease to appear. They then attempt to put an end to the activities of refugees and emigré organizations, and to dissuade Western countries from accepting refugees from the Soviet bloc states.

All these activities are aimed at reorienting the foreign policy of a West European country so that it begins by giving equal treatment to the Soviet Union and the United States, and then develops in a pro-Soviet direction until it accepts and supports many of the more important Soviet foreign-policy positions.

The Soviet leadership is not interested in transformation by revolution, a Communist seizure of power, or a Soviet military occupation of Western European nations. Rather, it desires a carefully measured, ever increasing acquisition of influence as described above.

In this process, the goal of the Soviet leadership is to thwart all undesirable activities within a Western nation while gradually drawing it away from the Western alliance and closer to the Soviet sphere of influence.

5

Can the Soviet System Change?

Internal Repression
and External Expansionism

Upon being awarded the Nobel Peace Prize, Andrei Sakharov said: "Peace, progress, human rights—these three goals are indissolubly linked: it is impossible to achieve one of them if the others are ignored."[37] And in his book *My Country and the World* he wrote:

> It is especially important to emphasize that the problems of disarmament cannot be separated from the other basic aspects of détente: overcoming the secretiveness of Soviet society, strengthening international trust, and weakening the totalitarian character of our country . . .
>
> A concern for greater openness in socialist countries—for the freedom to exchange people and information—must be one of the central tasks of the coordinated policy of the Western countries.[38]

In most discussions on peace and security policy, the interdependence between internal oppression and external expansionism is rarely taken into account. Soviet dissidents, both those who still live in the Soviet Union and those who are now in the West, deserve our gratitude for having drawn attention to this link. Andrei Amalrik has written:

> The democratization of the Soviet system is the only guarantee of security for the West. So long as questions of war and peace are decided by ten men who are not accountable to anyone, no accords, however favorable on paper, will allow the Americans and Europeans a good night's sleep.[39]

And Vladimir Bukovski has emphasized that "both aspects of totalitarianism, i.e., repression inside and aggression abroad, go hand in hand."[40]

Lev Kopelev, the well-known writer and literary critic, declared, upon receiving the prize of the International Book Fair in Frankfurt:

> It should be clear by now that the only real guarantee for East-West agreements is the respect for human rights in those countries that have the most lethal weapons. As long as Nobel Peace Prize winner Andrei Sakharov and all members of the Soviet Helsinki watch group, as long as the members of the Charter 77 group in Czechoslovakia, the leaders of Solidarity in Poland, and the peace activists in East Germany are persecuted . . . , nobody should feel safe on this continent. As long as diplomatic and economic negotiations exclude the problem of human rights because this problem belongs to the "internal affairs" of a country, the danger of war can only increase.[41]

I fully agree with these leading representatives of the civil rights movement in the Soviet Union. The security of the Western democracies does not depend only on the West's military strength or its ability to reach agreements with the Kremlin, but also on the extent to which internal transformations within the Communist-ruled countries can lead to liberalization and respect for human rights.

Changes in Communist Systems

The discussion of internal changes in the countries of the Soviet bloc meets with a lot of skepticism in the West. One often hears the following reasoning: The system will not tolerate any reforms, and all previous attempts in this direction have failed. One has to accept the Communist regimes as they are; at best, one can expect the leaders to take small steps to improve the situation. Besides, there is always the danger that domestic instability might prompt the leaders of these countries to step up repression or engage in international adventures to divert attention from their internal difficulties.

Such arguments are not new. For many years I have been collecting forecasts on possible future Soviet developments. These forecasts go back to the 1920s for the USSR, and to 1945 for the entire Soviet bloc. The overwhelming majority of these predictions overestimated the stability of Communist regimes and failed to detect the internal contradictions that have led to unexpected changes.

Such "surprises" include the June 1953 uprising in East Germany, which had been unthinkable only a few months earlier, the June 1956 workers' uprising in Poznan and other Polish cities, and the Hungarian Revolution in the autumn of 1956. As late as 1966, Czechoslovakia was generally considered a Stalinist model state; few observers in the West were prepared for the victory of the reformers in January 1968 that started the "Prague Spring."

The internal cohesion of the Soviet bloc has also been overestimated. Yugoslavia's break with Moscow in June 1948 took the whole world by surprise. Even highly respectable newspapers and journals wrote that after his break with Stalin, Tito would be able to maintain himself for a few weeks at most. Some even thought that Moscow and Belgrade had prearranged this break in order to mislead the West. Also, only few observers noticed the differences between the Soviet Union and China that had surfaced in the early 1950s. As late as the 1960s, some people were still speaking of a "Moscow-Peking Axis," as a break between the two Communist superpowers seemed utterly unimaginable. It took a lot of observers a long time to take note of the growing independence of a number of West European Communist parties, a development that has been termed "Eurocommunism."

It was, therefore, not surprising that most commentators overestimated the stability of Gierek's regime in Poland in the mid-1970s. Even those who were aware of oppositional tendencies did not consider them to be a serious force in society. When, in the summer of 1980, the strikers at Gdansk came forth with their demands and Lech Walesa's name became known, Western commentators often contended that the movement would not spread beyond the Baltic ports and would soon be put down anyway. As it happened, the Solidarity movement spread all over Poland, gaining 10 million members, and was followed by "Rural Solidarity," which had a membership of 3 million. This ground swell of opposition forced the government to make wide-reaching concessions for a while.

When Western observers finally do pay attention to oppositional movements in the Soviet bloc, they often impute these movements to the "national peculiarities" of this or that country and treat them as isolated cases. For these people, the Hungarian revolution was reminiscent of Hungary's struggle for national liberation in 1848–49, the "Prague Spring" echoed Czechoslovakia's two decades as a stable democracy in the interwar years, and Solidarity expressed the Poles' unbroken patriotism and the great influence of the Catholic Church.

As important as these national characteristics are, one should not overlook common elements in all the aforementioned movements. They all aim at instituting liberalizing reforms inside the country and making it more independent of the Soviet Union. There is reason to believe that such emancipatory developments could occur again in Eastern Europe—perhaps even in the Soviet Union.

The Soviet Union is an industrial state, and large sectors of the population are highly educated. They either personally remember or have heard older people speak of such momentous developments and events as the first Five-Year Plan, during which industrialization received a decisive push and agriculture was forcibly collectivized, the terror-ridden years of the Great Purges in 1936–38, the sudden U-turn of the Hitler-Stalin Pact in August 1939, the terrible suffering of the Second World War, the difficulties and the hunger of postwar reconstruction, Stalin's death in March 1953 and the hopes engendered by the subsequent de-Stalinization, Khrushchev's fall in 1964, and the period of authoritarian restoration under Brezhnev.

These experiences have shaped the thinking of Soviet citizens and sharpened their critical faculties. An intellectual opposition, the dissident movement, has emerged. The variety and quality of this opposition's underground publications, collectively known as *samizdat,* show the extent to which thoughtful Soviet citizens are reflecting on their system and on possible ways to liberalize and democratize their country.

Whenever one speaks about possible changes in Communist countries, one encounters opposition from two sides. For many traditional anti-Communists, all statements about reforms, de-Stalinization, or a "new course" are nothing but empty propaganda: in their view, there have never been genuine changes in a Communist dictatorship, and Communist systems can never change. According to this opinion, whoever speaks of transformations or even future liberalizations in the Communist world is naive and underestimates the dangers of Communist dictatorships.

But one also meets with opposition from those who were enthusiastic about the détente of the 1970s. These people are also skeptical about internal changes in the Communist world —but for different reasons. For them, reform movements in Eastern Europe have a destabilizing effect on East-West relations and therefore endanger peace. It is wiser, the argument continues, not to show too much concern for human rights: in order for détente to be durable, each side has to accept the other as it is. According to this view, the activists of the 1968 "Prague Spring" may have been *morally* right, but in practice they lost their sense of proportion. The same is true for Solidarity: it carried its demands too far. It should have been more realistic and adapted its tactics to concrete reality.

The exponents of this thesis warn against too much Western support for oppositional dissidents and reform movements in the Soviet bloc, as these might lead to "destabilizing developments" that would negatively affect East-West relations and the prospects for peace. They wish to improve East-West relations only by diplomatic means, and are often willing to have the West make unilateral concessions first. Somehow they are oblivious to the dictatorial nature of Soviet bloc countries.

Thus all those who discuss the possibility of change within Communist systems are criticized by both "traditional anti-Communists" and overoptimistic supporters of détente. It is important to break this double taboo. We have to examine under what conditions serious changes can occur in the Soviet Union and in other Communist countries, which forces in society favor such developments, and what the likelihood of their success is.

Reforms in the Soviet Bloc: Conditions and Forces

Socio-political transformations in the Communist countries of Central and Eastern Europe depend on a number of factors: the development of contradictions in the system; the relative strength of those social groups, tendencies, and forces that favor reform and change; the population's general mood and its attitude vis-à-vis the economic situation; and the cohesion of the political leadership and the bureaucratic power structure.

All Communist-ruled societies are marked by internal contradictions. They all contain forces that favor liberalization and reform, although these forces take different shapes from country to country.

- Industrial workers are becoming increasingly self-confident and would like to act as an autonomous social force, articulating their interests in independent trade unions.
- The non-Russian peoples of the USSR are critical of Russification, yearn for equality among the nationalities, and hope to gain more autonomy within the USSR.
- The younger generations in the Soviet Union, who have grown up in the post-Stalin era, are tired of the constant flow of official propaganda, have different values and goals, and would be ready to embark on a new course.
- Churches and religious movements of all kinds oppose the official atheism and demand more freedom of worship and freedom of conscience.
- The scientific and technological intelligentsia is confronted daily with outdated bureaucratic structures and therefore favors economic reforms and the lessening of official interference in scientific work.
- Artists (particularly writers and poets), who enjoy great prestige among the population, press for the freedom of creation and demand an end to censorship.
- There are relatively few *active* proponents of human rights and democratization in the Soviet Union, and their leverage is severely limited by official persecution. But they do express the yearnings of far wider strata and could serve to crystallize popular demands in the event of a beginning transformation of the system.

The history of Soviet and East European Communism has shown that economic pressure and the political dissatisfaction of the population can wrest concessions, reforms, and partial liberalizations from regimes. As Wolfgang Seiffert wrote:

Thorough, effective, and lasting reforms of the economic system in the countries of "real socialism" have so far only been carried out as a consequence of revolutionary developments. In other words, the bureaucratic leaderships of these countries have yielded to pressure only when societal developments confronted them with the alternative of either losing some hair or the whole head.

But economic reforms can only have a salutary influence on the entire system if they are coupled with political reforms. This confirms that in countries ruled by Soviet-type governments fundamental reforms come about only in the aftermath of deep political upheavals and have to face the resistance of the bureaucratic forces.[42]

The classic example of economic restraints and political dissatisfaction leading to reform is Lenin's New Economic Policy (NEP), of spring 1921. The civil war that had followed the Bolshevik Revolution was nearing its end. Most workers and peasants had supported the Bolsheviks in their fight against the Whites, and had suffered greatly as a result. As revolutionary fervor subsided and the dictatorial aspects of the new regime became ever more apparent, dissatisfaction and indignation spread among the working population. In Petrograd (today, Leningrad), Moscow, and in many other cities workers struck, there was peasant unrest in the countryside, and the fortress at Kronstadt, once a Bolshevik stronghold, became the focus of the famous sailors' rebellion. The young Communist regime was facing a serious crisis. In response, Lenin changed course dramatically. He eased the burden of the peasants, gave free rein to personal initiative and even private enterprise, and invited foreign capitalists to come and invest in Soviet Russia and contribute to reconstruction. With these measures he hoped to overcome the grave economic difficulties and the political crisis.

In the cultural sphere, the NEP inaugurated a period of unprecedented creative freedom that has never been reached since. For many Soviet citizens, the NEP era remains the relatively happiest time in Soviet history. Eight years later, the economic situation had stabilized and Stalin had consolidated his power. In 1929, he put a sudden end to the NEP and switched to a repressive line in the form of the first Five-Year Plan and the forced collectivization of agriculture.

A second example: When German troops attacked the Soviet Union on June 22, 1941, Soviet troops retreated in panic. As the Germans took Kiev and Kharkov, and were advancing on Moscow and Leningrad, Stalin's regime was facing the greatest crisis of its history. The change in the political line became immediately perceptible: the Communist Party and Marxism-Leninism were pushed into the background, and the Church received great leeway. As famine spread, the regime quietly tolerated a de facto extension of the private plots on the collective farms, without ever publicly announcing this policy shift. Stalin opened up cultural life, literature and the arts, to a degree hitherto unimaginable under his rule. In September 1941, he even asked for the deployment of British troops in the Soviet Union in order to stabilize the front lines—without posing the slightest preconditions! However, as soon as the military situation had improved at the end of 1943 and in early 1944, Stalin immediately switched back to a more repressive course: the Party became more prominent again, there were more arrests, a number of Caucasian nationalities were deported to Central Asia in the spring of 1944, Churches had their rights curtailed, and collectivization was once again dogmatically enforced.

A final example: After Stalin's death in March 1953, his heirs faced a deep crisis in the Soviet economy and especially in agriculture. Within the USSR, social and national tensions had become exacerbated, and internationally the country was isolated. To maintain the system, it was urgent to reduce tensions, to initiate reforms, to give the people new hope, and to overcome the international isolation of the Soviet Union. Anti-Western propaganda stopped only a few weeks after Stalin's death and the new leaders proclaimed their desire for improved relations with the West. In the summer of 1955, official statements spoke of the "spirit of Geneva." The regime relaxed its controls over the arts and literature, drastically toned down Russification, and brought increasing numbers of non-Russian officials into the system: there was a "thaw" everywhere. In economic policy a "new course" was proclaimed—emphasis would henceforth be on consumer industries. Enterprise directors received more prerogatives, and collective farms were given material incentives. On the international scene, the Soviet leaders demonstrated their new moderation by traveling to Belgrade and meeting with Tito, whom Stalin had excommunicated only seven years earlier. The Soviet Union also signed the Austrian State Treaty and evacuated its occupation zone in Austria. Perhaps the most important development of those years was the drastic reduction of the power of the secret police. Hundreds of thousands (according to some estimates, as many as three million) of people were released from jails and prison camps; de-Stalinization meant new hope for millions of Soviet citizens.

As soon as the regime had stabilized itself, Khrushchev switched back to a more hard-line policy. In the autumn of 1957, the Soviets had intercontinental missiles, and in October of that year, they put Sputnik into orbit. The spring of 1958 brought record harvests. Consequently, the anti-Western campaign was stepped up, and in October 1958 Khrushchev surprised the world with his Berlin ultimatum.

These examples speak for themselves. Under pressure, Soviet leaders shift gears and make concessions, both to their own population and to the outside world. As soon as the situation is under control, however, they intensify repression at home and resume their expansionism abroad.

Dissensions in the Nomenklatura

Discussions about internal contradictions and possible systemic changes in the Soviet Union often meet with the following objection: would the ruling elite tolerate such changes? Are the four power centers—the Party and the state administrations with their huge bureaucracies, the mighty military establishment, and the omnipresent KGB—not powerful enough to nip any reform attempts in the bud?

Of course, nobody would underestimate the power apparatus of the Soviet Union. But there are increasing signs that the apparatus is considerably less militant and monolithic than in former times. Within the four power centers—the Party, the government, the army, and the KGB—different groupings have emerged that sometimes disagree on policies. Also, differences of opinion are on the rise between the Soviet Union on the one hand, and its East European allies on the other.

The nomenklatura, too, is torn by internal strife. Although all nomenklatura officials share an interest in their continued rule, they differ on particular policies. On economic policy, there is a struggle between those who hope that an increased emphasis on labor discipline would be sufficient to overcome the Soviet Union's relative backwardness, and those who advocate a reform of the obsolete system of central planning of the economy.

In investment policy, proponents of heavy and defense industries vie for influence with the supporters of consumer industries. Regarding the nationalities, there are differences of opinion between the adherents of Russification and those who stress the multinational character of Soviet society. In foreign policy, we find "globalists," who want to maintain a Soviet role on a worldwide scale, and others who consider such a policy adventurous, and above all too costly, and who would like to limit Soviet activities. Some would like to improve and extend relations with the West out of economic and technological self-interest, while others take a more hostile and anti-Western position.

To these political disagreements one has to add institutional tensions. Cooperation among the four power centers is by no means devoid of friction. For instance, the Party is jealous of its prerogatives vis-à-vis the military. When, in 1983, army generals held press conferences on foreign policy issues, important Party officials interpreted this as an infringement on the leading role of the Party. In "normal" times, such jealousies remain innocuous, but when the situation becomes difficult they can lead to a polarization within the regime.

There are many instances of such polarization. After Stalin's death, proponents and opponents of de-Stalinization fought very hard at times. During the Hungarian Revolution in 1956 reformists led by Imre Nagy faced the Stalinist hard-liners around Matyas Rakosi and Ernö Gerö, and in 1967–68, the Czechoslovak Party was torn by struggles between supporters and opponents of reform. At times, this polarization has affected even the very top of the hierarchy, especially during succession crises when the new leaders struggle over the new "general line": after Lenin's death in 1924 and Stalin's death in 1953, after Khrushchev's fall in October 1964, after Brezhnev's death in November 1982, and, finally, in the last transition period that started with Gorbachev's nomination in March 1985.

Of course, it would be irresponsible to try to forecast the future of the Soviet bloc in detail. But in order to be prepared for whatever developments might occur, it is important to think about the alternatives. The following six possible tendencies and perspectives are not the product of the imagination of "Kremlin astrologists." Rather, they represent *possible* developments in the Soviet Union, and Western democracies should take them into account if they are to formulate effective long-term policies toward the USSR.

Economic Modernization

The term "economic modernizers" refers to those elements within the economic bureaucracy and the Party apparatus who are in favor of an economic reform—as long as it is initiated, planned, and controlled by the Party leadership. Its objective would be to overcome current supply problems, the serious situation in agriculture, the lag in modern technology (especially computers), and gradually to catch up with the West. The aim of the economic modernizers is to adapt the present system to a modern industrial society, to maximize economic efficiency and technological innovation, but at the same time keep Party control over political and cultural life so as to prevent a genuine democratization.

Given the tremendous difficulties of the Soviet economy, it is not inconceivable that Soviet leaders, or a majority of them, might finally decide to begin these long overdue reforms. Professor Jiri Kosta, one of the key figures of the "Prague Spring" and currently professor of economics at the University of Frankfurt, thinks that such a development is highly likely:

> Since the 1960s economic reforms have been increasingly brought about by economic difficulties . . .
>   Declining growth rates and lagging productivity gains in the COMECON countries, especially in the Soviet Union, will increase the pressure for reform. Wide-reaching decentralization and increasing integration into the world economy would be the logical response to the economic difficulties, but the interests of the ruling elite counteract such moves . . . In the long run the reform movement should prevail.[43]

The economic modernizers would probably start by giving the enterprises more autonomy and eliminating some of the bureaucratic shackles that hinder their dynamism. Each firm's performance would be evaluated on the basis of its profitability. A state-controlled trading system would have to replace the current bureaucratic method of resource allocation. Management would be allowed to develop more initiative; it would receive the right to make certain investment decisions. Many of the Central Planning Committee's decisional prerogatives would be transferred to the managers.

Horizontal links and arrangements among enterprises would take the place of the bureaucratically determined planning goals. Instead of having their investment determined by the state budget, companies would increasingly have to turn to the banking system and rely on their own capacities of self-financing.

If the economic modernizers prevail, one could also imagine what changes they would make in the way agriculture is organized. As in industry, they would eliminate the hundreds of often contradictory guidelines, decrees, orders, instructions, norms, and detailed production figures. The kolkhozi and sovkhozi themselves would offer their produce not only to the state, but, increasingly, also to the market. The state would still set some prices, but only to stimulate the production of certain goods and to encourage agricultural specialization. On collective and state farms, the current abstract system of determining wages would give way to a system in which wages would depend on the quantity and quality of the delivered agricultural products.

Although the economic modernizers are determined to limit reforms to the economic sector, they might be willing to initiate limited reforms in other fields in order to defuse simmering social problems. For the economic modernizers, modern and more flexible policies are the best means of reducing conflicts and contradictions while there is still time, so as to avoid explosions. Many of these policies would probably resemble those enacted in Hungary in the last decade.

Internal changes would also affect the Soviet Union's foreign policy. If the economic modernizers were to favor a more realistic foreign policy, they would probably lessen their country's costly involvement in the Third World. In their opinion, the occupation of Afghanistan was a mistake: Western computers matter more than do Afghan tribes. They prefer "political solutions" for the problems of Poland and other East European nations, and have more understanding for some of the moderate forces in these countries.

If the Soviet economy is to recover, and if the Soviet Union is to overcome its technological backwardness, East-West relations have to expand, say the economic modernizers. They would like to avoid all "unnecessary" conflicts with the West and to tone down anti-Western propaganda, because for them economic and technological cooperation have clear priority over constant threats and exaggerated armaments.

The hopes for economic modernization have increased since the nomination of Gorbachev in March 1985. He has repeatedly called for a "deep restructuring" of all spheres of Soviet society, and his call for "radical reform" at the Twenty-seventh Party Congress seemed to point in the same direction.

However, one cannot overlook that this call was not endorsed by any other Politburo members at that congress. Moreover, opponents of economic reform are by no means limited to the higher echelons of the Soviet political elite: they are particularly strong within the gigantic economic bureaucracies.

In the last two years, the long-standing taboo about the size of the Soviet bureaucracy has been broken. On May 13, 1984, the government newspaper *Izvestia* reported that the State Committee for Construction Affairs *(Gosstroi)* alone employs 160,-000 administrative officials, and in November 1984 (when Chernenko was still officially in charge, but Gorbachev was already number two in the top leadership), an article by M. V. Klimko in *Voprosy Istorii PSS* (Questions of History of the CPSU) revealed that the state economic apparatus employed 15.3 million civil servants.

The need for economic reform is obvious, and even the nomenklatura recognizes it, at least in part. Such an economic reform would, above all, aim at changing the current system of economic management, whereas a widening of the scope of private initiative is less important for now. It is very interesting that since Gorbachev's elevation references to Lenin's New Economic Policy have increased, particularly in discussions of agriculture. Perhaps this is an indication where economic reforms would begin.

The "Commercialization" of the System

Whereas the economic reform scenario stresses the change in the system of economic management without altering basic property relations, the concept of "commercialization" refers to the increased toleration of private enterprises and to the introduction of market-oriented mechanisms in agriculture, small industry, and the service sector.

Until now, state-ownership of the means of production and the state's central role in planning the economy have been unshakable dogmas of the Soviet system; they are ideologically justified and constitutionally mandated. But is there no possibility that these principles might be modified in the future?

Such a shift could take place only on the basis of a rapprochement between the nomenklatura officials and the increasingly self-confident "representatives of the second economy"; this rapprochement would be in the interest of both sides. The wide-ranging privileges of the nomenklatura have already been described. It bears repeating that these privileges are not given to the officials personally, but are part of the function each individual occupies. The loss of one's position in the nomenklatura usually entails the immediate withdrawal of all privileges. That is why officials are always looking for ways to increase their personal security, to give a permanent basis to their privileges, and to acquire personal property that they can pass on to their children.

The willingness of many nomenklatura officials to accept bribes is not due only to human weakness, but also reflects their desire to acquire genuine personal property so as to gain a measure of security. The representatives of the second economy are well aware of this, but they face a very different problem: their private activities are strictly illegal. Their "economic crimes" are heavily punished, and they can receive even the death penalty. But the discrepancy between theory and reality cannot last forever. Private enterprise in the Soviet Union is much more important than what the terms "black market" or "speculation" convey.

The more thoughtful officials understand that people who engage in private enterprise are not "criminal" outsiders, but have become a new social stratum in Soviet society. Given the increasing economic problems, especially in agriculture and in consumer goods industries, it will hardly be feasible to eliminate the "second economy": it provides too many badly needed services. Nomenklatura officials have learnt by experience that where economic interests clash with administrative measures, the former usually prevail: neither Khrushchev's much heralded "anticorruption campaign" nor similar initiatives by Andropov in 1983 and now by Gorbachev have succeeded in eliminating the second economy. It has become clear that it is much easier to crush the intellectual reform opposition than to limit the activities of private entrepreneurs, who enjoy the secret backing of nomenklatura officials at the highest Party and government levels.

It is true that the recent anticorruption campaign did have a few successes: a number of spectacular scandals came to light, those responsible for them were demoted, punished, sometimes even expelled from the Party and brought to court. But these successes only revealed the tip of the iceberg: it is no secret that Soviet authorities, with all their power, are incapable of coping with the second economy and corruption in official places. They are not dealing with a few thousand idealist intellectuals, but with powerful social strata: the nomenklatura officials are striving for personal property and wealth, and the representatives of the second economy are striving for unhindered freedom of enterprise.

In the event of a "commercialization" of the system, the first step would be the legalization of private enterprise in agriculture, small industries, and the service sector. This would very probably lead to a quick increase in the scope of private economic activity. Nomenklatura officials would get, or simply take, the right to participate in these private ventures as a reward for having legalized them. The integration of both strata might even go both ways, as representatives of the second economy might be brought into the apparatuses of Party and state.

In order to increase agricultural production, the collective farmers' private plots would have to be enlarged. One can imagine a dissolution of all unprofitable collective and state farms, perhaps even a complete reprivatization of agriculture. There are precedents for such a move; both Poland and Yugoslavia first collectivized agriculture in the late 1940s and then gave the land back to the farmers in the early 1950s. As in Lenin's New Economic Policy in the early 1920s and in today's Hungary, a legalized private sector would include commerce, small repair shops, and light industry, while state ownership would be limited to transportation and heavy industries. The semi-legal *tolkachi* could exercise their functions as official representatives of Soviet companies.

It would be relatively simple to justify such a development both politically and ideologically. All one would have to do would be to deemphasize certain Lenin quotations and replace them with others. Here is a sample: In October 1921, Lenin wrote that it was necessary to stress the component of "personal interest, personal incentive," since "personal interest increases production."[44] On October 17 of that year he stated:

> Every important branch of the economy must be built up on the principle of personal incentive . . .
>
> Get down to business, all of you! You will have capitalists beside you, including foreign capitalists, concessionaires and leaseholders. They will squeeze profits out of you amounting to hundreds percent; they will enrich themselves, operating alongside of you. Let them. Meanwhile you will learn from them the business of running the economy . . . we must undergo this training, this severe, stern and sometimes even cruel training, because we have no other way out.
>
> The state must learn to trade in such a way that industry satisfies the needs of the peasantry, so that the peasantry may satisfy their needs by means of trade.[45]

Soviet leaders could declare such a "commercialization" to be a new variation of the widely popular NEP. Of course, it would be somewhat embarrassing to introduce policies in the 1980s that Lenin had proclaimed more than sixty years ago, as such a move would amount to an admission that after fifty years of state-centered economic policies the Soviet Union had reached a dead end. But even this problem could be solved by giving the policy a new name: "mature new economic policy" suggests itself, and is analogous to the term "mature socialist society," which has been the official designation of the current stage of socialist development in the Soviet Union since 1977. Private firms could officially be called "cooperative-commercial enterprises"; the term "cooperative" has a socialist ring and is mentioned in the Soviet constitution, while "commercial" in Soviet usage usually refers to something positive, to a new development. All of these transformations could take place under the aegis of the ruling Party. In reality, the Party would function somewhat differently, but the changes in the Party rules would be relatively minor and hardly meet with much opposition from its members.

It is conceivable that such a transformation of the Soviet system might entail other, initially unintended changes in other areas. As a counterweight to the newly independent firms, free trade unions might emerge. Externally, the leaders of the Soviet Union would no longer need foreign adventures to divert domestic attention from internal difficulties; it is probable that after decades of stifling bureaucratic centralism the overwhelming majority of the population would be happy to concentrate on economic development and on the satisfaction of long neglected consumer demands.

Liberalization: Hope or Illusion?

A genuine liberalization, followed by a democratization of the Soviet system, would undoubtedly be the most desirable development for the future. Such developments could evolve gradually and on the basis of Soviet traditions. First, the terror apparatus would have to be dismantled. Economic reforms and the emancipation of the nationalities would follow. Finally, democratic rights would be granted and the Supreme Soviet would become a genuinely representative body. Of course, such developments could come only at the end of a very long process, but there are some factors that point in that direction.

Industrialization, urbanization, educational advances, and, above all, the people's social and political experience have combined to render Soviet citizens quite capable of actively taking part in political life. To this, one has to add the importance of generational change. That part of the population which bore the imprint of the Stalin era is dying out, and a new generation with different experiences and values has reached political maturity. The members of this generation have witnessed the revelations of the Twentieth Party Congress and de-Stalinization, and more than ever before they clamor for individual liberties and material goods. This generational shift has already begun at the higher Party echelons.

The growing influence and increasing importance of the scientific-technological intelligentsia has become quite palpable. The difficult problems that the Soviet Union is facing require that the regime reach out to natural scientists, engineers, economists, and sociologists and involve them in decision making. This could gradually lead to structural changes in the political hierarchy, and might conceivably prove to be the engine for liberalization and democratization.

Existing institutions could play a role in such a development. The political system of the Soviet Union maintains a number of fictions: According to the constitution, the Supreme Soviet is vested with wide-ranging powers, for example that of forming the government. As mentioned earlier, the true centers of power, the Politburo and the Central Committee, are not even mentioned in the constitution. Party rules clearly establish inner-Party democracy and the supremacy of Party congresses. Why should these institutions not acquire a life of their own some day in the future? This might come about as a result of disagreements among top leaders, who would turn to the Central Committee, perhaps even to the Party Congress, to break the deadlock. This would be the first step toward a democratization of the Party and might gradually spread to the population at large.

In the opinion of three democratic scientists, Sakharov, Valery F. Turchin, and Roy Medvedev, democratization would have to proceed cautiously and step by step, so as to avoid complications and sudden breaks. At the same time, democratization would have to be thorough and carefully planned. According to these three dissidents, Soviet society will not be able to solve its problems and evolve normally if there is no democratization.

The three envisage this process to begin with a "statement by the highest Party and Government organs on the necessity of further democratization." "Information on the state of the country" should initially be "restricted," but would be gradually increased until it would be "fully available to everyone." The authors add the following measures:

> Widespread organization of industrial establishments with a high degree of independence in questions of industrial planning and production processes, sales and supplies, finances, and personnel, and widening these privileges for smaller units . . .
>
> An end to jamming foreign broadcasts. Free sale of foreign books and periodicals. . . . Gradual (over three to four years) expansion and easing of international tourism on both sides. Freer international correspondence and other measures for the expansion of international contacts . . .[46]

Such a democratization would transform all aspects of Soviet society. The KGB would have to be reined in and controlled by elected bodies. All innocent inmates of prison camps, jails, and psychiatric clinics would have to be released and rehabilitated. The death penalty would have to be abolished, and conditions in the remaining prisons would have to be improved. New laws would prevent the misuse of psychiatric clinics for political purposes. Political trials would have to be open to the public. All constraints on the freedom of the press, of religion, and of conscience would have to be lifted; religious communities would receive the right to develop freely.

In the economic realm, emphasis would shift from the arms

industries to consumer industry, while gaps between social strata would be reduced to tolerable levels. Employees and workers would receive the right to form independent and self-governing trade unions that would represent their demands in public.

The transformation of the Supreme Soviet from a rubber-stamp assembly into a truly representative body would have to be complemented by internal changes in the Communist Party. Besides free discussion, there would have to be free and secret elections at all Party levels. Blind discipline and unconditional submission to an almighty leadership would have no place in a renovated Party. The transformation of the ruling Party would sooner or later make it possible for other independent organizations to appear, and eventually this might even lead to the emergence of other political parties. Thus a democratization of the CPSU could be the first step toward a democratization of the whole political system.

Until now, the history of the Soviet Union has been marked by one-party rule, but this option was a matter of debate at the dawn of Soviet rule, and need not necessarily last forever. Lenin himself, on December 4, 1917, i.e., one month *after* the Bolshevik Revolution, stated:

> The direct, consistent and immediate democratic principle, namely, the right to recall, must be introduced. . . . The transfer of power from *one party to another* then takes place peacefully, by mere *re-election.*[47] [Emphasis added]

One of Lenin's closest companions, Nikolai Bukharin, advocated the legalization of a second party during a visit to Paris in 1936:

> Some second party is necessary. If there is only one election slate and there is no contest, it is the same as Nazism. In order to differentiate ourselves in the minds of the peoples of both Russia and the West, we must institute a system of two electoral slates as opposed to the one-party system.[48]

Since the end of the 1960s, a number of Communist parties outside the Soviet bloc, including those of Italy, Spain, Sweden, and Japan, have clearly come out in favor of a multiparty system in a socialist society. The same development has taken place within the Soviet opposition. A group of Leningrad dissidents declared that "a true democratization of the bureaucratic regime is impossible without the existence of a legal opposition, i.e., some form of multiparty system."[49]

For Roy Medvedev, the well-known moderate dissident and advocate of socialist democracy, a multiparty system is necessary, since there are important social and political differences between various population groups and the Party and state apparatuses in the Soviet Union. According to Medvedev, these differences also exist within the working class, the intelligentsia, and among the officials. He writes: "Several of the political trends in our country already contain in embryo all the elements of political organization or parties."[50]

There are undoubtedly officials who, on the basis of their good education and their professional and human qualities, could function much more effectively in a free Soviet society. Should genuine economic reforms ever be implemented in the Soviet Union, a later democratization of the whole system could not be excluded.

Toward a Russian-Authoritarian State?

A future transformation of the Soviet system would not necessarily be liberal and democratic in nature: it could be a throwback to the authoritarianism of prerevolutionary Russia. In such a case, Marxism-Leninism would be officially replaced by Russian nationalism and the glorification of Russian traditions. The Russian hegemony in all walks of Soviet life would increase even further, and the regime would attempt to assimilate all nationalities in the "Great Russian empire." Authoritarian rule would at first be confined to the Russian heartland and later spread to the non-Russian areas of the Soviet Union and to Eastern Europe. However, unlike the present situation, there would be no lip-service to the ideas of a "Socialist Camp," "Socialist World System," "socialist internationalism," or "proletarian internationalism." The slogan "Workers of all countries, unite," and such symbols as the red flag with its hammer and sickle would disappear. Russian hegemony would take the forms of traditional Great Russian chauvinism. Political institutions such as the Communist Party, especially all its organs of world communism, would retreat into the background, or be dissolved altogether. It would be replaced by the traditional power centers of state and army, while the Orthodox Church (and perhaps other religious communities) would gain in influence.

The victory of authoritarian Russian nationalism would spell order, authority, and stability—without mass purges, vigilance campaigns, and ideological propaganda. The Russian nationalists would insist on the population's subordination to the leadership and prevent all critical discussions and publications, but the present preoccupation with political campaigns, mass meetings, and unanimous decisions would disappear. Key positions would devolve on the state apparatus, the army, and the Orthodox Church; instead of invoking Marxism-Leninism and socialism, the regime would legitimate itself by reference to the nation and its traditions.

Such developments would particularly affect cultural life. Russian literature would increasingly turn back to eternal Russian values with their particular emphasis on village life and rural bliss. Literary, political, historical, and philosophical writings would be infused with the idea that each nation has its own character and individuality, and that these factors determine the development of the people. Russia's evolution since 1917 would be termed an "aberration." The condemnation of the entire Soviet period would go hand in hand with a rejection of pluralist models of parliamentary democracy, which the Russian nationalists deem too "Western"—which for them is a negative term. The return to Slavophile themes would become the dominant current in intellectual life. Economic and social transformations would be of secondary importance: what matters most for Russian nationalists is spiritual change, i.e., the return to God, to national traditions, to national destiny, and to Russia's historical responsibility.

Moscow's foreign policy would change accordingly. Relations with the West would be limited, to avoid any kind of "westernization." Global activities in Africa, Asia, and Latin America would be toned down, but Russian domination in Eastern and Central Europe, and in all areas bordering on the Russian empire, would be consolidated. Such a policy would stress continuity with the foreign policy objectives of prerevolutionary Russia. Eurasian hegemonism would replace global expansionism.

This perspective, too, is not a product of the imagination, but emerges from clearly discernible Russian nationalist tendencies in today's Soviet Union. These tendencies exist in all social strata and on all political levels. In the markets of Russian towns, one often feels a definite antipathy toward the Uzbeks, Tajiks, Azerbaijanis, or Georgians, who sell their produce and thereby elicit the resentment of ordinary Russians. Andrei Sakharov has noted that "sometimes the striving toward a national revival takes on chauvinistic traits, and borders on the traditional 'everyday' hostility toward 'aliens.' Russian anti-Semitism is an example of this."[51]

Some Russian intellectuals, both at home and abroad, combine nationalism with a negative attitude toward both the Soviet experience and Western democracy. In their view, the present system cannot be overcome by liberalization and democratization, but by a return to the Orthodox faith and national Russian traditions. Arrogance, intolerance, and a profound disrespect for the experiences and traditions of other nations very often accompany this train of thought.

Russian nationalist ideas have found their way to the highest levels of the Soviet power elite. Mikhail Suslov, who was chief ideologue of the Soviet regime until his death in 1982, is said to have sympathized with them toward the end of his life. Economic officials have their own reasons to be responsive to Russian nationalism. In his book on the economic integration of Comecon countries, Wolfgang Seiffert recalls:

> It often happened to me in Moscow that otherwise very serious Russian scientists tried to explain the Russian people's low standard of living by pointing out that Russia would be far better off if it did not pour so much money, energy, and labor into the Asian republics, Azerbaijan, Armenia, and Uzbekistan. . . . [They] hoped that Russia's greatness would benefit if these ties could be loosened.[52]

Although Russian nationalist tendencies in contemporary Soviet life should be taken seriously, it is very doubtful whether Russian nationalists would by themselves be strong enough to take power in a country where half the population is not Russian. In a Russian authoritarian state, nationality problems would be far more exacerbated than they are now, and there would be a dangerous polarization between Russians and non-Russians.

Politically, Russian nationalists would confront very powerful adversaries. The Party and its apparatus would combat such developments by all available means, because its replacement by other groups (the state apparatus, the army, and perhaps the Orthodox Church) would signify the end of its power and privileges. Also, since the leaders could no longer invoke the "unity of the Socialist Camp," it would become increasingly difficult to maintain and legitimate Moscow's hegemony in Eastern Europe.

In the final analysis, therefore, the Soviet Union's transformation into a Russian authoritarian state is not very likely. At most, Russian nationalists could play a role by allying themselves with other factions within the leadership, which would allow them to have some influence over the course of events.

The Danger of Neo-Stalinism

Economic reforms, liberalization, and a return to Russian nationalism are not the only alternatives for the future. Critical observers of Soviet developments, both in the West and among Soviet intellectuals, also discuss the dangers of a neo-Stalinist restoration. If it came to that, repression at home would intensify, while Soviet foreign policy would become more hard-line.

A possible scenario follows: After adequate preparations, a neo-Stalinist faction manages to seize power. It would use the next (perhaps extraordinary) Party Congress to proclaim a new general political line. For the first time since 1952, gigantic portraits of Stalin would appear in public places, all newspapers and journals would publish pictures and quotations of Stalin, and Stalin-era films would be shown again. His *Collected Works* would be reedited and enter official curricula.

Many important decisions that affected post-1953 events would be officially condemned. All writings that contain such key terms of the post-Stalin era as *socialist legality, collective leadership, criticism of the personality cult,* and *détente* would disappear from libraries. The new leadership would lay the blame of all current difficulties on the erroneous, even treacherous policies of Khrushchev, Brezhnev, and their successors. These men would be depicted as having betrayed Stalin's heritage and tradition.

In their criticism of post-Stalin developments, the new leaders of the Kremlin would more readily invoke Stalin's name, which still plays a greater role in collective consciousness than the moribund tenets of Marxism-Leninism. One can easily imagine what the line of argument would be: The country needs a stable leadership again, everything was better under Stalin, and it is time to reestablish order again. Show trials of scapegoats would consolidate the new power structures, while vigilance campaigns and purges would intimidate the population. In domestic policies, "screws would be tightened again." On the economic front, the neo-Stalinists would attempt to improve productivity and continue industrialization by making increased use of forced labor. Order, stability, authority, purges, mass arrests, all under the banner of loyalty to Stalin's heritage, would be the hallmarks of neo-Stalinist domestic policy. Foreign policy would be affected, too: The neo-Stalinists might argue that the détente of the 1970s neither enabled the Soviet Union to catch up with the West technologically, nor did it bring any other economic advantages worth mentioning. All détente did was to leave the Soviet Union with a huge foreign debt and contribute to its becoming "too soft."

One could expect such a regime to propagate the unconditional unity of the Soviet bloc, coupled with threats against Romania's independent foreign policy, Hungary's economic reforms, and Yugoslavia's nonalignment. In Poland, General Jaruzelski would be chided for not being tough enough, and, as a warning to the rest of Eastern Europe, repression against the supporters of Solidarity would drastically increase.

Cultural contacts with the West would be sharply limited, and economic links would be reduced to a minimum. The new leaders would argue, "For fifty years we industrialized successfully without Western capitalists. Why do we need them now?"

This dire picture of a neo-Stalinist future is by no means a figment of the imagination. Supporters of this tendency can currently be found in both the Party and the state apparatuses, and also in the KGB and the army. Given the Soviet Union's internal difficulties, such a "return to the past" cannot be excluded. In fact, there are no guarantees *against* such a development: The legal system is still subject to manipulation by a small power elite, and there are no other institutional checks to restrict this small elite's scope of action.

The economic and technological progress that the Soviet Union has achieved since Stalin's death does not necessarily increase the chances for a liberalization of the system. Some Soviet intellectuals fear that modern technology and computers are precisely what could enhance the repressive nature of the dictatorship by allowing it to keep a tighter control over citizens both at work and at home. Moreover, new psychological and medical techniques could facilitate the neutralization of dissent. In this context, some critical intellectuals are already apprehensive about "Stalinism with computers."

The possibility of a neo-Stalinist restoration is frequently discussed, mainly because among some groups in the Soviet Union one can observe a kind of "Stalin nostalgia." The explanation for this rather surprising development lies in the fact that there has been no systematic and critical debate about the past, and that even de-Stalinization did not change the structures of power. Stalin's crimes were briefly discussed only twice: first in the immediate aftermath of the Twentieth Party Congress, in February 1956, and later after the Twenty-second Party Congress, in October 1961. In both instances, bureaucratic forces soon proved strong enough to put an end to Khrushchev's initiatives.

Since Khrushchev's fall, in October 1964, all criticism of Stalin and of Stalinism has ceased. When discussing the lives of great Bolshevik leaders who were killed during Stalin's purges, Soviet authors have to gloss over the real causes for their deaths. There are no official systematic accounts of Stalin's crimes or of the system he built. Thus people's memories of the terror, the purges, the vigilance campaigns, the show trials, and the millions of labor camp victims were pushed into the background, while Stalin himself became a "man of order" in the minds of many people.

Many Western correspondents have noted the emergence of a "Stalin nostalgia." Hedrick Smith, who represented the *New York Times* in Moscow from 1971 to 1974, was dismayed at the many positive appraisals of Stalin he encountered in the Soviet Union. An Azerbaijani taxi driver in Baku, when asked about the photograph of Stalin that adorned his windshield, told him: "We love Stalin here. He was a strong boss. With Stalin, people knew where they stood." A factory director in his fifties, whom Smith met on the train from Odessa to Moscow, told him, after complaining about the long hair and untidy look of Soviet youth and the unruliness and unreliability of workers in his plant, "They are all slackers. We have no discipline now. We need a strong leader. Under Stalin, we had real discipline. If someone came five minutes late to work . . ." and here the factory director ran a finger across his throat.

A young metallurgical worker in his twenties said, "You want to know what the workers think? . . . Russians need a leader who is strong . . . like Stalin." And a linguist in his fifties told Smith, "Stalin knew how to impress people. When he was alive, other countries respected and feared us more."

A writer in his sixties, who spent eight years in Stalin's labor camps, tried to explain the nostalgia for Stalin among the working people: "They feel that he built the country and he won the war. Now they see disorganization in agriculture, disorganization in industry, disorganization everywhere in the economy and they see no end to it. They are bothered by rising prices. They think that when there was a tough ruler, like Stalin, we did not have such troubles. People forget that things were bad then, too, and they forget the terrible price we paid."

The poet Yevgeny Yevtushenko told Smith how one summer he had sat around a campfire in Siberia with some students. One of them had shaken him by proposing a toast to Stalin, as "all the people believed in Stalin and with this belief, they were victorious." It turned out that the students did not know about Stalin's crimes. When Yevtushenko asked them how many people they thought had been arrested during Stalin's rule, one said twenty to thirty people, another estimated their number at 200, and a third admitted that there had been 10,000. When the poet told them that the figure is reckoned in the millions, they did not believe him.[53]

In the years 1978–82, the end of the Brezhnev era, one could increasingly see Stalin's picture in private apartments and even in public, such as on the windows of taxicabs.[54] In Georgia, where "the native son" has never lost his popularity, pictures of Stalin could be bought on the black market for one ruble; from Georgia they found their way to the rest of the Soviet Union.

During the summer and autumn of 1984, under Chernenko, the Stalin issue gained new saliency. On July 5 of that year, ninety-four-year-old Vyacheslav Molotov, who had been the second most important Soviet leader throughout Stalin's rule, was readmitted into the Party and received by Chernenko. Also, such Soviet publications as *Sovietski Patriot, Literaturnaya Gazyeta,* and *Krasnaya Zvezda* ("Red Star," the army paper) repeatedly printed positive assessments of Stalin, often accompanied by wartime pictures of him. In February 1985, *Victory,* a film that praises Stalin both as diplomat and as military leader, reappeared on Soviet screens.

In February 1985, shortly before Gorbachev took over, some World War II veterans requested that the city of Volgograd be renamed Stalingrad, which had been its official name until 1961. Under Chernenko, a decision to that effect was prepared. But at the instruction of the new General Secretary, Deputy Defense Minister Vassili Petrov politely but firmly rejected the request at a press conference in Moscow on May 6.

Two days later, on May 8, 1985, Gorbachev gave an official speech commemorating the fortieth anniversary of the Soviet victory in World War II. On this occasion, he drew attention to the importance of the "State Committee for Defense," which had been chaired by the General Secretary of the CPSU, Joseph Vissarionovich Stalin. As soon as Gorbachev had pronounced Stalin's name, the 5000 Party officials, army officers, and war veterans broke into stormy applause. Twice Gorbachev tried to continue, but was stopped by the continuing ovation. He succeeded only on his third attempt, visibly irritated by the unexpected demonstration of sympathy for Stalin.

There can be no doubt that the Stalin issue is still alive. Until now, Soviet leaders have tried to propagate a positive image of Stalin as statesman and military leader, while at the same time cautiously distancing themselves from the domestic aspects of his regime. This is not easy. Not a few Soviet citizens, especially among intellectuals, would welcome a clear repudiation of Stalinism, but there are also those, particularly among the functionaries, who favor an explicit adherence to Stalin's traditions.

In spite of these tendencies, the danger of a neo-Stalinist development has decreased. It seems hardly possible to force the Stalinist system of the 1930s on a Soviet Union that has changed considerably since then. The adoption of Stalinist methods would only aggravate the existing economic problems and exacerbate national and social tensions. Furthermore, the current leadership would not sit by idly while neo-Stalinists rise to power. Today's leaders would be tomorrow's scapegoats, which would be a very powerful incentive for them to oppose a full-scale return of Stalinism.

How Likely Is a Military Dictatorship?

The possibility of a military takeover in the Soviet Union has been the object of interesting discussions for many years. The proclamation of martial law in Poland in December 1981 by General Jaruzelski made many people wonder whether similar developments would be possible in the USSR. According to this scenario, in the Soviet Union a military dictatorship could come about either gradually, by the armed forces increasing their influence in the government, or by an outright military coup. The domestic political and economic difficulties facing the regime might damage its legitimacy to such an extent that the top leaders might come to regard the army as the only force that can maintain the regime. Military leaders might then decide to take power themselves, either alone or in alliance with some Party leaders who would agree to play second fiddle to the army. If such a scenario were to come true, one could imagine an increase of repression at home and expansionism abroad; some even see the possibility of such developments being accompanied by economic reforms.

Since the 1960s, the army's growing influence on decision making in the Soviet Union has been a clearly discernible fact. Its visibility in public life increased steadily during the Brezhnev period (1964–82), coinciding with the Soviet Union's transformation into a superpower. Soviet arms exports to the Third World, the presence of military advisors in distant countries, the building of military bases, and the expansion of the Soviet navy have allowed the military to become a major factor in the formulation of Soviet foreign policy. The growing importance of nuclear weapons and the interaction between security issues and foreign policy have compelled the Soviet leadership increasingly to seek the advice of military experts. This, in turn, has enabled the military to gain thorough insights into the Party leadership's foreign policy plans and to influence decision making.

After Khrushchev's fall, the army's growing influence has made itself felt in other areas, such as cultural life and education. Since 1966, "military-patriotic education" has played an important role. All official publications emphasize military traditions in addition to the standard references to "the leading role of the Party."

In the Politburo, the importance of the Defense Minister rose steadily from the 1960s to the mid-1980s. The military's influence in Soviet affairs became much more pronounced after the Twenty-sixth Party Congress, in 1981, a year and a half before Brezhnev's death. Events in Poland certainly affected this development. The Polish United Workers Party was not only utterly discredited in the population but also torn by internal strife: One third of its members actively participated in Solidarity. The army was the regime's last recourse, although it should be noted that the Polish security service cooperated closely in the crackdown of 1981. Since that time high Soviet officials have been known to discuss the merits of a "Polish solution."

After Brezhnev's death in November 1982, leading representatives of the armed forces stepped up their public appearances. By the time the Soviets shot down KAL 007 on September 1, 1983, the army had become strong enough to manipulate all official statements and communiqués in such a way that its direct responsibility was never openly touched upon.

When Andropov hinted at the Soviet Union's willingness to

be more flexible at the Geneva disarmament talks, the military foiled his attempts by publicly issuing hard-line declarations that neutralized the effect of the General Secretary's efforts. It is no exaggeration to say that the army's overall influence in Soviet politics was never as great as during the first months of Andropov's rule from November 1982 to the summer of 1983. But it appears that after the shooting down of the Korean airliner on September 1, 1983, important forces within the Communist Party were willing and able to reduce the growing influence of the military in Soviet decision-making. The decisive change occurred after the death of Defense Minister Marshal Ustinov in December 1984.

The two most obvious candidates to succeed him, Sergei Akhromeyev, the Chief of Staff, and Marshal Kulikov, Commander-in-Chief of the Warsaw Pact forces, were passed over in favor of the relatively colorless seventy-three-year-old Marshal Sergei Sokolov. Sokolov was only a simple member of the Central Committee then, and he had to wait until 1985 to be admitted to the Politburo as a candidate member. Until then, the armed forces had been represented in the Soviet Union's highest decision-making body by a full member, and only the future will tell if, in the long run, they accept this relative demotion.

This leaves us with the question of whether the army is either willing or able to seize power in the Soviet Union. Three factors militate against such a development:

First, it is very doubtful whether the military actually *want* total power. They already have more influence than ever before over all those areas which are of direct interest to them. At the same time, they have the distinct advantage of not being responsible for the remaining areas, such as the economy. Therefore, it stands to reason that the military's main objective is to consolidate its current position, perhaps strengthening it here and there; they do not want responsibility for solving the Soviet Union's economic, social, and nationality problems.

Second, the army does not enjoy a degree of autonomy that

would enable it to prepare and carry out a military coup. The Party's and the KGB's control over it are still extensive enough for any coup attempt to be uncovered on time.

Third, a military takeover presupposes a degree of unanimity within the armed forces that does not exist in reality. The various branches of the armed forces have diverging interests, and among the officers there is a cleavage between those who served in World War II and were profoundly influenced by that experience, and the younger, more technocratically oriented generation. Under these conditions, it would be very difficult to achieve the unity of motivation necessary for a coup.

Consequences for the West

These short scenarios are, of course, not alternative blueprints for future developments. The list is by no means complete. Moreover, different factions within the Soviet elite favor one or the other of the six tendencies we have identified. This means that economic constraints, political dissatisfaction, and the tug of war between different factions within the Soviet elite could lead to a combination of elements from two or even three of the mentioned tendencies. Nevertheless, all six perspectives are based on existing factors and forces; they are, therefore, also of interest for the future of East-West relations.

A harsher or more moderate line in the Soviet Union would undoubtedly influence East-West relations. Domestic changes in the Soviet Union always have an immediate effect on its foreign policy. The general rule is that the more modern, pluralist, flexible, and moderate the Soviet Union becomes, the more hope there is for a genuine and trustworthy détente. And, conversely, the harsher the repression inside, the greater the danger of a confrontational policy abroad.

As a practical consequence, all Western analyses, political evaluations, statements, and other activities should take into account the domestic balance of forces in the Soviet Union. The

West must not be content merely to react to Soviet initiatives, but should include all potential long-term changes in its calculations.

In the final analysis, of course, it is domestic factors that determine internal developments in the Soviet Union and the other Communist-ruled states. But the question remains: what policies should the Western democracies pursue to strengthen reformist forces and thus facilitate liberalization in the Soviet bloc?

6

How Can the West Support Liberalizing Tendencies?

O
ur short overview of possible transformations of the Soviet system has shown that a political liberalization and an opening up of Soviet society would not only benefit the peoples of Soviet bloc, but also pave the way for a genuine improvement in East-West relations and thus lay the foundation of a lasting peace. But how can the West exert influence on the Soviet Union and its allies, and encourage reforms (or at least not hinder reformist forces) without interfering in the internal affairs of these countries?

The Struggle for Human Rights

Human rights are, of course, the most important aspect of such a long-term strategy. The question of whether Western democracies have a right (or obligation) to support human rights in the countries of the Soviet bloc (and, of course, in all other dictatorships), and how this could be done best, has led to a number of public controversies.

During the détente of the 1970s, there were those who wanted to keep away from the whole issue. Unfortunately, this attitude persists here and there even today. Three arguments are used: First, any public support for human rights would only harm the dissidents. This is clearly not the case: experience has shown that when Western public opinion consistently expresses concern for the dissidents and encourages efforts on behalf of human rights, repression actually decreases. International solidarity *can* help the dissidents.

According to the second argument, "quiet diplomacy" is far more effective in helping people in individual cases, and public support for human rights would only hamper these diplomatic efforts. This view overlooks the fact that the two parts of this argument are not mutually incompatible. Of course, one should use all available channels to ease the plight of certain groups on a case-by-case basis, but public opinion in a Western democracy cannot leave it at that. It is our duty to report regularly and objectively on arbitrary arrests of dissidents and their suffering in jails, prison camps, and psychiatric clinics.

Lastly, some fear that any open concern for human rights might be seen in the countries of the Soviet bloc as an interference in their internal affairs. This, too, is wrong. The leaders of these countries signed the so-called Helsinki Declaration in the summer of 1975, and, perhaps more importantly, the United Nations Covenant on Civil and Political Rights of September 1966. In both these documents, they took it upon themselves to respect their provisions.

All those who take an active interest in human rights were greatly encouraged by President Carter's open letter to Andrei Sakharov. On January 21, 1977, the Nobel Peace Prize laureate had pleaded with a certain number of Western heads of state to help Soviet dissidents by showing public support for them. On February 5, Carter responded as follows:

Dear Professor Sakharov,

I received your letter of January 21, and I want to express my appreciation to you for bringing your thoughts to my personal attention.

Human rights is a central concern of my administration. In my inaugural address I stated: "Because we are free, we can never be indifferent to the fate of freedom elsewhere." You may rest assured that the American people and our government will continue our firm commitment to promote respect for human rights not only in our country but also abroad.

We shall use our good offices to seek the release of prisoners of conscience, and we will continue our efforts to shape a world responsive to human aspirations in which nations of differing cultures and histories can live side by side in peace and justice.

I am always glad to hear from you, and I wish you well.

Sincerely,

Jimmy Carter

This correspondence between a leading representative of the Soviet civil rights movement and the American President is proof not only of the dissidents' personal courage, but also of their increasing self-confidence. How did this development come about?

Almost forty years have passed since the United Nations proclaimed the Universal Declaration of Human Rights on December 10, 1948. The Cold War had reached its first climax—the West was still shaken by the Berlin blockade, and the East chafed under Stalin's rule. The Soviet bloc's isolation from the rest of the world was almost total. The U.N. declaration was published neither in the Soviet Union nor in the other Communist states. I was then a teacher at the Karl Marx Party Academy in Klein-Machnow, near Berlin, but in spite of the privileged access to information that my position gave me, I cannot remember the event. The Soviet bloc countries had, in fact, little reason to publish the declaration, having abstained during the crucial General Assembly vote—together with South Africa and Saudi Arabia!

The Soviet population at large became conscious of the need for systematic protection of human rights only after Stalin's death, when the millions who returned from the camps told about the extent of the terror they had faced. The hopes that de-Stalinization had generated were dashed when Khrushchev was deposed and the regime returned to a harder line. However, the discussions about human rights that the short-lived "thaw" had engendered formed the basis of an independent and opposi-tional reform movement.

Since April 1968, the *samizdat* publication *Chronicle of Cur-rent Events* has been the Soviet civil rights movement's main forum for intellectual exchange. The front page of each issue features Article 19 of the United Nations Covenant on Civil and Political Rights, which the Soviet Union has signed:

Everyone has the right to freedom of opinion and expression; this right includes freedom to hold opinions without interfer-ence and to seek, receive and impart information through any media and regardless of frontiers.

In their quest for human rights, Soviet dissidents as a rule avoid double standards. Time and again they repeat that who-ever defends human rights violations in South Africa or Chile, but protests against similar violations in Communist countries, acts in as one-sided a manner as those who pay attention to human rights violations in only the Western world and do not care about the Soviet bloc, or even think that speaking up on behalf of the dissidents in the East would endanger peace.

The civil rights movement received a new impetus on Septem-ber 18, 1973, when the Soviet Union officially ratified the afore-mentioned United Nations covenant. Now the dissidents could turn their full attention to the concrete application of its provi-sions. These are legally binding on the signatories.

After the conclusion of the 1975 Helsinki Conference on Secu-rity and Cooperation in Europe, to give its full title, the argument that support for human rights in the Soviet Union constitutes interference in that country's internal affairs can no longer be sustained. Point VI of the conference's Final Act limits the scope of "non-intervention in internal affairs" to "armed intervention or threat of such intervention," acts of "military, . . . political, economic, or other coercion," and "assistance to terrorist activities, or to subversive or other activities directed towards the violent overthrow of the regime of another participating State."

Contrary to a widespread misconception, the Final Act does not deal with human rights only in "Basket 3." In "Basket 1," which deals with questions of security in Europe, we find under Point VII:

> The participating States will respect human rights and fundamental freedoms, including the freedom of thought, conscience, religion or belief, for all without distinction as to race, sex, language or religion.
>
> They will promote and encourage the effective exercise of civil, political, economic, social, cultural and other rights and freedoms . . .

In the often quoted "Basket 3," all signatories commit themselves to facilitating human contacts across borders by allowing "persons to enter or leave their territory temporarily, and on a regular basis if desired, in order to visit members of their families." "The preparation and issue of [travel documents] and visas will be effected within reasonable time limits: cases of urgent necessity—such as serious illness or death—will be given priority treatment." Authorities will "ensure that the fees for official travel documents and visas are acceptable."

The publication of the Helsinki Declaration in 1975 led to developments that caught the Soviet leadership by surprise. The reform movement now had an even clearer goal: Communist states had signed the declaration, and human rights groups now intended to work for its realization. But the dissidents' hopes did not last long. Even the Helsinki Watch Groups that had been formed for no other purpose than to monitor official compliance with the Helsinki accord were suppressed and their members persecuted.

Repression did not spare even Sakharov. On October 20, 1975, he requested an exit visa to go to Norway and receive his Nobel Peace Prize. The Soviet authorities refused. His wife, Elena Bonner, read his acceptance speech:

> Détente can only be assured if from the very outset it goes hand in hand with continuous openness on the part of all countries, an aroused sense of public opinion, free exchange of information, and absolute respect in all countries for civic and political rights.

Mrs. Bonner added that since Helsinki, human rights violations in the Soviet Union had actually increased: "In the Soviet Union today many thousands of people are both judicially and extrajudicially persecuted for their convictions."[55] In this context, Sakharov mentioned the psychiatric clinics, the political trials, and the arrests of human rights activists. He knew what he was talking about: as his wife was reading his speech in Oslo, he himself and a few friends were on their way to Vilnius, the capital of Soviet Lithuania, where they wanted to attend the trial of fellow dissident Sergei Kovalyov, a biologist.

As the regime increased pressure on the civil rights movement, it became imperative that Western democracies provide some outside help. Over and over, Sakharov and others tried to draw Western attention to the plight of Soviet dissidents. The letter to President Carter was part of these efforts.

On February 10, 1977, CBS interviewed Sakharov on the subject of the letter. He said:

> The new president's moral, courageous position evokes my respect and hope. It is not interference in other countries' internal affairs to conduct a decisive, consistent, and principled defense of human rights throughout the world. . . .
> I have neither the right nor the opportunity to give advice to the new administration about how it should act in any particular situation. I can only permit myself to say that any

disagreement, uncertainty, or partial retreat will give the Soviet authorities the impression that the new administration is
giving in to blackmail and pressure. I am deeply convinced
that will not actually occur, for any appearance of weakness
will affect all aspects of East-West relations, including disarmament negotiations.[56]

In the beginning, it seemed as if Sakharov's fear that the West
might yield too easily were unfounded. On March 1, 1977, the
U.S. government invited Vladimir Bukovski, a civil rights activ-
ist who had been expelled from the Soviet Union, to visit the
White House. He was received first by Vice-President Walter
Mondale, later by President Carter himself. In his memoirs,
Bukovski remembers:

> I did not ask him for any special favors, I just tried to make
> a convincing argument that the campaign for human rights
> had to be obstinate and consistent if we were to have any
> success. One had to take into account the special features of
> the Soviet system and the Soviet psyche. One should not
> expect any rapid results and not change policy if there were
> no immediate successes. Of course Soviet leaders would try
> to prove that they were unaffected by open pressure. They
> might even temporarily increase repression, so as to provoke
> criticism of the new Western attitude, but such a move should
> not deter the West. If the West maintained its human rights
> policy for a number of years, the Soviet Union would have no
> choice but to yield.[57]

Many commentators showed, sadly enough, little understanding for President Carter's initiative, and much derision and
mockery was heaped on it. The few positive reactions that the
move had elicited were drowned by general rejection, both in
the United States and in Western Europe. The dominant opinion
stated that it was dangerous to combine foreign policy with
moral principles, as this would lead to all sorts of problems and
dead ends. The opponents of this policy made a number of

arguments: The U.S. government had been too idealistic; Carter's letter to Sakharov and his meeting with Bukovski had created new risks and would play into the hands of the hawks in the Kremlin; the "Sunday preacher" from Plains was jeopardizing the fruits of détente; one had to consider whether public criticism of conditions in other countries did not actually worsen the plight of the dissidents; and, finally, the West could not force its own conception of human rights on the Soviet leadership.

In the face of widespread and, in my view, completely unfounded criticism, the human rights initiative gradually lost its momentum, as Sakharov had feared. World public opinion lost interest, the Helsinki watch groups in the Soviet Union and the signatories of Charter 77 in Czechoslovakia felt abandoned, and East European nomenklatura officials had gained a major victory.

The waning of public interest in the West made it easier for the Soviet authorities to settle their account with the civil rights movement, as they had planned to do for a long time. In January 1980, Sakharov was arrested in Moscow and deported to Gorki; since then, he has lived under the close guard of the KGB, whose agents have completely isolated him, constantly bother him, and even confiscate his manuscripts. All Helsinki groups have been exposed, and their members have been arrested and put into jails, psychiatric clinics, or prison camps.

In the West, the deterioration of the situation in the Soviet Union was hardly noticed, as attention has been focused on arms control. Only gradually did many people come to realize how closely Western security and repression in the Soviet Union were connected. Human rights figured prominently on the agendas of the succeeding Belgrade and Madrid conferences, and on September 20, 1983, the final document of the Madrid conference again emphasized the importance of human rights.

The awarding of the 1983 Nobel Peace Prize to the Polish labor leader Lech Walesa (again, the laureate had to have his wife represent him in Oslo), and public activity in the West demanding the return of Sakharov from his exile in Gorki can perhaps be interpreted as signs that more and more people in the West are realizing just how important it is to support human rights abroad.

A long-term, resolute, and patient strategy for the defense of human rights in the Soviet bloc, supported by Western governments and by international public opinion, would very probably yield positive results. It might conceivably lead to the liberation of thousands of political prisoners, a development that would facilitate an opening up of Soviet bloc societies, and ultimately create the foundation for improved East-West relations.

East-West Trade

Since 1972, the Soviet Union has each year been forced to import considerable quantities of grain from the United States, Argentina, Canada, and Australia. The figures vary from 5.5 million tons in 1974–75 to 45 million tons in 1981–82. For the Soviet leaders, these imports constitute not only an economic but also a political problem. These imports affect the economy in that they have to be paid for in hard currency or, sometimes, in gold. Politically, they amount to an admission that Soviet agriculture is in a deep crisis. It is ironical that the Soviets have to buy their grain from capitalist countries, whose economic system the Soviets never tire of deriding as being "rotten" and going through a "profound crisis."

The political significance of these grain imports is such that Soviet leaders have given strict orders that the fact never be mentioned publicly. So far they have succeeded: only those Soviet citizens who listen to foreign radio broadcasts know that they are saved from famine by Western grain deliveries.

Next to grain imports, the transfer of technology is the second most important aspect of East-West economic relations. Of course, the Soviet Union has an enormous industrial potential and sizable reserves of raw materials. However, many of these reserves are located in distant Siberia and their exploitation necessitates great capital expenditure and modern technology. Although the industrialization of Siberia is a top priority, it cannot be adequately achieved without the economic and technological cooperation of the West. The widespread claim that the Soviet Union could, if necessary, do without Western technology, contradicts the Kremlin's decades-long attempts to gain access to Western know-how. Even under Stalin, when autarchy was the order of the day, the Soviet Union never stopped trying to import Western technology and actively recruited Western engineers and technicians. Khrushchev's "chemicalization" campaign of the late 1950s would have been unthinkable without the participation of Western engineering firms. The industrial plants constructed by Western enterprises in the Soviet Union during the détente era have also been of great importance for that country's economic development.

Most experts agree that the technological gap between the Soviet Union and the West amounts to between fifteen and twenty years. With few exceptions, East-West technological transfer is thus a one-way affair. Soviet trade representatives are, above all, interested in investment goods. Compared to the licenses and the technological know-how that flow to the Soviet Union, Western machinery and "key-in-hand" enterprises are of lesser importance. For instance, when Fiat built the Togliatti automobile factory in the Soviet Union, the company had to train 2,500 Soviet technicians. Italian engineers had to adapt the making of the Fiat 124 model (known as *Zhiguli* in the USSR, and as *Lada* abroad) to Soviet conditions. The widespread view that Soviet industry can easily imitate Western products overlooks the simple fact that such imitation takes several years to accomplish, and that by the time the production of the imitated goods can begin, the original technology may already be obsolete.

Also, one should not exclude the possibility that products ostensibly imported for civilian purposes might later be put to military use by the Soviets. This especially applies to computers: a 1100-10C computer officially bought from the United

States for use in a chemical factory in the Volga region was later used by Soviet engineers to improve decisively the Backfire strategic bomber. Of course, large computers can also be used for the steering of intercontinental missiles. Since 1950, the Coordinating Committee for East-West Trade (COCOM), has controlled and coordinated all transfer of technology to Communist countries; all NATO countries (with the exception of Iceland) and Japan belong to it. Although COCOM cannot declare an embargo on a certain type of product, it does regulate exports of strategically important goods on the basis of very precise criteria. Nevertheless, the Soviets have managed a number of times to acquire products that they wanted to put to military use.

Finally, the gas pipeline deal has played an important role in East-West trade relations. On November 20, 1981, two days before then General Secretary and head of state Leonid Brezhnev went to Bonn, Soviet foreign trade officials and representatives of Western enterprises signed the most important East-West trade agreement of all times in the West German city of Essen. At issue was the construction of gas pipelines and compressor stations with a total value of 20 billion deutsche marks. Transporting the gas over a distance of 3,000 miles presented such difficulty for the Soviets that they suggested that European companies build the pipelines and then accept natural gas as payment.

Shortly after the gas pipeline deal was signed, Polish authorities declared martial law on December 13, 1981. In response, the Reagan administration imposed a number of economic sanctions first on Poland and later on the Soviet Union. The gist of these sanctions was an embargo on the export of electronic products and other high technology. On June 18, 1982, the United States government extended this policy to all foreign subsidiaries of American companies and to firms producing goods under U.S. licence: the goal was to force the West European allies and Japan to adopt policies similar to those of the United States. In addition, the American government demanded a reduction of the total volume of credit extended to the Soviet bloc, and also a tightening of credit conditions in East-West trade.

These measures had a visible effect on the Soviet gas pipelines. Two American companies, Caterpillar and General Electric, were prevented from delivering important equipment. A Japanese firm stepped in for Caterpillar, but the Soviets ended up falling half a year behind schedule.

The gas pipeline deal led to intense arguments between supporters and opponents of the pipeline project. The opponents felt that Western industrialists had come to the rescue of the Soviet leadership at a time of unprecedented economic difficulties. These opponents argued that the long terms of the credits had enabled the Soviets to undertake a gigantic project without making any financial commitment of their own. After gas deliveries started, the argument went on, the Soviets would earn $10 billion in hard currency per year, income that they could use for the import of high technology that could then be used for armaments. The final objection to the deal was that it put Western Europe, especially West Germany, in a position of dependency on the Soviet Union, as it enabled the Soviet leaders to cut off energy supplies.

The supporters of the deal countered that it was precisely in times of worsening East-West relations—brought about by the occupation of Afghanistan and the declaration of martial law in Polar l on the Soviet side, and by the imposition of economic sanctions on the American side—that trade relations had to be nurtured so as to prevent a return to a "new ice age," to the Cold War. Also, Soviet gas supplies accounted only for a small part of total consumption in Western Europe, which meant that fears of European dependency were exaggerated.

It is indeed unlikely that the Soviets might one day cut off gas deliveries to Europe, as such a move would harm them more than anybody else. But it is conceivable that they will make adroit use of their favorable position in order to extract political concessions from some Western European countries. Mere threats to cut off gas supplies might impel some governments to inflect their policies in a direction desired by the Soviets.

The debate over the gas pipeline deal soon spread to the issue of economic sanctions in general. Given the market orientation of the Western democracies and the competition among individual companies both within a country and on the international level, it is indeed very difficult for Western countries to pursue effective common trade policies, especially in times of high unemployment.

To draw attention to practical difficulties, however, is not tantamount to accepting unconditionally the arguments of the supporters of extensive East-West trade. It has been repeatedly argued that East-West trade works for peace. This is hardly true. In the détente era, 1969–79, trade expanded significantly, yet the Soviets increased their armaments efforts. Then came the invasion of Afghanistan and the military suppression of Solidarity.

The claim that East-West trade leads to more liberal domestic policies is not sustained by the facts either. On the contrary: by the end of the 1960s, the Soviet leadership was already in such dire straits that economic reform seemed inevitable. However, the rapid expansion of East-West trade, the delivery of key-in-hand factories by the West, and technology transfer led the leaders of the Soviet Union to believe that they could avoid reforms. Nor did they relent on the repression of the dissidents. So long as all economic decision making is in the hands of an unelected dictatorial elite, East-West trade and technology transfer will, above all, benefit the regime, not the people.

Finally, it is often said that the American sanctions against Poland only increased General Jaruzelski's dependence on Moscow. This is not true. On the contrary, these sanctions acted as a clear warning to the leaders of other East European countries not to take repression too far. After he was arrested in the wake of the December 13, 1981, crackdown, Adam Michnik, a leading representative of Solidarity, wrote about the sanctions against

Poland: "The economies of Communist countries cannot survive without Western technology and raw materials. . . . Can one blame Western politicians for making further credits contingent on the restoration of civil rights in Poland?" He called the West's reaction "a happy surprise" that could "contribute to limiting repression." He went on to say; "for jailed and persecuted people [these sanctions] are an injection of hope, a light at the end of the dark tunnel that is everyday life in Poland under martial law."[58]

Serious thought should be given to the idea of including political questions in important trade negotiations. Economic agreements could perhaps be complemented by political arrangements. For instance, the West might insist that the Soviet press publish details about Western grain deliveries and deals involving advanced technology. Such news would certainly have a lasting effect on the Soviet population.

I would like to illustrate the importance of this often neglected aspect of East-West trade by a personal recollection. I spent the Second World War in the Soviet Union. In those days of widespread famine, our meager food rations included a peculiar egg powder that played a vital role in keeping us alive. Here and there we heard rumors that this powder had been provided by our Western allies, who sent not only weapons but also other necessities, including food. But nobody knew any details. On June 11, 1944, a day I will never forget, all major Soviet newspapers suddenly published lists of all allied deliveries to the USSR from October 1, 1941, to April 30, 1944. With great surprise we found out what the United States alone had sent: 6,430 airplanes, 3,734 tanks, 206,771 cars, 245,000 telephones, 5.5 million pairs of boots, and—most impressive of all—more than two million tons of foodstuff.

The impact of this news was overwhelming. For weeks, I heard people commenting that without the help of the Western allies the country would have faced not only a very difficult military situation, but also widespread starvation. The memory of this decisive Western aid was so strong that even at the start of the Cold War in 1947 the Soviet authorities had great trouble arousing the people against the United States and the other former Western allies. I have no reason to believe that reaction today would be different. The possibility of linking East-West trade with realistic political agreements deserves some thought.

The Importance of
Western Radio Broadcasts

For the people of the Soviet Union, foreign radio broadcasts are the only window to the rest of the world. When Andrei Amalrik arrived in the West in the summer of 1976 after his Siberian exile, he immediately stressed the importance of Western radio stations. Amalrik called them an important instrument for transforming the Soviet Union, since they provided people with a contrast to their daily lives, and, moreover, acted as multipliers for the civil rights movement.[59]

Even in distant Kolyma, where the exiled lived, many people listened to Western broadcasts:

> The use of radio receivers was forbidden in the camp, but transistor sets found their way in from the outside, just as vodka did, and I was able to listen to the Voice of America for almost a month until they confiscated my set. Of all the Western broadcasting stations, the Voice of America was the only one that reached Kolyma. All the free workers in Talaya listened to it . . .[60]

Two Soviet civil rights activists, the pharmacist and writer Victor Nekepilov and the poet Felix Serebrov, both of whom are members of the Helsinki movement and have been arrested several times, wrote a memorandum about what these broadcasts meant to them:

> We are very thankful to these Western radio stations for providing us with varied information about world events, un-

stereotyped commentaries, and interesting reports about life in Western countries. We are also grateful that the literary, economic, scientific, and musical programs enable us to feel what is most important for us: the pulse of our own lives, that non-official pulse of a culture that has to live under ice. . . . The Western radio broadcasts are not only an important source of information and an intellectual voice for millions of our compatriots. They are also a unique school of democracy, a door to the Russia of tomorrow. . . . The importance of Russian language programs is immeasurable. Without claiming to possess detailed statistics, we venture to state on the basis of our personal experiences that anybody who has a short wave radio listens to Western broadcasts. Today all classes of Soviet society listen to them: students, workers and farmers, former political prisoners, and government officials. Increasingly even Party officials, journalists, members of the judiciary, and army officers tune in to these programs.[61]

The Soviet Union and the Communist states of Eastern Europe beam far more programs to the West than vice versa. Radio Moscow, the world's largest foreign broadcasting service, emits 2,094 hours of programming in more than eighty languages per week. More than three hundred shortwave radio stations are spreading Soviet propaganda around the world. North America receives 112 weekly program hours, Western Europe, 1,236 program hours. During the détente era, foreign-language broadcasts were expanded considerably. At present, Radio Moscow alone broadcasts more program hours than Voice of America, Radio Free Europe, and Radio Liberty combined.

Among Western radio stations, Radio Liberty and Radio Free Europe (both located in Munich), the BBC, and Voice of Germany (Deutsche Welle), in Cologne, are of particular importance. They provide alternative sources of information for more than 300 million people living in countries whose governments control all telecommunications.

The most important task of Voice of America consists of reporting and commenting on events from an American perspective. Emphasis is on discussing U.S. domestic and foreign policies and reporting on cultural life in America.

For listeners in Eastern Europe, Radio Liberty and Radio Free Europe are of greater importance. Their task is to report about events in the countries targeted by their broadcasts, that is to say, Radio Free Europe for Eastern Europe, and Radio Liberty for the Soviet Union.

A research department employing seventy experts who sift through several hundred Soviet and East European publications provides detailed analyses concerning political, economic, cultural, and other developments in the Soviet bloc. The research department's archives comprise 96,000 volumes in fifty-five languages, and 8 million press clippings in 40,000 categories. Radio Liberty broadcasts in Russian around the clock, and, in addition, several hours a day in fifteen other languages of the Soviet Union. The station has forty-six transmitters in Germany, Spain, and Portugal. Radio Liberty and Radio Free Europe do not limit themselves to reporting news and analyzing developments in the Soviet Union and in Eastern Europe: philosophical, religious, and historical themes are also given air time.

The two stations also inform their listeners about dissident publications. They thus stimulate public debates about a variety of political, economic, cultural, and social issues. Such broadcasts do not neglect the problems Western societies face, and they also take into account their listeners' views concerning their own countries.

The BBC plays a very important role, too. Maurice Latey, who for many years headed the Russian-language section of that station, has stated that it is the BBC's task to carry out the wishes of its listeners and provide objective news, honest commentary, and background information about events. According to Latey, many listeners are interested in what goes on in the democratic countries, be it work or vacation, arts or science and technology, sports or music. The BBC's official policy is to avoid any kind of propaganda, as listeners are already saturated with that.

The Voice of Germany's broadcasts to the Soviet Union are in Russian only. Botho Kirsch, the director of the station's Russian-language program, is convinced that objectivity, topicality, and credibility are the three qualities that Russian listeners value most about the varied programs from Germany, regularly listened to by more than 2 million Soviet citizens.

Of all the programs devoted to life in the West, those which deal with social and economic themes meet with the greatest interest among Soviet listeners. They want to know how many hours workers and employees in Western countries have to work, how much they earn, how many weeks of paid vacation they get, and what services social security provides. Other listeners request that the radio stations provide information about Western educational systems. Some want to find out more about health care and workers' rights. Others send in questions about Western electoral systems, about the judiciary and its independence, about legal systems and prison conditions. Often the stations receive letters requesting that they broadcast something about the programs of various political parties, as it is impossible in the Soviet Union to get hold of these—even the party programs of such independent Communist parties as those of Italy, Spain, Japan, and Yugoslavia are unavailable.

The extraordinary popularity of the Western radio broadcasts has induced the Soviet regime to try to combat their influence. Soviet diplomats use their personal connections to Western politicians to ask that these "survivals of the cold war" be silenced. They claim that these stations constitute an "interference in the internal affairs" of the Soviet bloc, and that they therefore "jeopardize peace." The assertion that the radio stations are "survivals of the cold war" conveniently overlooks the fact that for more than twenty-five years they have avoided all cold-war propaganda and concentrated on providing information that would be otherwise unavailable to people in the Soviet bloc. The reproach concerning "interference in internal affairs" is doubly grotesque: first, because, as stated earlier, far more broadcasts go from the East to the West than vice versa, and second, because in 1973 the USSR, by ratifying the Covenant on Civil and Political Rights, explicitly approved the free flow of information.

During the decade of détente, 1969 to 1979, Soviet efforts to lessen the impact of Western radio stations unfortunately met with some success. In some countries, including West Germany, there were attempts to "tame" the broadcasts. This led to an immediate decrease in the numbers of listeners. In the meantime, however, the true nature of these Soviet efforts has been understood in the West.

Since the "taming" method did not produce the desired effect, the Soviet leadership resolved, in August 1980, to fall back on a time-honored practice going back to Stalin: they decided to jam Western broadcasts. An estimated 2,500 jamming stations have been set up to "cover" the programs of Radio Liberty, Radio Free Europe, Voice of America, the BBC, and Deutsche Welle. This enormous technical and financial effort notwithstanding, it has not been possible to cut people in the Soviet Union off completely from receiving independent information. All the radio stations mentioned suddenly increased the number of their frequencies when the jamming stations began affecting radio signals in August 1980.

As long as the regimes in the Soviet bloc prevent their citizens from reading books, newspapers, and magazines of their own choice, and from informing themselves freely about developments at home and abroad, it is urgently necessary that Western radio stations provide the peoples of the Soviet bloc with all the information to which they have a right as citizens.

7

Proposals for a New Western Approach to the Soviet Union

In the West there are two opposing views concerning policies toward the Soviet Union. Traditional anti-Communists, known as hawks, regard the Soviet Union as an adversary and a threat. They stress (correctly) the Soviet expansionist activities from 1939 to the present and the military buildup during détente. But often their evaluations are one-sided. They believe in a "master plan" or "blue print" of Soviet leaders for world domination. They overestimate the monolithic nature of systems, underestimate differences, contradictions, and possibilities of change. They see the Soviet Union primarily or almost solely as a military threat, and advocate a military buildup in the West to counter the Communist menace, seeing no other alternatives than an uninterrupted arms race.

In contrast to this group, the doves, undoubtedly with justification, stress that the Russians and the West are confronted with the danger of a nuclear war, which has to be avoided at all costs. Through confidence-building, cooperation and mutual trust, disarmament negotiations, increasing East-West economic cooperation, and regular summit meetings, the doves hope to achieve peace. However, they completely overlook the dictatorial and expansionist nature of the Soviet regime.

Both the hard-liners and the foreign policy liberals take little notice of what is going on on the Soviet side. The hawks project their fears and hostility toward the Soviet Union, the doves their good will, good intentions, hopes, and illusions.

It is time to overcome these outdated concepts, take into consideration the reality of the Soviet dictatorship, the aims of the nomenklatura, the internal contradictions, the forces of change, and to confront our own aims and values with Soviet reality.

The policy of the United States and its European allies toward the Soviet Union and the countries of the Soviet bloc should be based on sober and realistic assumptions. These policies should be free of the exaggerated hopes and optimistic illusions that were prevalent during the era of détente, but they should also avoid a return to the Cold War and the primitive undifferentiated anti-Communism of the 1950s.

In my opinion the following nine points should form a realistic approach to the Soviet Union:

Leadership and Population

We should never forget that we have to deal with a bureaucratic centralist dictatorship that denies its citizenry elementary civil rights. The expansionist nature of the Soviet Union is inherent in the aims of the Soviet nomenklatura. This has very little to do with the Soviet population, neither with the Russians nor with the numerous non-Russian nationalities, who, as a whole, desire peace and friendship with Western democracies.

The widespread use of the term "the Russians" tends to blur the issue: it gives the impression that we are dealing with a people, a nation, whereas in reality we are dealing only with the nomenklatura. One always has to keep in mind that the Politburo is not the Soviet Union, Husak is not Czechoslovakia, General Jaruzelski is not Poland, and Zhivkov is not Bulgaria: this would remain true even if the leaders changed. It would be a big step forward if politicians of Western democracies differentiated clearly between Soviet leaders and the Soviet population.

This clear distinction is more than a semantic device. It implies that the Western democracies are confronted simultaneously with the problem of having to deal with the Soviet power elite, and of having to think about how to build bridges to the Soviet population.

Our Realistic Aim: Businesslike Relations

In our relations with the Soviet Union we should be clearly aware of both the possibilities and the limitations of East-West relations. The nomenklatura's expansionist tendencies notwithstanding, it also carefully takes risks into account, tries to avoid military confrontations, and is interested in economic and technological cooperation. For the Soviet nomenklatura, we are representatives of the "capitalist countries" and therefore considered enemies—we cannot change this perception whatever we do, however we behave, and however conciliatory we are. But there are possibilities.

It is worthwhile to look at how the Soviet leaders themselves define relations with what they call the "capitalist countries." Official Soviet statements often speak of *dyeloviye otnosheniya* which means "sober, businesslike relations." This corresponds exactly to what is both realistically possible and desirable; there should be no return to the Cold War and undifferentiated anticommunism, but also no illusions about "sincere cooperation" or "friendship" with the nomenklatura.

"Businesslike relationship" implies neither threats nor illusions, but the careful study of the areas in which limited understanding is possible. The possibilities for cooperation arise out of the nomenklatura's desire to avoid military conflicts, and its interest in technology and economic-technological cooperation. The West should take advantage of these opportunities but never press its wish for cooperation or friendship on the nomenklatura. There should be a serious commitment to avoid armed conflicts, but also a clear understanding of the qualitative differences between the two systems, democracy and dictatorship.

Differentiation Between Eastern Europe and the Soviet Union

Six Central and East European countries have been under Soviet domination since the end of World War II: Poland, East Germany (the German Democratic Republic), Czechoslovakia, Hungary, Romania, and Bulgaria. However, these countries are no longer mere satellites; although they are still largely subordinated to the Soviet leadership, they have increasingly developed certain independent interests. One can no longer overlook the growing efforts of national leaderships, prompted by the populations' yearning for more independence, to gain greater autonomy from the Soviet Union. The Soviet model is challenged more frequently and more openly than ever before. Even the leaderships of some of these countries are trying to gain more freedom of action for themselves. Therefore the Western democracies should clearly differentiate between the Soviet Union on the one hand, and the Central and East European members of the Warsaw Pact on the other.

Moreover, the differences among the individual Central and East European countries should also be given careful consideration. While Hungary has for almost two decades engaged in economic reforms that have gradually led to a certain liberalization in other areas, in Poland and Romania the leaderships are putting increased emphasis on the countries' national traditions to bolster their own legitimacies. Certain, albeit minimal, tendencies in that direction can also be discerned in Bulgaria and East Germany.

It is necessary for the West to take different trends among the Central and East European countries into account, to stress the principle of self-determination of nations, to pursue policies that will increase the scope of action of the leaderships of these countries, and at the same time promote liberalization and human rights.

Negotiations with Communist Leaders

Western governments should welcome opportunities to meet and negotiate with the leaders of Communist-ruled countries, especially on the important field of arms control, but they should not seek such opportunities at any price. These negotiations should be conducted without the slightest illusions concerning the nature of the dictatorial regime.

Public opinion in the West often tends to expect too much of East-West summits or state visits. Unfortunately, no miracles occur on such occasions. Moreover, experience has shown that insufficiently prepared summit meetings are hardly conducive to a long-term improvement in East-West relations. Negotiations with leaders are and will remain necessary, but not at all times, under all conditions, and about all subjects. A pause can sometimes be quite fruitful in negotiations, and a more low-key realistic assessment of East-West summit conferences can avoid deep and long-term disillusionments. East-West relations are protracted processes. Successful negotiations and subsequent agreements come about only as a result of careful, laborious, and patient preparatory work.

In all negotiations with leaders of the Soviet Union or the Soviet bloc, the Western side should avoid giving the impression that it is acting under time pressure and that it needs quick breakthroughs. Hasty declarations to the effect that the forthcoming talks will produce this or that agreement mean that the negotiations will have failed before they have really begun.

The West must avoid unilateral concessions, because rather than reciprocate, the Soviet negotiators are more likely to react by formulating new demands and hardening their positions.

Western representatives should insist on absolute equality between them and their Communist counterparts. The principles of reciprocity should guide all their actions, even if this causes a delay or slowdown in the negotiations.

During negotiations, the Western side should express its views consistently and not tire of repeating them. It should avoid changing proposals constantly, as this undermines the Western negotiators' credibility and predictability, which in turn weakens their positions.

It happens not infrequently that, after protracted negotiations, the Soviet side will propose an "agreement in principle" that does not lay down exact conditions of implementation and verification. The West should avoid these "agreements in principle" at all costs. It should insist on including details concerning implementation and verification in the text of the agreement or treaty itself, rather than in supplementary declarations or "letters."

Success in negotiations should not be measured by the number of treaties or agreements the Western statesmen or diplomats bring home from their visits to Moscow, but rather by their ability to avoid signing unclear treaties (which lead to constant dissensions about what the wording actually meant) or agreements with too many one-sided Western concessions.

Western negotiators who enunciate their country's positions clearly and firmly earn the true respect of their Soviet colleagues. Such a negotiating strategy enables both sides to have a clear understanding of the issues and problems that separate them.

The more clearly the Western negotiators formulate their objectives, the more consistently they pursue them, and the more precisely the agreements and the conditions of their implementation and verification are worded, the more lasting and effective the agreements and treaties will be.

Military Aspects:
Arms Control and Disarmament

In Western democracies, particularly in the United States, there is a tendency to concentrate on military aspects of East-West relations, sometimes to such a degree that this aspect is seen as the dominant factor, which leads to its isolation from the economic and political considerations. Such an attitude reflects the interest of the Western analysts but completely disregards the perceptions and aims of the Soviet nomenklatura. The main concept "international correlations of forces," which is the guideline for the Soviet nomenklatura, does not separate military relationships from other relationships. Rather, it includes economic, political, military, and moral-ideological forces of both systems as well as the capacity of the two systems' leaders to make use of these forces in a politically fruitful manner. This has to be taken into consideration, both by the Western governments and by Western public opinion: The West must learn not to reduce East-West relations to their military dimension.

In the area of military relations, arms control, and disarmament talks, the West should couple its unavoidable defense efforts with a serious willingness to reduce armaments. Military threats and "saber rattling" should be avoided, but it is also necessary to carry out decisions once they are taken—such as NATO's double-track decision. Consistency and predictability are of the essence for relations with the Soviet bloc.

The West must always remember that the nomenklatura needs foreign policy successes to shore up its flagging legitimacy at home, but that it also tries to avoid the risks of military confrontations with serious adversaries. The leaders of the Soviet Union fear that their country might not be able to sustain the economic cost of an escalating arms race. With a GNP only half the size of that of the United States, the Soviets have managed to achieve strategic near-parity, but there are, nevertheless, clear limits to how far they can go in an arms race.

In evaluating arms control negotiations and agreements, one

also has to take into consideration the Soviet nomenklatura's insistence on the prestige and the role of the Soviet armed forces, not only as a counterweight to the West, but also as a means for solidifying its authority within the Soviet bloc, for underlining the Soviet Union's role as superpower, and for diverting attention of the Soviet population from the economic and social difficulties by emphasizing the country's military power.

Economic Relations

Economic ties between the Western democracies and the Soviet Union and countries of the Soviet bloc are of great importance but they are not of equal significance to both sides. The Soviet Union's leadership needs technology and grain to a much greater degree than the Western democracies need the markets of the Soviet Union.

The importance of East-West trade for the Soviet leadership cannot be calculated in percentage points or tonnage, but must be seen in the light of the Soviet leaders' desperate need for products that their own centralized economies cannot always provide. The Soviet Union and other countries of the Soviet bloc are dependent on Western know-how, transfer of technology, and grain delivery to an extraordinary degree. In many important technologies, the Soviet Union lags behind the West by fifteen or more years. Even for the exploitation of its own natural resources, it is often dependent on Western know-how and credit.

Under these circumstances, economic sanctions and embargoes can by no means be ruled out in certain exceptional cases, for instance in response to a Soviet aggression. The results of such sanctions in the past few years have been more significant than Soviet propaganda would have us believe. The Soviet Union's economic dependency notwithstanding, the West should apply economic sanctions only in exceptional cases. Given the market-oriented economies of Western countries, generalized embargoes or long-term economic sanctions are hardly feasible, least of all in periods of economic downturn and widespread unemployment. Nothing would harm Western positions more than announcing sanctions with a lot of fanfare and then proving incapable of enacting them.

Instead, Western countries should try to coordinate their trade policies more, be less forthcoming with credit, and exercise tighter control over the transfer of advanced technology that the Soviets can use also for military purposes. As mentioned elsewhere in this book, the Soviet press as a rule does not report on East-West economic agreements, and often presents foreign-built enterprises as achievements of the regime. The West should insist that details of all economic agreements be publicized in the Soviet Union, a general practice everywhere else in the world. This would positively affect the population's perception of the West.

Furthermore, it is time to think about how to combine East-West economic cooperation with political and human rights agreements. An attempt should be made to balance technology transfer and grain sales with political-humanitarian agreements, i.e., an end to the jamming of Western radio broadcasts, the easing of emigration, the establishment of clear, permanent yearly quotas for the release of political prisoners from camps and psychiatric clinics, and an improvement of visitor exchanges.

It is not suggested here that these aims (or proposals) be put forward as preconditions or ultimatums before negotiations begin, but, rather, that they be incorporated during the course of the negotiations. This may not always be easy to achieve, but it is by no means impossible, especially since the Soviet leaders are dependent upon Western technology and grain deliveries; the success would depend upon the Western ability to endure and persist in its proposals.

Building Bridges to the Population

The relations of Western democracies with the Soviet Union cannot be limited solely to the dealings with the Kremlin leaders, with the leading representatives of the nomenklatura. As important as diplomatic and economic relations and arms control negotiations between East and West may be, it is equally important to build bridges to the peoples on the other side and to do everything possible to ease repression.

This is not only, as often assumed, a moral obligation, as it cannot be overlooked that external expansion of the Soviet nomenklatura is inseparably linked with internal repression. The harsher the repression inside the Soviet Union (and other countries of the Soviet bloc) the more the nomenklatura emphasizes an imaginary external threat of "imperialist forces." This then leads to strained East-West relations, increasing the danger of a return to a Cold War. On the other hand, a loosening up of the system and reforms and liberalizations are the preconditions for improving East-West relations. Any liberalization of the regime in the Soviet Union and other countries of the Soviet bloc is therefore not only in the interest of the Soviet population but of the Western democracies as well. The Western democracies are thus confronted with the task of building bridges to the Soviet population and of supporting liberalization, reforms, and human rights.

The governments of Western democracies should insist that the leaders of the Soviet Union and of the other states of Eastern Europe respect the provisions of the Helsinki Declaration and the United Nations pact on civil and political rights.

The importance of Western radio broadcasts was pointed out in the previous chapter. Since 1980, these broadcasts have been jammed by the Soviet Union, Czechoslovakia, East Germany, and Poland (but not by Hungary!), while Soviet bloc radio stations transmit freely to the West. It is incumbent upon the West to insist that the jamming cease, in accordance with the principle of reciprocity and the above mentioned agreements. Western broadcasts in Russian and other languages of the Soviet population should be increased—which is perfectly permissible because the Soviet Union and the Soviet bloc countries transmit more in the languages of the Western alliance than the West does in the languages of the Soviet Union and Eastern Europe.

These Western broadcasts are not a side aspect of our relations with the Soviet Union, but are one of their most important components. They are the main instrument of our contact to the populations of these countries, providing them with the information their own leadership withholds from them. In these broadcasts, our respect and admiration for the great cultural and scientific achievements, for the historical traditions of Russians and non-Russian nationalities should be as pronounced as our criticism of the bureaucratic dictatorial regime and our insistence on democratic rights.

Finally, the West should insist that the Soviet bloc countries ease restrictions on travel to the West. Such a move would fulfill the wishes of many citizens in these countries, and also contribute to an improvement of East-West relations by allowing people in Eastern Europe to get to know the West first hand and thereby reduce whatever prejudices they may have.

Western support for human rights can, however, be only successful if one does not expect results in a few weeks or months. A long-term approach, persistence, and endurance are the preconditions for success. Only if the Soviet leaders become aware that the Western democracies are serious about their aims and will not give up in their endeavor will they be ready for concessions and adapt themselves to the new situation.

Greater Emphasis on Long-Term Objectives

It is regrettable that public opinion often concentrates only on the current situation, while long-term perspectives, including possible internal transformations in Soviet bloc countries, receive only little attention.

Although they may appear monolithic at first sight, the stability of these countries is widely overestimated. The various emancipatory movements in Eastern Europe, Khrushchev's de-Stalinization, the "Polish October," the Hungarian Revolution of 1956, the Prague Spring of 1968, and the Solidarity movement in Poland in 1980–81, show to what extent socio-political forces have been striving for change in the Soviet bloc.

This applies more particularly to transition periods, since these are often characterized by conflicts between various forces. Here, too, the West should pursue differentiated policies. We should make clear to the neo-Stalinist hard-liners in the Soviet leadership that there are limits to their power and that their expansionist activities would meet with a firm response by the West. But at the same time we should let the moderate and more realistic forces know that if they succeeded in imposing a more moderate course in domestic and foreign policy, they could count on our interest and understanding.

Solidarity with the Reform Movements

The democratic countries of the West have both the right and the duty to express their solidarity with all those groupings and currents in the Soviet bloc that advocate liberalization and democratization and that struggle for the respect of human rights. This means, above all, Solidarity in Poland, Charter 77 in Czechoslovakia, and Sakharov's civil rights movement in the Soviet Union. The West must not relent in its demands that Sakharov be allowed to return to Moscow from his exile in Gorki and express his opinions freely.

Support for human rights in Communist-ruled countries is morally justifiable and likely to succeed if any kind of one-sidedness is avoided. Public opinion in the Western democracies must speak out equally on human rights violations in the Soviet Union and other Communist-ruled countries, and on similar problems in certain Latin American dictatorships or in South Africa. East-West relations in fields of interest to Moscow

—trade and arms control—must be made contingent on an improvement of the human rights policy of the Soviet leadership. Quiet diplomacy in individual cases is a valid option. But in the long run, a strong public campaign is necessary to achieve concrete results. Public displays of respect such as the conferral of the Nobel Prize on Andrei Sakharov in 1975, and on Lech Walesa in 1983, should not remain exceptions but should be followed by similar measures benefitting other activists.

The voices of dissidents in the Soviet Union and in other Soviet bloc countries should be taken more seriously into account in the Western democracies. Their works should be published, discussed, and also included in the academic studies of the Soviet Union and Eastern Europe.

The opinion of dissidents emigrating to the West should be listened to and discussed. Increasingly at conferences, congresses, and public meetings it has become usage to invite "a Russian," but for some strange reason, the invited "Russian" is always a representative of the nomenklatura. Why not invite an emigrated dissident? Or invite both an official Soviet nomenklatura representative and a dissident? We should get used to having to deal both with the official Soviet regime and with spokesmen of reform and human rights movements in the USSR.

At important public meetings and events such as party and trade union congresses, scientific and cultural conferences, and church meetings, it would be appropriate for participants to express their support of the civil rights movements in the Soviet bloc by inviting exiled representatives of such movements to attend and to briefly address the audience.

Insistence on human rights and self-determination implies support for all those groups in the Soviet population that are striving for change, for liberalization, and for moderation. It encourages a search for alternatives to the present dictatorial system from within the Soviet experience by striving for a peaceful evolution toward greater freedom and pluralism.

Naturally, one cannot expect results in a few weeks or months. A long-term policy is called for, one that combines serious and realistic negotiations at top government levels with support for those popular forces striving for liberalization and greater freedom within the Soviet Union.

In sum, any Western attempt to better relations with the Soviet Union should balance high-level negotiations with support for Soviet dissidents and all reforming, democratic forces with an insistence on human rights and self-determination. Ultimately, liberalization and reforms within the Soviet Union will have much broader effects, laying the foundation for improved East-West relations.

Notes

1. "Introduction," in *Sakharov Speaks* (New York: Alfred A. Knopf, 1974), p. 43.

2. The nomenklatura system was first systematically presented by Boris Lewytzky, *Osteuropa* 11/1961, and B. Harasymiv in *The Canadian Journal of Political Science*, 2 (1969), pp. 493–512.

3. *Nomenklatura: the Soviet Ruling Class* (Garden City, New York: Doubleday, 1984), especially chapters 5 and 6. See also Konstantin M. Simis, *U.S.S.R.: The Corrupt Society* (New York: Simon and Schuster, 1982), pp. 35–64.

4. Karl Marx and Friedrich Engels, *The Communist Manifesto* (Harmondsworth: Penguin, 1985), p. 83.

5. J. V. Stalin, "The Political Strategy and Tactics of the Russian Communists," in *Works*, vol. V (Moscow: Foreign Languages Publishing House, 1953), p. 73.

6. *Kommunist*, no. 10, July 1982, pp. 6–21.

7. Heinrich Böll, Lev Kopelev, and Heinrich Vormweg, *Antikommunismus in Ost und West* (Cologne: Bund, 1982).

8. No. 4, 1982.

9. Wolfgang Leonhard, *Child of the Revolution* (Chicago: Henry Regnery Company, 1957), pp. 131–35.

10. Böll and Kopelev, *Antikommunismus*, p. 70.

11. A. Sakharov, "Die Menschenrechtsbewegung in der Sowjetunion und Osteuropa," in *Furcht und Hoffnung* (Vienna and Munich: Molden, 1980), p. 254.

12. George F. Kennan, *Memoirs*, vol. 1 (Boston: Atlantic-Little Brown, 1967), p. 560.

13. An English translation can be found in *The Russian Menace to Europe* by Karl Marx and Friedrich Engels, essays edited and selected by Paul W. Blackstock and Bert F. Hoselitz (Glencoe, Illinois: The Free Press, 1952).

14. Ibid, pp. 26, 51–55, passim.

15. *Yearbook on International Communist Affairs, 1984,* Richard F. Staar, ed. (Stanford, Calif.: Hoover Institution Press, 1984), pp. 426–27.

16. *The Russian Menace,* p. 26.

17. Kennan, *Memoirs,* p. 562.

18. " 'Left-Wing' Communism—An Infantile Disorder," in V. I. Lenin, *Collected Works,* vol. XXXI (Moscow: Progress Publishers, 1966), pp. 70–71.

19. The figures are from *Yearbook,* pp. 427–35.

20. Wolfgang Seiffert, *Kann der Ostblock überleben? Der Comecon und die Krise des sozialistischen Weltsystems* (Bergisch Gladbach, 1983), p. 21

21. "Report on the Review of the Program and on Changing the Name of the Party" to the Seventh Extraordinary Congress of the RCP(B), *Collected Works*, vol. XXXVII, pp. 132 and 135.

22. "Report on the Party Program" to the Eighth Congress of the RCP(B), March 19, 1919, *Collected Works,* vol. XXIX, p. 175.

23. "Speech Closing the Debate on the Party Program" at the Eighth Congress of the RCP(B), March 19, 1919, *Collected Works,* vol. XXIX, p. 192.

24. "The Third International and Its Place in History," April 15, 1919, *Collected Works,* vol. XXIX, p. 311.

25. " 'Left-Wing' Communism—An Infantile Disorder," *Collected Works,* vol. XXXI, p. 21.

26. *Pravda,* September 26, 1968. For the full English text, see *Current Digest of the Soviet Press,* no. 39 (October 16, 1968), p. 11.

27. L. I. Brezhnev, "Speech at the Fifth Congress of the Polish United Workers' Party," November 12, 1968, *Pravda,* November 13, 1968; L. I. Brezhnev, *Following Lenin's Course* (Moscow: Progress Publishers, 1972), p. 145.

28. Cf. Ceauşescu's speech to the graduates of Romanian military academies on August 15, 1968, and Tito's declaration in *Borba* (Belgrade), March 13, 1969.

29. *Peking Review,* no. 13 (March 28, 1969), p. 23.

30. In his book *Nightfrost in Prague: The End of Humane Socialism,* tr. Paul Wilson (New York: Karz, 1980), Zdenek Mlynar, who was Secretary of the Central Committee of the Czechoslovak Communist Party, left a graphic account of the atmosphere in which these talks took place.

31. "Russlands Schwäche und innere Konflikte—Gespräche mit dem Sowjet-Kenner George Kennan," in *Epoche,* June 1982, p. 8.

32. See *Pravda,* February 24, 1981.

33. "Report of the Commission on the National and Colonial Questions to the Second Congress of the Communist International," July 26, 1920, *Collected Works,* vol. XXXI, p. 244.

34. *Pravda,* February 15, 1956.

35. V. Afanasyev, M. Makarova, and L. Minayev, *Fundamentals of Scientific Socialism* (Moscow: Progress Publishers, 1969), p. 183.

36. Mikhail S. Gorbachev, *A Time for Peace* (New York: Richardson & Steirman, 1985), p. 248.

37. Andrei Sakharov, "Peace, Progress, and Human Rights," in *Alarm and Hope*, p. 4.

38. Andrei D. Sakharov, *My Country and the World*, tr. Guy V. Daniels (New York: Vintage Books, 1975), pp. 63–64, 106.

39. Andrei Amalrik, *Notes of a Revolutionary*, tr. Guy V. Daniels, with an introduction by Susan Jacoby (New York: Alfred A. Knopf, 1982), p. 291.

40. Wladimir Bukowski, *Dieser stechende Schmerz der Freiheit* (Stuttgart, 1983), p. 428.

41. *Die Zeit*, March 18, 1983.

42. W. Seiffert, *Kann der Ostblock überleben?* pp. 87 and 109f.

43. Jiri Kosta, "Die ökonomischen Reformen in den Ländern Osteuropas," in H. Vogel, ed., *Wirtschaftliche Probleme Osteuropas* (Berlin, 1982).

44. V. I. Lenin, "Fourth Anniversary of the October Revolution," October 14, 1921, *Collected Works*, vol. XXXIII, p. 58.

45. V. I. Lenin, "The New Economic Policy and the Tasks of the Political Education Departments—Report to the Second All-Russia Congress of Political Education Departments," in *Collected Works*, vol. XXXIII, pp. 70–72.

46. "Manifesto II," in *Sakharov Speaks*, p. 127.

47. V. I. Lenin, "Report on the Right of Recall at a Meeting of the All-Russia Central Executive Committee," November 21 (December 4), 1917, *Collected Works*, vol. XXVI, pp. 339–40.

48. Quoted in *Power and the Soviet Elite: "The Letter of an Old Bolshevik" and Other Essays* by Boris I. Nicolaevsky, edited by Janet D. Zagoria, (New York: Praeger, 1965), p. 15.

49. Cornelia Gerstenmaier, *Die demokratische Bewegung in der Sowjetunion* (Stuttgart, 1971), pp. 323–27.

50. *On Socialist Democracy*, tr. and ed. Ellen de Kadt (New York: Alfred A. Knopf, 1976), p. 99.

51. "Introduction," in *Sakharov Speaks*, p. 43.

52. W. Seiffert, *Kann der Ostblock überleben?* p. 96.

53. Hedrick Smith, *The Russians* (New York: Times Books, 1974), pp. 250–51.

54. Zhores A. Medvedev, *Andropov* (Harmondsworth: Penguin, 1984), p. 53.

55. "Peace, Progress, and Human Rights," in *Alarm and Hope*, pp. 10 and 14.

56. Andrei Sakharov, *Alarm and Hope*, pp. 48–49.

57. W. Bukowski, *Dieser stechende Schmerz der Freiheit*, pp. 87f.

58. *Der Spiegel*, March 3, 1982, p. 135.

59. *Die Welt*, March 5, 1977.

60. Andrei Amalrik, *Notes of a Revolutionary*, p. 206.

61. Quoted in *Die Welt*, February 27, 1980.

62. For the most recent formulation of Soviet foreign policy objectives, see "The Soviet Communist Party Congress on the International Situation and Soviet Foreign Policy," an advertisement that appeared in the *New York Times*, March 21, 1986, p. 18.

Index

Afghanistan, 120, 126
  Soviet occupation, 83, 119, 127,
    137
agreements in principle, 89–90,
    205
agriculture:
  administrative bureaucracy, 45–46
  collective and state farms, 46–47,
    49–50
  machinery problems, 47
  private plots, 48–49
  productivity in, 46–47
  reform proposals for, 49–50,
    157–58, 161–62
  transportation problems, 47
  worker impressment, 47–48
Akhromeyev, Sergei, 140, 178
Albania, 111, 118
alcoholism, 58
Algeria, 123, 127
Aliev, Geidar, 16, 31
Amalrik, Andrei, 146, 195
Andropov, Yuri, 16, 54, 83, 113, 161,
    177–78
Angola, 123, 126, 127, 128, 129
anti-Semitism, 53

appliances, production of, 59–60
arms control process:
  missile deployments and, 135–36,
    139
  resumption of talks (1984), 140
  Soviet manipulation of, 138
  Western strategies, 206–7
  see also negotiating strategy
    headings
arms industry, 43–44
the Army, 13, 154–55
  Central Committee, representation
    on, 25
  foreign policy role, 83
  officers, 13, 15
  political influence, 176–78
  the State's control of, 15
  takeover of government, possible,
    176–79
  titles and decorations, 21
Association of Free Trade Unions of
    Soviet Toilers, 62–63

Baibakov, Nikolai, 35
BBC, 196, 197
Beria, Lavrenty, 83

Berlin Wall, Soviet explanation for, 92–93
Biryukova, Aleksandra, 36
Bishop, Maurice, 129
black market, *see* second economy
Bolshevik (Soviet journal), 74
Bonner, Elena, 186
bourgeoisie, Marx's definition of, 22–23
Brezhnev, Leonid, 15, 33, 109–10, 119, 138
Bukharin, Nikolai, 166
Bukovski, Vladimir, 146, 187
Bulgaria, 102, 111, 117, 203

Cambodia, 119, 120
Can the Soviet Bloc Survive? (Seiffert), 105
Carter, Jimmy, 137, 182–83, 187–88
CC, *see* Central Committee
Ceauşescu, Nicolae, 110
Central Committee (CC):
  age and nationality structure, 26–27
  apparatus of, 27–28
  foreign policy role, 78, 82
  industrial departments, 40
  international communism, contacts with, 78
  meetings of, 24
  member privileges, 26
  membership of, 24–26
  responsibilities of, 24
Central Committee Secretariat, 28, 33
  functions of, 30
  laws re, 29
  membership of, 30
Central Political Administration of the Soviet Armed Forces, 15
changes in Soviet system, possible:
  democratization, 146, 163–67
  East-West trade and, 193–95, 207
  economic management reforms, 156–59
  economic pressures, effects of, 151–54

  foreign policy and, 179
  generational shift and, 164
  liberalization forces, 149, 150–51
  military takeover, 176–79
  multiparty system, 166–67
  nationalistic authoritarianism, return to, 167–70
  neo-Stalinism, 171–76
  nomenklatura polarization and, 154–56
  oppositional movements and, 147–49
  political dissatisfaction, effects of, 151–54
  private enterprise (commercialization), 159–63
  radio broadcasts from the West and, 195–96
  Western skepticism re, 147–48, 149–50
  see also human rights
Chebrikov, Victor, 16, 35
the Cheka, 16
Chernenko, Konstantin, 140, 175
Chicherin, Georgi, 83
China, People's Republic of, 110, 117, 147–48
  Soviet Union, relations with, 118–20
Christianity, 58
Chronicle of Current Events (*samizdat* publication), 184
classless society, 56
coexistence doctrine, 130–32
collective farms (kolkhozi), 46–47, 49–50, 157–58
Comecon, *see* Council for Mutual Economic Assistance
Communist Manifesto, 22–23
Communist Party of the Soviet Union (CPSU), 154–55
  admission procedures, 9
  apparatus of, 13–14
  as association of loyal and obedient citizens, 11
  Central Committee, representation on, 24–25

congresses of, 24
democratization of, 166
foreign policy role, 125, 126
member duties, 9–11
member personality changes, 12
member privileges, 12
membership of, 8
model citizen, tasks of, 10–11
negotiating strategy, role in, 86–87
Party duties, 10
rules of, 10, 12, 24
socializing function, 11–12
Soviet bloc parties, contacts with, 106–7
the State, relations with, 14, 15
see also Central Committee
Communist Youth Organization (Komsomol), 14
see also Komsomol
computers, Soviet use of, 190–91
Congo, 123, 126, 127
Coordinating Committee for East-West Trade (COCOM), 191
corruption and bribery:
campaigns against, 161
in education, 65
food shortages and, 64–65
in medical care, 65
podarki (bribes), 65
see also second economy
Council for Mutual Economic Assistance (Comecon), 103, 104–6, 112
Council of Ministers of the Soviet Union, see the State
CPSU, see Communist Party of the Soviet Union
cruise missiles, NATO deployment of, 136, 139
Cuba, 102, 103, 120, 123, 125, 126, 130
Soviet model, adoption of, 128–29
cultural life, nationalism and, 168–69
Czechoslovakia, 102, 103, 111, 117, 203
"Prague Spring" movement (1968), 81, 83, 104, 114–15, 147, 148

Declaration on Liberated Europe (1945), 89–90
democratization of Soviet system, 146, 163–67
de-Stalinization, 15, 52, 56, 153–54, 173, 184
détente:
agreements reached through, 133
economic cooperation, 132, 133
human rights and, 134–35, 149–50, 181–82
political aspects, 132–33
Western public opinion re, 133, 134–35
dissident movement, 149, 183–84, 185–86, 188, 211–12
Dobrynin, Anatoly, 36
Dolgikh, Vladimir, 29
double-track strategy (NATO), 136, 139

East-West trade:
changes in Soviet system and, 193–95, 207–8
computers, 190–91
economic sanctions, 137, 191, 193–94, 207–8
gas pipeline construction, 191–93
human rights and, 208
political arrangements and, 194–95, 208
Soviet grain imports, 189
technology transfers, 189–91
economic sanctions by the West, 137, 191, 193–94, 207–8
economic system:
administrative apparatus, 40–41
bonus system, 43
employment and, 43
hoarding promoted by, 42
industrialization successes, 40
management reforms, possible, 156–59
ministries, 40
plans, yearly, 41–42
private enterprise, toleration of, 159–63

economic system (*continued*)
quality of products, 42
reform, official resistance to, 37, 45, 159
technological innovation and, 44
tolkachi, role of, 41, 42–43, 45, 162
worker morale in, 43
see also second economy
Economy of Agriculture (Russian journal), 49
education, corruption in, 65
Egypt, 126, 127
Engels, Friedrich, 73, 74–76, 80, 107
Estonia, 53, 81
Ethiopia, 123, 126, 127, 128, 129

factories, working conditions in, 61–62
Fiat automobile factory, 190
Finland, 81
food industry, 59
food shortages, 59, 64–65
Foreign Affairs, Ministry of, 82–83
foreign policy:
the Army's role, 83
Central Committee's role, 78, 82
centralized direction and coordination of activities, 101
changes in Soviet system, effects of, 179
CPSU's role, 125, 126
decision-making process, 82–84
economic concerns, 81, 82
economic modernization and, 158
front organizations, use of, 97–101
historical influences, 72–76
human rights and (internal repression-external expansion), 73, 75–76, 145–46, 209
ideology and, 77
international class struggle and, 131, 132
international communism, use of, 77–79
international correlation of forces doctrine, 79–80, 206

KGB, role of, 83
language manipulation, 91–95
messianism in, 73
miscalculation in, 84
nationalism, effects of, 169
negotiating strategy, 86–91, 205
neo-Stalinism and, 172
non-bloc socialist countries, relations with, 118–20
non-governmental contacts, 95–97
power politics in, 72–76, 79
proxies, use of, 82, 125–26
risk-consciousness in, 81–82
Soviet people's attitude toward, 7
world revolutionary process, 76–79
see also hegemony; Soviet bloc, policies re; Third World, policies re; the West, policies re
"The Foreign Policy of Russian Czarism" (Engels), 74–76, 80
foreign service, 25
front organizations, 97–101
functionaries, *see* officials

gas pipeline construction, 191–93
general laws of the building of socialism, 108–9
General Secretary, 30, 32–33
Gorbachev's appointment as, 33–34
succession and change issue, 33–34
see also specific secretaries
Georgia, 53–54, 174
German Democratic Republic (East Germany), 102, 103, 104, 111, 113–14, 117, 125, 126, 147, 203
German invasion (1941), 153
Germany, Federal Republic of (West Germany), 139
Gerö, Ernö, 156
Ghana, 127
Gorbachev, Mikhail, 31, 47, 175
antialcohol campaign, 37, 58
anticorruption campaign, 161

economic reforms, promotion of,
36–37, 158–59
General Secretary, appointment
as, 33–34
as hardline modernizer, 37
Politburo changes, 30, 35–36, 37
political rise of, 34–35
the West, policies re, 140–41
the government, *see* the State
Grenada, 127, 129
Grishin, Victor, 34, 35
Gromyko, Andrei, 34, 35, 36, 83, 140
Guinea, 123

hegemony, 107–8
doctrines of, 108–10
nationalism and, 167–68, 170
Helsinki Conference on Security and
Cooperation in Europe (1975),
182, 184–85
historical materialism, 55–56
Honecker, Erich, 117
housing shortage, 60
human rights:
détente and, 134–35, 149–50,
181–82
dissident movement re, 149,
183–84, 185–86, 188, 211–12
East-West trade and, 208
foreign policy aspects, 73, 75–76,
145–46, 209
international actions, 182–83,
184–85
quiet diplomacy and, 134, 182
West's support for, 182–83, 186–89,
209–10, 211–12
Hungarian Revolution (1956), 81, 83,
104, 112–13, 147, 148, 156
Hungary, 74, 102, 103, 106, 111,
116–17, 203
Husak, Gustav, 117

ideology:
classless society concept, 56
contradictions of, 56–57
decline of, 56–59

in early years of the Soviet Union,
55–56
foreign policy and, 77
historical materialism, 55–56
instruction in, 57
Politburo and, 31–32
popular alternatives to, 58–59
India, 126
International Association of
Democratic Lawyers, 98, 99, 100
international class struggle, 131, 132
international communism, 77–79
international correlation of forces
doctrine, 79–80, 206
International Organization of
Journalists, 98, 99, 100
International Union of Students, 98
Iran, 128
Iran-Iraq war, 127–28
Iraq, 126
Israel, 117
Izvestia, 159

Jaruzelski, Wojciech, 117, 176
Jews, 53

Kadyrov, Firidun, 68
Kennan, George, 72–73, 90–91, 118
KGB, 13, 22, 25–26, 83, 154–55
political importance of, 15–16
Khrushchev, Nikita, 24, 31, 33, 56,
154, 161, 184
coexistence doctrine, 130–31
de-Stalinization, 15, 52, 56, 173
Kirsch, Botho, 198
Klebanov, Vladimir, 62
Klimko, M. V., 159
Komsomol (Communist Youth
Organization), 17
see also Communist Youth
Organization
Kopelev, Lev, 48, 53, 146
Korea, Democratic People's Republic
of (North Korea), 118
Kosta, Jiri, 157
Kovalev, Sergei, 109

Kovalyov, Sergei, 186
Krasnaya Zvezda (Army paper), 175
Kulikov, 178
Kunayev, Dinmukhamed, 35

labor discipline problems, 37
language manipulation:
  context, importance of, 93–94
  negative connotations for Western
    actions, 91–92
  positive connotations for Soviet
    actions, 92–93
  semantic differentiation, 94–95
Laos, 120
Latey, Maurice, 197
Latin America, 128–30
Latvia, 81
Lenin, V. I., 32, 76
  on democracy, 166
  on foreign policy, 95–96, 121
  on hegemony, 107–8
  New Economic Policy, 152
  on personal incentive, 162
Libya, 123
  U.S. attack on (1986), 128
Ligachev, Yegor, 30, 35, 36
limited sovereignty doctrine, 109–10
Literaturnaya Gazyeta, 175
Lithuania, 53, 81
Litvinov, Maksim, 83

Madrid conference (1983), 188
Marx, Karl, 22–23, 73, 107
Marxism-Leninism, *see* ideology
medical care:
  corruption in, 65
  for officials, 20
  shortcomings of, 60–61
Medvedev, Roy, 164–65, 167
Michnik, Adam, 193–94
military takeover, possible, 176–79
missile deployments in Europe
  (NATO), 136, 139
"model citizen," 10–11
Molotov, Vyacheslav, 83, 175
Mondale, Walter, 139, 187

Mongolia, 102, 103, 119, 123
Morosov, M., 63
Mozambique, 123, 126, 127, 128
multiparty system, 166–67
Muslim republics, 54
My Country and the World
  (Sakharov), 145

Nagy, Imre, 113, 156
nationalistic authoritarianism,
  return to, 167–70
nationality problem, 50–51
  anti-Semitism, 53
  birthrates and, 52
  deported nationalities, 52–53
  non-Russians, national identity
    among, 53–54
  official recognition of, 54
  passport system, 51
  reform proposals, 54–55
  Russification policies and, 51, 53,
    54
NATO, 136, 139
negotiating strategy:
  agreements in principle, 89–90,
    205
  concessions, attitude toward,
    90–91
  CPSU's role in, 86–87
  long-term focus, 88–89
  opening speeches, 87–88
  principle of initiative, 88
  time pressures, lack of, 90
negotiating strategy for the West,
  90–91, 204–5
Nekepilov, Victor, 195–96
neo-Stalinism, 171–76
New Economic Policy (NEP), 152,
  159
Nicaragua, 126, 127, 129–30
Nikitin, Alexei, 63
nomenklatura:
  bourgeoisie, comparison with,
    22–23
  as executive authority, 18
  as feudal system, 23

Gorbachev's appointment as
  General Secretary, 33–34
hierarchy of, 21
KGB surveillance of members, 22
member loyalty, 23
member privileges, 19–21, 160
member promotions, 23
polarization of, 154–56
power as goal of, 19
private enterprise, toleration of,
  160–61
as ruling class, 19
titles and decorations, system of,
  21
Western understanding of, 38
noncapitalist development doctrine,
  121–23, 126

OBKSS (Department for the Struggle
  Against Theft of Socialist
  Property), 68
ochkovtiratelsvo (official coverups),
  17–18
October Revolution, 108
officials:
  age and nationality of, 26–27, 30
  capitalists, comparison with, 22
  common characteristics, 13
  education of, 17, 31
  failure coverups by, 17–18
  itinerary of, 31
  loyalty, importance of, 16, 23
  medical care for, 20
  nomenklatura officials, 19–21, 22,
    23, 160
  Politburo officials, 31
  privileges of, 19–21, 26, 160
  second economy, involvement in,
    68–69
  socio-political activity, 17
  State officials, 13, 14–15
  success criteria for, 17
  support groups, 18
  titles and decorations for, 21
Ogarkov, Nikolai, 140
opinion polls, 4

Palestine Liberation Organization,
  128
the Party, *see* Communist Party of
  the Soviet Union
Party language, 11–12
passport system, 51
peace movement in the West, 138,
  139
Pershing II missiles, NATO
  deployment of, 136, 139
Petrov, Vassili, 175
plans, economic, 41–42
podarki (bribes), 65
Poland, 62, 74, 81, 102, 103, 104, 111,
  113–14, 117, 147, 148, 161–62, 203
  martial law in, 83, 137, 176, 177
Polish United Workers Party, 177
Politburo, 28, 33
  age structure, 30
  changes under Gorbachev, 30,
    35–36, 37
  decision-making process, 32
  ideology and, 31–32
  laws re, 29
  members' education, 31
  members' itinerary, 31
  membership of, 29
  power of, 29, 31
  press coverage of, 29
"Prague Spring" movement (1968),
  81, 83, 104, 114–15, 147, 148
private enterprise:
  toleration of, 159–63
  see also second economy
Problems of Peace and Socialism
  (journal of international
  communism), 77–78

"Questions of History of the CPSU"
  (Klimko), 159
quiet diplomacy by the West, 134,
  182

radio broadcasts, Soviet, 196
radio broadcasts from the West,
  209–10

radio broadcasts (*continued*)
  changes in Soviet system and,
    195–96
  Soviet government's reaction to,
    198–99
  stations, 196–98
  topics of interest to listeners, 198
Radio Free Europe, 196, 197
Radio Liberty, 196, 197
Radio Moscow, 196
Rakosi, Matyas, 156
Reagan, Ronald, 137, 139, 140
Romania, 102, 111, 115, 117, 203
Romanov, Nikolai, 34, 35
Russification policies, 51, 53, 54
Ryzhkov, Nikolai, 30, 31, 35

Sadat, Anwar el-, 126
Sakharov, Andrei, 146, 169, 186, 212
  Carter's letter to, 182–83, 186–87
  on change in Soviet system, 145,
    164–65
  on dissatisfaction of Soviet
    people, 5–6
  exiling of, 137, 188, 211
  on ideology, 57
SALT I, 135
samizdat (underground
  publications), 149, 184
scientific-technological intelligensia,
  57, 151, 164
second economy:
  labor for, 66–67
  legitimization of, possible, 160–61
  officials involved in, 68–69
  origins of, 66
  quality of products, 67
  State use of, 67–68
Secret Police, *see* KGB
Seiffert, Wolfgang, 105, 151–52, 170
Serebrov, Felix, 195–96
shabashniki (second economy
  workers), 67
Shcherbitzky, Vladimir, 35
Shevardnadze, Eduard, 30, 31, 35, 83,
  140, 141

Shultz, George, 140
Smith, Hedrick, 173–74
SMOT (trade union), 63–64
socialist camp, *see* Soviet bloc
  headings
Sokolov, Sergei, 29, 36, 178
Solidarity movement, 62, 104, 117,
  134, 137, 148, 177
Somalia, 126, 127
Soviet bloc:
  Communist Parties in, 106–7
  countries of, 102–3
  limited independence for, 116–18
  resistance to Soviets in, 103–4,
    112–13, 114–15, 147–48, 203
  Soviet hegemony over, 107–10
  Soviet troops in bloc countries,
    113–15
  trade within, 105
  see also specific countries
Soviet bloc, policies re:
  economic coordination, 104–6
  goals of, 103, 104
  military cooperation, *see* Warsaw
    Pact
  political-ideological cooperation,
    106–10
Soviet people:
  alcoholism among, 58
  dissatisfaction among, 4–6
  Eastern Europe, attitude toward, 7
  foreign policy, attitude toward, 7
  ideology and, 55–59
  nationalities, 50
  national pride, 5
  political influence, 8
  reform efforts, 6–7
  religiosity of, 5–6, 58
  rights, lack of, 7–8
  standard of living, 59–61
  trade unions and, 62–64
  West's recognition of, 38, 201–2,
    209–10
  working conditions, 61–62
  see also nationality problem
Sovietski Patriot, 175

SS-20 missiles, deployment of, 135–36, 138
Stalin, Joseph, 23, 33, 52, 74–75, 152, 153
Stalin nostalgia, 173–76
the State, 13, 154–55
  apparatus of, 14
  the Army, control of, 15
  Central Committee, representation on, 25
  CPSU, relations with, 14, 15
  functioning of, 28
  officials of, 13, 14–15
  second economy, use of, 67–68
state farms (sovkhozi), 46–47, 49–50, 157–58
Strategic Defense Initiative (SDI), 139–40
summit meetings, 204
Supreme Soviet, 8, 28, 164
Suslov, Mikhail, 169
Syria, 123, 126, 127, 128

Tanzania, 123
technological innovation, 44
Third World, policies re:
  anticolonialism, 124
  economic assistance, absence of, 120, 127, 130
  failures of, 127–28
  goals of, 120–21
  Latin America, interest in, 128–30
  military influence, 125–26
  national liberation movements, use of, 124–25
  noncapitalist development doctrine, 121–23, 126
  political parties, contacts with, 125, 126
  political problems, focus on, 120
  proxies, use of, 125–26
  socialist orientation countries, 123–24
  treaties of friendship and cooperation, 126
Tikhonov, Nikolai, 34, 35

Tito, 110, 147, 154
tolkachi, 41, 42–43, 45, 162
tonnage ideology, 41–42
trade, *see* East-West trade
trade unions, 62–64, 163
travel abroad, 7–8, 210
Turchin, Valery F., 164–65

United Nations Covenant on Civil and Political Rights (1966), 182, 184
Universal Declaration of Human Rights (1948), 183
Ustinov, Dmitrii, 178

Victory (film), 175
Vietnam, 102, 103, 119, 120, 123
Voice of America, 195, 196–97
Voice of Germany, 196, 198
Vorotnikov, Vitaly, 31
Voslenski, Mikhail, 19

Walesa, Lech, 62, 148, 188, 212
warehouse ideology, 42
Warsaw Pact, 102–3
  changes in, Soviet proposals re, 115–16
  internal movements, suppression of, 112–13, 114–15
  member countries, 110–11
  military maneuvers, 114
  organs of, 112
  Soviet troops in bloc countries, 113–15
  time limit of, 115
  treaty text, 111
the West, policies re:
  businesslike relations, 202–3
  coexistence doctrine, 130–32
  détente, 132–35
  economic objectives, 142–43
  front organizations, use of, 97–101
  Gorbachev's policies, 140–41
  influence, acquisition of, 144
  military objectives, 141–42
  miscalculation in, 84–86

the West (*continued*)
  political objectives, 143–44
  public opinion, use of, 95–96
  rapprochement (1984), 140
Western policies regarding the
    Soviets:
  Afghanistan invasion and, 137
  arms control, 206–7
  businesslike relations, 202–3
  conservative versus liberal
    policies, 200–201
  dissident movement, support for,
    211–13
  East European countries,
    recognition of, 203–4
  human rights, support for, 182–83,
    186–89, 209–10, 211–12
  long-term objectives, 210–11,
    212–13
  military aspects, 206
  missile deployments in Europe,
    136, 139
  negotiating strategy, 90–91, 204–5
  nomenklatura, understanding of,
    38
  peace movement and, 138, 139
  quiet diplomacy, 134, 182
  Soviet people, recognition of, 38,
    201–2, 209–10

  see also East-West trade; radio
    broadcasts from the West
Women's International Democratic
    Federation, 98, 99
working conditions in factories,
    61–62
World Economy (Hungarian
    journal), 47
World Federation of Democratic
    Youth, 98, 99
World Federation of Trade Unions,
    98
World Peace Council, 98, 100
world revolutionary process, 76–79

Yakovlev, Aleksander, 36
Yalta Conference, 89
Yeltsin, Boris, 29, 36
Yemen, People's Democratic
    Republic of (South Yemen), 123,
    126, 127, 128
Yevtushenko, Yevgeny, 174
Yugoslavia, 147, 161–62
  Soviet Union, relations with,
    118–19, 120

Zaikov, Lev, 30, 31, 36
Zhivkov, Todor, 117